Not a Sound

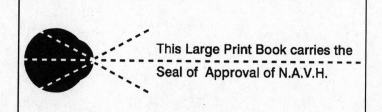

NOT A SOUND

HEATHER GUDENKAUF

THORNDIKE PRESS
A part of Gale, Cengage Learning

GALE
CENGAGE Learning

Farmington Hills, Mich • San Francisco • New York • Waterville, Maine
Meriden, Conn • Mason, Ohio • Chicago

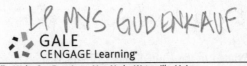

GALE
CENGAGE Learning

This is a work of fiction. Names, characters, places, and incidents either are the product of the author's imagination or are used fictitiously, and any resemblance to actual persons, living or dead, business establishments, events, or locales is entirely coincidental.

Thorndike Press® Large Print Basic.
The text of this Large Print edition is unabridged.
Other aspects of the book may vary from the original edition.
Set in 16 pt. Plantin.

LIBRARY OF CONGRESS CATALOGING-IN-PUBLICATION DATA

Names: Gudenkauf, Heather, author.
Title: Not a sound / by Heather Gudenkauf.
Description: Large print edition. | Waterville, Maine : Thorndike Press, 2017. | Series: Thorndike Press large print basic
Identifiers: LCCN 2017017309 | ISBN 9781410498090 (hardcover) | ISBN 1410498093 (hardcover)
Subjects: LCSH: Large type books. | GSAFD: Suspense fiction.
Classification: LCC PS3607.U346 N68 2017 | DDC 813/.6—dc23
LC record available at https://lccn.loc.gov/2017017309

Published in 2017 by arrangement with Harlequin Books, S.A.

Printed in the United States of America
1 2 3 4 5 6 7 21 20 19 18 17

For Erika Imranyi — who knows how
to make lemonade from lemon squares

Prologue

I find her sitting all by herself in the emergency waiting room, her lovely features distorted from the swelling and bruising. Only a few patients remain, unusual for a Friday night and a full moon. Sitting across from her, an elderly woman coughs wetly into a handkerchief while her husband, arms folded across his chest and head tilted back, snores gently. Another man with no discernable ailment stares blankly up at the television mounted on the wall. Canned laughter fills the room.

I'm surprised she's still here. We treated her hours ago. Her clothing was gathered, I examined her from head to toe, all the while explaining what I was doing step-by-step. She lay on her back while I swabbed, scraped and searched for evidence. I collected for bodily fluids and hairs that were not her own. I took pictures. Close-ups of abrasions and bruises. I stood close by while the police officer interviewed her and asked deeply personal private questions. I offered her emergency contraceptives and the phone number for a domestic abuse shelter. She didn't cry once during the entire process. But now the tears are falling freely, dampening the clean scrubs I gave her to change into.

"Stacey?" I sit down next to her. "Is someone coming to get you?" I ask. I offered to call someone on her behalf but she refused, saying that she could take care of it. I pray to God that she didn't call her husband, the man who did this to her. I hope that the police had already picked him up.

She shakes her head. "I have my car."

"I don't think you should be driving. Please let me call someone," I urge. "Or you can change your mind and we can admit you for the night. You'll be safe. You can get some rest."

"No, I'm okay," she says. But she is far from okay. I tried to clean her up as best I could but already her newly stitched lip is oozing blood, the bruises blooming purple across her skin.

"At least let me walk you to your car," I offer. I'm eager to get home to my husband and stepdaughter but they are long asleep.

A few more minutes won't matter.

She agrees and stands, cradling her newly casted arm. We walk out into the humid August night. The full moon, wide faced and as pale as winter wheat lights our way. Katydids call back and forth to one another and white-winged moths throw themselves at the illuminated sign that reads Queen of Peace Emergency.

"Where are you staying tonight? You're not going home, are you?"

"No," she says but doesn't elaborate more. "I had to park over on Birch," she says dully. Queen of Peace's lot has been under construction for the better part of a month so parking is a challenge. It makes me sad to think that not only did this poor woman, beaten and raped by her estranged husband, have to drive herself to the emergency room, there wasn't even a decent place for her to park. Now there are five open parking spaces. What a difference a few hours can make in the harried, unpredictable world of emergency room care.

We walk past sawhorse barriers and orange construction cones to a quiet, residential street lined with sweetly pungent linden trees. Off in the distance a car engine roars to life, a dog barks, a siren howls. Another patient for the ER.

"My car is just up here," Stacey says and points to a small, white four-door sedan hidden in the shadows cast by the heart-shaped leaves of the lindens. We cross the street and I wait as Stacey digs around in her purse for her keys. A mosquito buzzes past my ear and I wave it away.

I hear the scream of tires first. The high-pitched squeal of rubber on asphalt. Stacey and I turn toward the noise at the same time. Blinding high beams come barreling toward us. There is nowhere to go. If we step away from Stacey's car we will be directly in its path. I push Stacey against her car door and press as close to her as I can, trying to make ourselves as small as possible.

I'm unable to pull my eyes away from bright light and I keep thinking that the careless driver will surely correct the steering wheel and narrowly miss us. But that doesn't happen. There is no screech of brakes, the car does not slow and the last sound I hear is the dull, sickening thud of metal on bone.

1

Two Years Later . . .

Nearly every day for the past year I have paddle boarded, kayaked, run or hiked around the sinuous circuit that is Five Mines River, Stitch at my side. We begin our journey each day just a dozen yards from my front door, board and oar hoisted above my head, and move cautiously down the sloping, rocky bank to the water's edge. I lower my stand-up paddleboard, the cheapest one I could find, into the water, mindfully avoiding the jagged rocks that could damage my board. I wade out into the shallows, flinching at the bite of cold water against my skin, and steady it so Stitch can climb on. I hoist myself up onto my knees behind him and paddle out to the center of the river.

With long even strokes I pull the oar through the murky river. The newly risen sun, intermittently peeking through heavy, slow-moving gray clouds, reflects off droplets of water kicked up like sparks. The late-October morning air is bracing and smells of decaying leaves. I revel in the sights and feel of the river, but I can't hear the slap of my oar against the water, can't hear the cry of the seagulls overheard, can't hear Stitch's playful yips. I'm still trying to come to terms with this.

The temperature is forecast to dip just below freezing soon and when it does I will reluctantly stow my board in the storage shed, next to my kayak until spring. In front of me, like a nautical figurehead carved into the prow of a sailing vessel, sits Stitch. His bristled coat is the same color as the underside of a silver maple leaf in summer, giving him a distinguished air. He is three years old and fifty-five pounds of muscle and sinew but often gets distracted and forgets that he has a job to do.

Normally, when I go paddling, I travel an hour and a half north to where Five Mines abruptly opens into a gaping mouth at least a mile wide. There the riverside is suddenly lined with glass-sided hotels, fancy restaurants, church spires and a bread factory that fills the air with a scent that reminds me of my mother's kitchen. Joggers and young mothers with strollers move leisurely along the impressive brick-lined river walk and the old train bridge that my brother and I played on as kids looms in the distance — out of place and damaged beyond repair. Kind of like me.

Once I catch sight of the train bridge or smell the yeasty scent of freshly baked bread I know it's time to turn around. I much prefer the narrow, isolated inlets and sloughs south of Mathias, the river town I grew up in.

This morning there's only time for a short trek. I have an interview with oncologist and hematologist Dr. Joseph Huntley, the director of the Five Mines Regional Cancer Center in Mathias at ten. Five Mines provides comprehensive health care and resources to cancer patients in the tristate area. Dr. Huntley is also on staff at Queen of Peace Hospital with my soon-to-be ex-husband, David. He is the head of obstetrics and gynecology at Q & P and isn't thrilled that I might be working with his old friend. It was actually Dr. Huntley who called me to see if I was interested. The center is going to update their paper files to electronic files and need someone to enter data.

Dr. Huntley, whom I met on a few occasions years ago through David, must have heard that I've been actively searching for work with little luck. David, despite his grumblings, hasn't sabotaged me. I'll be lucky if he can muster together any kind words about me. It's a long, complicated story filled with heartache and alcohol. Lots of alcohol. David could only take so much and one day I found myself all alone.

I come upon what is normally my favorite part of Five Mines, a constricted slice of river only about fifteen yards wide and at least twenty feet at its deepest. The western bank is a wall of craggy limestone topped by white pines and brawny chinquapin oaks whose branches extend out over the bluff in a rich bronze canopy of leaves. Today the river is unusually slow and sluggish as if it is thick with silt and mud. The air is too heavy, too still. On the other bank the lacy-leaf tendrils of black willows dangle in the water like limp fingers.

Stitch's ears twitch. Something off in the distance has caught his attention. My board rocks slowly at first, a gentle undulation that quickly becomes jarring. Cold water splashes across my ankles and I nearly tumble into the river. Instead I fall to my knees, striking them sharply against my board. Somehow I manage to avoid tumbling in myself but lose my paddle and my dog to the river. Stitch doesn't appear to mind the unexpected bath and is paddling his way to the shore. Upriver, some asshole in a motorboat must have revved his engine, causing the tumultuous wake.

I wait on hands and knees, my insides swaying with the river until the waves settle. My paddle bobs on the surface of the water just a few feet out of my reach. I cup one hand to use as an oar and guide my board until I can grab the paddle. Maybe it's my nervousness about my upcoming interview, but I'm anxious to turn around and go back home. Something feels off, skewed. Stitch is oblivious. This is the spot where we usually take a break, giving me a chance to stretch my legs and giving Stitch a few minutes to play. I check my watch. It's only seven thirty, plenty of time for Stitch to romp around in the water for a bit. Stitch with only his coarse, silver head visible makes a beeline for land. I resituate myself into a sitting position and lay the paddle across my lap. Above me, two turkey vultures circle in wide, wobbly loops. The clouds off in the distance are the color of bruised flesh.

Stitch emerges from the river and onto the muddy embankment and gives himself a vigorous shake, water dripping from his beard and moustache or what his trainer described as *facial furnishings,* common to

Slovakian rough-haired pointers. He lopes off and begins to explore the shoreline by sniffing and snuffling around each tree trunk and fallen log. I close my eyes, tilt my face up toward the sky and the outside world completely disappears. I smell rain off in the distance. A rain that I know will wash away what's left of fall. It's Halloween and I hope that the storm will hold off until the trick-or-treaters have finished their begging.

Stitch has picked up a stick and, instead of settling down to chew on it like most dogs, he tosses it from his mouth into the air, watches it tumble into the water and then pounces. My stepdaughter, Nora, loves Stitch. I think if it weren't for Stitch, Nora wouldn't be quite as excited to spend time with me. Not that I can blame her. I really screwed up and I'm not the easiest person in the world to communicate with.

I'm debating whether or not to bring Stitch into the interview with me. Legally I have the right. I have all the paperwork and if Dr. Huntley can't be accommodating, I'm not sure I want to work for him. Plus, Stitch is such a sweet, loving dog, I'm sure the cancer patients that come into the center would find his presence comforting.

My stomach twists at the thought of having to try and sell myself as a qualified, highly capable office worker in just a few short hours. There was a time not that long ago when I was a highly regarded, sought-after nurse. Not anymore.

Stitch has wandered over to where the earth juts out causing a crooked bend in the river, a spot that, lacking a better word, I call the elbow. I catch sight of Stitch facing away from me, frozen in place, right paw raised, tail extended, eyes staring intently at something. Probably a squirrel or chipmunk. He creeps forward two steps and I know that once the animal takes off so will Stitch. While nine times out of ten he'll come back when I summon him, he's been known to run and I don't have time this morning to spend a half an hour searching for him.

I snap my fingers twice, our signal for Stitch to come. He ignores me. I row closer. "Stitch, *ke mne*!" I call. *Come.* His floppy ears twitch but still he remains fixated on whatever has caught his eye. Something has changed in his stance. His back is rounded until he's almost crouching, his tail is tucked between his legs and his ears are flat against his head. He's scared.

My first thought is he's happened upon a skunk. My second thought is one of amusement given that, for the moment, our roles have reversed — I'm trying to gain his attention rather than the other way around. I snap my fingers again, hoping to break the spell. The last thing I need is to walk into my new job smelling like roadkill. Stitch doesn't even glance my way.

I scoot off my board into knee-deep water, my neoprene shoes sinking into the mud. I wrestle my board far enough onto land so it won't drift away. Maybe Stitch has cornered a snake. Not too many poisonous snakes around here. Brown spotted massasauga and black banded timber rattlers are rare but not unheard of. I pick my way upward through snarls of dead weeds and step over rotting logs until I'm just a few yards behind Stitch. He is perched atop a rocky incline that sits about five feet above the water. Slowly, so as to not startle Stitch or whatever has him mesmerized, I inch my way forward, craning my neck to get a better look.

Laying a hand on Stitch's rough coat, damp from his swim, I feel him tremble beneath my fingers. I follow his gaze and find myself staring down to where a thick layer of fallen leaves carpets the surface of the water. A vibrant mosaic of yellow, red and brown. "There's nothing there," I tell him, running my hand over his ears and beneath his chin. His vocal chords vibrate in short, staccato bursts, alerting me to his whimpering.

I lean forward, my toes dangerously close to the muddy ridge. One misstep and I'll tumble in.

It takes a moment for my brain to register what I'm seeing and I think someone has discarded an old mannequin into the river. Then I realize this is no figure molded from fiberglass or plastic. This is no Halloween prank. I see her exposed breast, pale white against a tapestry of fall colors. With my heart slamming into my chest, I stumble backward. Though I try to break the fall with my hands, I hit the ground hard, my head striking the muddy earth, my teeth gnashing together, leaving me momentarily stunned. I blink up at the sky, trying to get my bearings, and in slow motion, a great blue heron with a wingspan the length of a grown man glides over me, casting a brief shadow. Slowly, I sit up, dazed, and my hands go to my scalp. When I pull my fingers away they are bloody.

Dizzily, I stagger to my feet. I cannot pass out here, I tell myself. No one will know where to find me. Blood pools in my mouth from where I've bitten my tongue and I spit, trying to get rid of the coppery taste. I wipe my hands on my pants and gingerly touch the back of my head again. There's a small bump but no open wound that I can feel. I look at my hands and see the source of the blood. The thin, delicate skin of my palms is shredded and embedded with small pebbles.

The forest feels like it is closing in all around me and I want to run, to get as far away from here as possible. But maybe I was mistaken. Maybe what I thought I saw was a trick of light, a play of shadows. I force myself back toward the ridge and try to summon the cool, clinical stance that I was known for when I was an emergency room nurse. I peer down, and staring up at me is the naked body of a woman floating just beneath the surface of the water. Though I can't see any discernable injuries on her, I'm sure there is no way she happened to end up here by accident. I take in a pair of blue lips parted in surprise, an upturned nose, blank eyes wide-open; tendrils of blond hair tangled tightly into a snarl of half-submerged brambles keeps her from drifting away.

Pinpricks of light dance in front of my eyes and for a moment I'm blinded with shock, fear, dread. Then I do something I have never done, not even once at the sight of a dead body. I bend over and vomit. Great, violent heaves that leave my stomach hollow and my legs shaky. I wipe my mouth with the back of my hand. I know her. Knew her. The dead woman is Gwen Locke and at one time we were friends.

2

Gwen Locke. Nurses, the both of us. Friends at one time. Good friends. Once again my stomach clenches and I retch, but this time nothing comes up. Stitch's trance has been broken and he paces in agitation, his powerful jaws opening and closing with what I'm sure are sharp yips and barks. I fumble with my FlipBelt, a tubular band with a series of pockets where I keep all the items that I have to carry with me when I'm on the river. Safely ensconced in a waterproof case is the cell phone that I promised my cop friend Jake I would carry with me at all times. Never mind that it would do me little or no good in emergency situations, like this one. Nine-one-one via text message hasn't reached my silent little world yet so I dial the three numbers and hope for the best. I wait three seconds and begin to speak. "My name is Amelia Winn," I say, I'm sure my voice is high and shrill and nasally. "I found a body. Please send help. I'm on Five Mines River, two miles north of Old Mine Road. I'm deaf and can't hear you."

Phone clutched between my fingers, I repeat the same message over and over before disconnecting. *I found a body. Please send help. I'm on Five Mines River, two miles north of Old Mine Road. I'm deaf and can't hear you.*

Frantically, I turn around and around, my heart thrumming, the air squeezed from my chest. I try to swallow up each inch of the landscape with my eyes. The sway of switch-grass along the bank, each shiver of a tree branch, each shadowy crag and crevice in the bluffs could be concealing someone. Each whisper of a breeze across my neck, the killer's touch. Nothing. No one there. The sun is slipping in and out from behind the clouds and every shift in light seems ominous. Finally, dizzy and exhausted, I sink to the ground and lean my back against the curly white bark of a paper birch. Though I'm afraid, I'm not fearful of someone noiselessly sneaking up on me. Stitch, snuggled up against me, his bearded chin resting on my lap, will alert me of any new presence. I just don't know what I'm going to do if someone steps into the clearing to confront me. Do I run? Do I stay and fight? Would Stitch stay by my side to protect me? I don't know.

Just when I think I have my breathing under control, the chills start in. Gwen lies only a few yards away from me. I pull the pepper spray that Jake gave me from another FlipBelt pocket.

Jake Schroeder is a Mathias police detective and best friend of my brother, Andrew, from when we were growing up. I've had a bit of a crush on Jake since I was eight. He thinks of me as a pesky little sister who still needs looking out for since my brother moved to Denver and my dad, fed up with Iowa winters, retired to Arizona.

Jake was the first one I saw when I opened my eyes in the hospital after a hit-and-run driver struck Stacey Barnes. Stacey was killed on impact and I suffered a broken leg, a severe head injury and the complete annihilation of the tiny bones and neural pathways of my inner ears. I was sure that the driver was the bastard who abused Stacey, but it wasn't. So with no leads the case remains unsolved.

Two years later, I'm almost divorced, unemployed, profoundly deaf, probably an alcoholic and still a little pissed. Okay, an alcoholic. No *probably.* I still find it hard to admit. The only people in Mathias who haven't given up on me are my stepdaughter, Nora, because she's seven and I'm the only mother she remembers and Jake, who's no stranger to heartache himself. Jake's the one who hauled my drunk ass out of bed, got me to my first AA meeting, and made me take an American Sign Language (ASL) class at the local college with him. Even before my accident he was already proficient in ASL. Two counties over, a policeman shot and mistakenly killed a deaf teenager when he didn't hear the command to stop. Local law enforcement, hoping to avoid future tragedies, arranged for training and Jake learned the basics. To top it all off he showed up at my house one day with a Czech dog trainer named Vilem Sarka and Stitch — a reluctant service dog.

Stitch came to me with his own baggage. A thick, zipper-like scar extends vertically from the bottom of his belly to just below his throat. Hence his name. "Some sick fuck. Over one hundred stitches," Vilem wrote on a pad of paper when I asked what had happened.

I stroke Stitch's head and wait for help, knowing that it could arrive in a matter of minutes or not for up to an hour. There are only three ways to get to our remote location: by boat, by four-wheeler or by foot. I focus my attention on Stitch's ears; if they start to twitch I know he hears something. My bet is help will come via the river and a Department of Natural Resources officer with a boat. Up until now I have never been afraid around the dead and now I'm terrified.

I can't believe Gwen is dead and I can't help but think of my own accident, which I'm not convinced was an accident, after all. What if Gwen's murder and my attempted murder are connected? Crazy, I know. But Gwen and I both treated patients who were abused by very bad, very dangerous people. Is it such a stretch to think they would come after the nurses who were trying to gather the forensic evidence to put them in jail for a very long time?

Stitch raises his head and looks at me with worry. I must have whimpered or spoken out loud. I do that sometimes without even knowing it. "It's okay," I tell him. My throat is sore and I figure I must have been shouting while I was talking to the 9-1-1 dispatcher. What if the person on the other end of the line couldn't understand me? What if they don't know where to send help and no one is coming?

I'm just about ready to call 9-1-1 again

when Stitch scrambles to his feet and faces north and up the river. "Two if by sea," I say, holding on to Stitch's collar so he won't run off.

Sure enough, a heavyset man of about sixty, steering a small boat with the Iowa DNR logo emblazoned across its side motors toward us. Stitch looks up at me for reassurance, and I gently pat his back. The boat slows and the DNR officer says something, but he's too far away and I can't read his lips.

"I can't hear you," I say, and the officer's mouth widens in a way that tells me he's shouting.

"No, I'm deaf," I say, cupping my ear. "I can't hear you. Come closer." He looks at me suspiciously, hand on his sidearm. I can't say that I blame him. I'm sure I sounded like a maniac on the 9-1-1 call. The dispatcher most likely added "approach subject with caution" when passing on the details.

"I can read lips," I say. "I just need to see your face."

He drives the boat up to the shore and with some difficulty climbs over the side and joins us beneath the birch. "Is he friendly?" the officer asks, glancing nervously down at Stitch.

"Very," I assure him. I turn to Stitch and palm upward, bring my hand toward my shoulder. Immediately, he sits down. I reach into my pocket and pull out a dog treat and Stitch snags it with his long pink tongue. "Good boy." That trick took three weeks to master.

The officer takes another cautious step forward. "I'm DNR Officer Wagner. Are you okay?" His lips stretch wide with each word. He's overenunciating. I'm used to this when people first find out about my hearing loss.

"I'm fine," I say with more confidence than I feel. "She's over there." I point to the maple tree. "Just over the ridge, in the water."

"Stay here," he orders. I pretend I don't understand him and follow him up the incline, both of us grabbing onto low-hanging branches to avoid slipping on the slick decaying leaves that litter the ground. When we reach the crest my eyes immediately go to where Gwen's body sways with the gentle current. Officer Wagner's head swivels from left to right, searching. When his spine goes rigid I know he finally sees her. He gropes into his pocket and pulls out a cell phone and presses it to his ear.

I bend at the waist, again light-headed. I was an ER nurse for eighteen-odd years.

I've seen people come in with injuries beyond comprehension. I've seen dead bodies before, have had people die from catastrophic injuries in my care. But always at the hospital, in a sterile, antiseptic setting.

I force myself to stand upright and take a deep breath. I feel useless. If there was a chance Gwen was still breathing I could have given her CPR, but it's clear that she's dead. Gwen is a bit younger than I am, and she's fit — has the slim physique of a serious runner. Was she running or hiking the trails and then waylaid by a predator who dragged her off the path, raped and then killed her, finally tossing her into the river like trash?

From our vantage point, I can't see any obvious injuries. No bullet holes, no gaping wounds, no scavengers have discovered her. She can't have been in the river long. I think of the waves that knocked Stitch off my paddleboard and sent me to my knees just before I found Gwen's body. I wish I saw what the boat looked like. I wish I had more information to offer the police. I wonder if her husband, Marty, has missed her yet. Or worse, could he have been the one to do this? I don't know him well, but I met him several times. Gwen never mentioned having any problems in their marriage and he seemed like a nice man. And then there is their daughter, Lane. She will be devastated when she learns that her mother is never coming back home.

I swallow back my tears, pull my eyes from the body and scan the earth around me. Muddy footprints everywhere. I think I can discern three different shoe treads. Most likely my own and the DNR officer's, and possibly the killer's. There are also the imprints of Stitch's large paws zigzagging the ground chronicling his agitation. Off in the brush is a discarded glass beer bottle. It could have belonged to one of the ever-growing number of weekend warriors who have discovered this length of river due to the opening of Five Mines Outfitters, located right next door to my house. The outfitter offers an array of outdoor services including canoe, kayak, paddleboard and in the winter, snowshoe and ice skate rentals.

Below us Stitch waits, wiggling impatiently while somehow remaining in a seated position. I gesture for him to settle and stay and he complies. Officer Wagner tugs on my sleeve and nods toward the woods below us. Emerging from the trees is a small troupe of four-wheelers. Unable to contain himself, Stitch leaps to his feet and begins to spin around in excitement.

Five of the six people on the ATVs are law enforcement officers, including Jake. The lone civilian I recognize as my new neighbor, the proprietor of Five Mines Outfitters. We've never officially met, but I hate him anyway. The day he opened his business he brought a steady stream of unwanted strangers into my backyard, disrupting my solitude. The four-wheelers most likely belong to my neighbor and the Mathias Police Department commandeered them and asked him to lead the way through the woods so they could get to the scene as quickly as possible. Jake and the four other officers slide from their ATVs and begin to move toward us, leaving my neighbor behind.

Stitch knows Jake so he greets him with an enthusiastic wag of his bottle brush tail and attaches himself to Jake's side. When the officers reach the bottom of the bluff, Jake says something to the group and they remain below as he and Stitch make the short climb to where Officer Wagner and I wait.

Jake still has the same boyish good looks that he did thirty years ago. Seeing him in his detective's uniform of a suit and tie makes me smile at the incongruity of how I remember him as a kid. He was a constant at our house, preferring ours to his own. His father was volatile, unpredictable, mean. Daily, he'd show up with his mussed sandy-brown hair, smelling of fresh cut grass and bubble gum, dressed in grubby jeans, scuffed tennis shoes and a purple-and-gold Minnesota Vikings T-shirt in search of my brother.

Jake's normally cheerful face is now set in rigid seriousness and he's oblivious to the mud that has caked his dress shoes and splattered onto his suit pants. He's not even out of breath when he reaches us, a testament to the great physical shape he's in. Instead of first asking where the victim is, he eyes me up and down. He winces at the sight of my bloodstained shirt, extends the index finger of both his hands and brings them toward each other, the right hand twisting one way and the left hand the other, making the ASL sign for *hurt.*

"I tripped," I explain, holding up my hands. "It looks worse than it is." He takes my hands in his and turns them over to examine my cut and scraped palms. His grasp is warm against my chilled fingers and I realize just how cold I am.

"Her name is Gwen Locke. I know her. We worked together. She's been to my house," I say. "I've been to hers."

Jake looks surprised but doesn't ask me if I'm sure of the woman's identity. He releases my hands, and I immediately miss his warmth. He turns his attention to the DNR officer. Wagner points to the water, and a muscle in Jake's jaw twitches and once again he becomes all business.

"Go back down by your paddleboard," he signs. "We have to seal off this area. I'll be right down to take your statement and Officer Snell will make sure you get home safely." I nod, and Jake gives me a wisp of a smile as if to let me know that everything will be all right. I want to believe him.

Officer Snell, with his closely cropped hair and smattering of acne across his forehead, looks to be barely out of his teens. He's waiting, pen and pad already in hand by the time I reach him. Cold has seeped through my pants, still damp from wading through the water and from my tumble to the ground and I begin to shiver.

"Just a few questions, ma'am," Snell begins, but I quickly lose the thread and stop him.

"Maybe we should wait for Jake. Detective Schroeder," I amend. "He knows sign." Officer Snell nods his understanding and we stand around awkwardly until Jake makes his way down to us.

Jake knows how to talk to me. Not only does he know sign, he looks me right in the eye and keeps his sentences short. I answer out loud while Snell writes down my answers. He covers all the expected questions: name, address, phone number, age.

"You say you know her?" Jake signs.

I nod. "Her name is Gwen Locke. She's a county sexual assault nurse and last I knew was a nurse at Queen of Peace and Mathias Regional." I try to keep one eye on Stitch who grows bored and wanders away. His attention is on a black squirrel that looks curiously down from a tree branch at the drama unfolding before him.

"Do you have any contact information for her? Know her next of kin?" Jake signs as Snell flips his notebook to an empty page.

I haven't used the phone number I have for Gwen in almost two years. After my accident she reached out to me, came by the hospital and to the house to visit but I refused to talk to her. To anyone. "Her husband's name is Marty and she has a daughter named Lane. She grew up here." I pull out my phone and find Gwen's number. Snell adds it to his growing list of notes.

Jake has me take him, step by step, through my morning right up until Stitch discovered Gwen in the river. Beyond his shoulder I see Stitch wander toward my neighbor who is waiting next to a four-wheeler, his hands stuffed in the pockets of his jacket. He bends down to scratch Stitch's ear. "Stitch, *Ke mne*!" I call. *Ke mne* is Czech for *come* and pronounced as *khemn yea.* Stitch leisurely trots back to my side. Stitch's trainer, Vilem, who is originally from Prague, trained all of his police and rescue dogs using Czech commands, including Stitch and Jake's K-9.

Jake shifts so that his face is once again in front of mine. "You going to be okay?" he asks. "Do you want me to call someone for you?"

That's when I realize I'm late for my interview with Dr. Huntley. I've forgotten all about it.

"Oh, shit!" I say. I check my watch. It's close to ten thirty. I'm already a half an hour late. By the time I get home, cleaned up and to the clinic I'll be well over two hours late. I tell Jake about the interview and that I have to get home.

"Sorry," he signs. "Officer Snell will get you home as soon as possible. You'll have to come to the police station at some point and we'll have you sit down with a certified interpreter to take your official statement.

I'll check in with you later." Then he moves back up the bluff toward Gwen's body.

I check my phone and find two texts from Dr. Huntley's office manager. The first reading, Dr. Huntley is running behind schedule and will be about thirty minutes late for your interview.

For a moment I'm hopeful that I'll still be able to get to the clinic in time to catch him but then I read the second message and my stomach sinks. Dr. Huntley has to leave for another appointment. He will contact you if he'd like to reschedule. Great. The professional equivalent of "don't call me, I'll call you."

There's a third text from David. It's only one word but it speaks volumes.

Typical.

3

Jake orders me not to share any details about my discovery with anyone so I send a text to Dr. Huntley's office manager, apologizing for my absence. I explain that I have a good reason for missing the interview and that I will tell her all about it later. My fingers itch to respond to David's smart-ass text with something equally snarky, but my attorney, Amanda, has advised me to keep all my communications with David cordial so I shove my phone into my pocket before I change my mind.

Because I'm not Nora's biological mother I have absolutely zero rights when it comes to custody or visitation. If and when I get to see Nora is completely in David's hands.

I clearly remember the day, even though I was completely sloshed, that David finally had enough. He had come home from his shift at the hospital and found me sitting on the floor of our bedroom with a bottle of

Smirnoff and my coffee mug with "Cute enough to stop your heart and skilled enough to restart it" written across the side. A Valentine's Day gift from David. I couldn't be that bad off if I was still using a glass. At least I wasn't chugging directly from the bottle, never mind that I was holed up in my bedroom with the shades drawn, lights off, drinking vodka and watching closed captioned episodes of *Judge Judy* at four in the afternoon on a Tuesday.

Of course I didn't hear David come into the room, but once he turned on the light and I saw the look on his face I knew things were bad. "You forgot to pick up Nora," he said, pointing to his watch as I rolled the Smirnoff beneath the bed.

"Sorry," was all I could offer. "I'll go get her now." I got unsteadily to my feet. My face felt numb and I almost didn't care that I couldn't actually hear what David was saying.

"No, Amelia, you won't. You can't get in a car and drive like this." I couldn't stand seeing the anger, the disappointment in his eyes, so I averted mine. David grabbed my chin. Not hard, but firmly, so that I couldn't help but look at him. "You will never drive with Nora again. Do you understand?"

"You can't tell me what I can and can't

do," I said, my chin still cupped in his hand. I remember actually being glad that his hand was there, I was having trouble keeping my head steady. I kept wanting to lie down, close my eyes.

"I can and I will," David said through clenched teeth, making it difficult for me to read his lips. "I en an I ill," it looked like he was saying, and for some reason this struck me as funny and I started to laugh.

"Dammit, Amelia!" David said, his fingers now digging into my cheeks so hard that tears sprang into my eyes. "You will not get into a car with my daughter. If you do, I'll call the police, I swear, I will. Once you sober up, I want you out. Out of my house. Do you understand?" David's face was pale and he was nearly vibrating with rage.

I wrenched away from his grasp, the half-filled mug still in my hands. "Now Nora's *your* daughter? I knew you would do this," I spat. "I knew you could never deal with me being deaf. I'm not your perfect little wife anymore so you're going to just throw me away," I slurred.

"I'm not doing this because you're deaf, Amelia. I'm doing this because you are a fucking drunk." This I understood. No need for my husband to repeat these words. I read his lips perfectly.

The mug was out of my hand before I even realized that I had thrown it. The mug struck the wall, exploding into shards just as Nora came into the room. Vodka sprayed in all directions. Nora's mouth made a perfect O as she clamped her hands over her ears and then ran from the room. David gave me a look filled with pure hate and rushed after her.

"Trista wasn't perfect, either, was she? You ran her off too!" I shouted. "No wonder she got as far away from you as possible." I slammed the door, locked it, and with shaking hands I rooted around beneath the bed in search of the bottle of vodka. When my fingers found the cool smooth glass, I sat with my back against the wall, the carpet wet beneath me, and drank until the tremors slowly subsided.

Officer Snell tugs on my sleeve and points to an opening in the trail. The EMTs arrive in a six-wheeled contraption that's a cross between an ATV and a short bed truck. It has a yellow stretcher strapped to the back and I realize that this is how they plan to transport the body out of here. It's not enough that Gwen has been found murdered, nude and dumped like refuse into the river, now she has to be unceremoniously hauled out of here by a mud-splattered OHV — off-highway vehicle. I know my irritation is misplaced. This isn't the first time that a body has been found in a rural, hard-to-get-to spot but usually it's due to a hunting accident or a drowning or someone collapsing on the trail, not murder.

I decline the offer from an EMT to tend to my hands even though they are still oozing blood and sting. Officer Snell is deep in conversation with my new neighbor so I find a rock to sit on while Stitch explores the muddy banks. I take this opportunity to survey the man who moved into the cabin next to my home. The two-story luxury stone-and-log home with its wide windows and wraparound decking puts my ragtag cabin to shame. The previous owners lost the home to foreclosure and it sat empty for the last three years. My new neighbor bought the property at the beginning of summer and opened Five Mines Outfitters. Now my once quiet road has a regular flow of traffic. Even worse, my stretch of river and the trails that have been my safe haven have been invaded by strangers. To be fair, we're not exactly next-door neighbors, either. The outfitters is settled nearly out of sight behind thick foliage atop a bluff and well above the river, safe from any flooding while my somewhat shabby A-frame sits dangerously close to the river's edge and is one heavy rain away from being swept into Five Mines by floodwaters.

This is the closest I've actually come to meeting my neighbor. I've only seen him from a distance when he lugs canoes or kayaks down to the access ramp he installed on the property for his customers. Seeing him up close, I realize that he's older than I thought. Midforties, I'd say. He is tall and very fit with jet-black hair, dark eyes and Asian features. As far as I can tell, he lives alone and runs the outfitters on his own.

"Officer . . . take . . . home . . . four-wheeler." I'm able to fill in the gaps and figure out that Officer Snell is letting me know that I'm going home on one of the four-wheelers.

"What about my board?" I ask, knowing that to worry about my paddleboard is petty under the circumstances, but I'm convinced that this board saved my life on more than one occasion, whisking me away from the bottle of Jack Daniel's I have stashed in the cabinet beneath my sink. I know I should just dump it out, along with the bottle of red wine I have hidden, but I can't bring myself to do it. Instead, when the need hits, I grab my board and Stitch and get the hell out of the house and paddle until I'm exhausted and the urge fades. At least for the time being.

"We can strap it on the back of one of the . . ." my neighbor says and then moves toward my board so that the rest of the sentence drops away when I can no longer see his lips. Expertly he lifts the board above his head in one smooth motion, turns back to face me, his mouth still moving. He has no idea I can't hear him and I don't have any desire to educate him, so I just nod. He retrieves a knot of bungee cords from a small storage box on the ATV and secures the board lengthwise so that half of it projects off the back.

Snell is talking to an officer, who if possible, is younger than he is. From the look on the boy's face he is disappointed about having to leave what is likely the most exciting crime scene he'll ever encounter in his career in law enforcement so that he can accompany us home. I feel a little sorry for him but it dawns on me that if I don't act fast I'm going to end up sitting behind my neighbor or the officer with my arms wrapped around their midsection as they drive me home. No way. I get onto the four-wheeler with my board strapped to it, staking my claim, and signal to Stitch to hop up behind me. I pretend not to notice Okada's slightly irritated expression as he climbs on behind the young officer.

It's about a forty-minute trek back to my house by four-wheeler and not that much faster on foot. I would have just walked home if I didn't have my board with me. The maze of trails, which are maintained by the DNR, have mine-era names that echo back to Mathias's mining history: Prospector Ridge, Galena Gulch and Knife Claim Hollow. We take Dry Bone Loop, a trail that winds like a corkscrew up one side of the bluff and then down the other. A delicate shower of gold and crimson leaves wafts down, littering the trail and catching in my hair. Stitch, from his spot behind me on the ATV, cranes his neck, jaws playfully snapping as he tries to snag each leaf that floats near. After about ten minutes of sitting patiently behind me as I navigate the rocky terrain, Stitch leaps from his seat and decides to run on ahead of us, pausing every few minutes to let us catch up.

I'm eager to get home to try and contact Dr. Huntley directly. I'm hoping he'll be able to reschedule our interview for this afternoon or at least some time this week. I'm sure David is fuming self-righteously and will try to find a way to use my absence against me. If finding a body in the river isn't a valid enough reason to miss my appointment, I don't know what is. The thing is, I'm not allowed to tell Dr. Huntley just why I stood him up.

Up ahead of us Stitch has wandered off the trail and is pawing tentatively at something in a twist of barberry dripping with red berries. My heart rate quickens and I bring the ATV to a stop. Stitch continues to bat at whatever has captured his attention, and I jump when I feel a brush at my elbow. The officer and my neighbor have parked their ATV behind mine and have come to my side, curiously watching Stitch. For a beat I'm afraid that Stitch has discovered another body and I find myself frozen in place. My eyes lock with the officer's and I know the same thought is skittering across his brain.

I slide from my seat and we all start to walk toward Stitch. Startled by the sudden movement, Stitch darts away from us, a colorful object dangling from his muzzle. Stitch thinks we're playing a game with him. He allows us to get just a few steps from him and then he dashes away, then stops short to see if we're still in pursuit.

"Stitch, *ruce vzuru*!" *Stand still,* I call, and instantly Stitch freezes and rolls his eyes toward me to make sure I'm serious. I look at him sternly and signal for him to come, and he slinks to my side. I show him my closed fist and open it, his cue to drop whatever is in his mouth. He grudgingly complies.

The three of us gather in a tight circle and bend forward to get a closer look at the item dispatched at our feet. It's a woman's running shoe. Beneath the layers of dirt, the shoe is brightly colored with fuchsia and neon green stripes. An expensive brand that only the most serious of runners seem to own. The thought of Stitch playing keep away with something that Gwen may have been wearing makes my stomach roil. We stand upright, and the officer pulls a phone from his pocket.

"Could belong to anyone," I read his lips, but the crease in his forehead lets me know he's not so sure. "We'll tag it just in case." I nod and move out of the way so that he can make his phone call.

There has to be a logical explanation as to why a running shoe has been abandoned in the weeds, though nothing I come up with makes much sense. An involuntary shiver runs through me. Gwen was a serious runner. Could the shoe belong to her?

My neighbor approaches. He's tall, about six feet, and I have to tilt my head back to get a good look at his sharply planed face. "Evan Okada," he says, holding out his hand. ". . . live next door . . . I wish . . . meeting under better . . ."

"Amelia Winn," I say and take his hand. His fingers wrap around mine — a warm cocoon.

Evan goes on to speak and from what I can decipher and from the wary look on his face he is telling me that he's tried to stop over to my house but the dog runs him off.

"Really?" I ask as if dumbfounded. "He's normally so friendly." In reality, when Stitch alerts me that someone is at the door I pretend to not be home or if I see my neighbor walking down the path from his house toward mine I let Stitch out the back door with the order to *stekje* and *scok* — to jump and bark, sending Evan scurrying back to the top of the bluff. My little revenge for all the unwanted foot and river traffic his business has brought to my backyard.

He turns away from me and gestures toward the trail. I have no idea what he's saying and I should probably tell him that I can't hear but I don't particularly want to share any personal information with him. Though I'm fully capable of taking care of myself, I don't advertise that I'm a single woman living all alone. My ex, David, used to say that I have a thin layer of ice encasing my heart that makes it hard for people to get to know me and that the warm temperature in the room when we first met must have melted it enough for him to be able to wriggle his way in. I would laugh, because it was true. Ever since my mom passed away when I was thirteen, I've been guarded, cautious of getting close to others. When David came along I let him in, let myself trust him. Now, once again, the thin layer of ice has thickened and has developed a bad case of freezer burn.

Thankfully, the officer has finished his phone call and though Evan is still chattering away I take the opportunity to extract myself from his side.

"Can I head on home?" I ask the officer. "It's not far, just down this side of the ridge. I really need to get home," I say. "I have an appointment that I'm already late for." He hesitates and I know he's grappling between following the order that he was given to make sure Evan and I get home safely and securing what could be a new part of the crime scene after Stitch unearthed the woman's shoe. "Please," I add. "Officer Snell has all my contact information. And I'm freezing," I add for good measure. The officer reluctantly nods.

Without meeting Evan's eyes, I lift my hand in farewell and make a wide berth around where the shoe lies atop a pile of jewel-toned leaves. I climb back on the ATV and summon Stitch to join me. I turn the key and make sure the engine stop switch is in the run position, engage the clutch and start the engine. The scent of diesel fuel assaults my nose. Slowly, we begin the descent down the bluff.

I have no idea if the officer has allowed Evan to leave too and I don't look behind me to check to see if he's following on his ATV. Periodically, Stitch lays his chin on my shoulder, his silver eyes imploring me to let him run ahead. *"Zustan,"* I say. *Stay.* The trip down the bluff goes more slowly than the first half. The rocky trail tapers and is so steep in spots that I'm afraid that the four-wheeler might tip over. If I didn't have my board and paddle strapped to it, I would abandon the ATV altogether and walk the rest of the way. Though I'm glad to be rid of the officer and Evan, I find that I'm feeling a little bit exposed and vulnerable. Without my hearing, I have to rely on my vision to gauge the world around me.

I have to so fully concentrate on maneuvering down the trail in front of me that I can't be as cognizant of my surroundings as I usually am. I have no idea if someone is hiding in the woods, watching and waiting. Every shadow, each sway of a tree branch seems ominous.

I mentally scold myself. I'm sure I'm perfectly safe. As an emergency room and sexual assault nurse examiner or SANE I know more than most people; I know that assaults are much more likely to be committed by an assailant familiar to the victim. But something nags at me. I've worked enough domestic assaults to know that most violence occurs in the home — not in a remote, wooded location. Could Gwen and Marty have been hiking the trails, gotten into an argument that escalated, resulting in her death? But that would mean that Marty would have removed her clothing and deposited her in the river to cover his tracks, destroying any evidence that might lead back to him. I only met Marty a few times, but he seemed like such a nice guy. I just don't see it.

It's unnerving to know that a murderer may have recently been walking this very trail. I release my right hand from the steering wheel and reach behind me to rub Stitch's head. He's accepted his plight in having to remain on the four-wheeler and is contentedly surveying his surroundings. I know that he will immediately alert me if something's not right.

Finally, we reach the base of the trail and I can see my A-frame through the trees and much to Stitch's delight I release him and he darts toward the house. Right now I'm living in a house that belongs to my dad. It's just a simple fishing cabin where we would spend summer weekends when Andrew and I were kids. For now, this is the perfect place for me. The remote location keeps me out of the bars, the dozens of windows let the light in and the river is just yards from my door.

I drive past three police cars and Jake's unmarked vehicle that are parked along the gravel road that runs right up to my driveway. I stop the four-wheeler next to my storage shed. I don't have a garage, just a covered car park where I keep my old Jeep. It's one of the few things I came into my marriage with that was completely my own and one of the few I left with. I thumb into place the correct numbers on the padlock in order to unlock the door to the shed, unload my board and paddle and set them inside next to my kayak, cross-country skies and snowshoes.

I drive the four-wheeler to where Evan

has constructed a garage-like structure from log-cabin wood. This is where he stores his four-wheelers, canoes, kayaks, life jackets and other outdoor gear. I know this because all summer I've seen the wannabe outdoorsmen and women emerge from behind the hewn logs with all manner of outdoor gear. They are dressed in their two-hundred-dollar hiking boots, neoprene bodysuits and GoPro cameras.

The garage is locked up tight so I leave the four-wheeler where I'll at least be able to keep an eye on it from my house. I may not want to be in a coffee klatch with my neighbor but I also don't want to be the one who let his four-wheeler get stolen.

I trudge back to my house, about a football field away. My muscles feel heavy and achy. I'm chilled through and all I want to do is take a hot shower and curl up on the couch with Stitch and a cup of coffee. I kick off my water shoes, unlock the front door and call to Stitch. *"Ke mne!"* Stitch comes to my side as I open the door, waiting for me to enter first.

I refill Stitch's water dish that I keep in the tiny laundry room right next to my stacked washer and dryer, peel off my damp clothes and drop them to the floor and push open the door that leads to the only bathroom in the house. If I end up getting this job, if I still have a chance considering I missed the interview, the first thing I'm going to do is gut this area so that I can have the biggest, most luxurious bathtub I can find. Right now all I have is a primitive shower, and no matter how much I bleach and scrub it, the mold and mildew always return, creeping ominously up the walls. I turn the water to full throttle and step beneath the showerhead, letting hot spray wash away the mud and dirt and the chill of my morning trek.

As my sore muscles relax under the stream of water I think back to the crime scene. I know that the police will probably want to interview me again about what I saw. Did I mention the beer bottle? I don't think I did. I know I didn't say anything about the extra set of footprints in the mud. Even though it will probably amount to nothing I should have mentioned it. The killer could have brought her through the thicket of prickly brambles, forced her over the piles of fallen timber. He could even have deposited her in the river somewhere upstream and she floated to the spot where I found her. None of these scenarios quite add up for me. Though Gwen was mostly submerged, the parts of her that were exposed — her face, her breasts, her feet, were remarkably unscathed.

What did that mean? That she came willingly with him and he killed her on the scene? That would make most sense if they had been a couple that had been hiking. But wouldn't there be another set of footprints? Surely there would be signs of some sort of struggle.

Unlike most showers, the water in mine doesn't gradually grow colder to let you know that the water heater isn't keeping up. Instead, it goes from scalding, which is how I like it, to frigid. Usually I have it timed perfectly so I exit the shower before the water turns to ice, but today I am so deep in my thoughts about my discovery, I lose track of time and the icy water pours over me in full force.

I slap the handle down and the flow stops. I step from the shower dripping wet, grab a towel from the dryer and wrap it round my midsection, then scurry up the steps to my bedroom that takes up the entirety of the second-floor loft. Teeth chattering, I stand in front of my open closet door where my interview outfit, still swathed in dry cleaner's plastic, hangs.

I reach into the closet past my interview outfit, hoping that I'll still get a chance to wear it, and snag a sweatshirt and a pair of jeans from the top shelf. I hastily dress, and as I blow-dry my hair I run my fingers over the thick scar, courteous of my hit-and-run driver, that runs nearly ear-to-ear just above the base of my skull. My hair still won't grow there but I'm able to cover it by keeping the top layers long.

Through my glass door I see that the dark clouds are swelling and heavy with moisture. It looks like the kids of Mathias will be trick-or-treating carrying umbrellas and wearing rain gear over their costumes. Not that I'm going to have any trick-or-treaters knocking on my door tonight. It's too rural, too remote out here. But I still put together a goodie bag and a few extra candy bars just in case David decides to bring Nora over so I can see her in her costume. I even slapped some of those window cling-on Halloween decorations in the shapes of ghosts and cobwebs and bats on my sliding glass door in a weak attempt to be festive.

Jake has a fit about my sliding door every time he comes to visit me. "Any half brain can break into one of these. It's a burglar's wet dream," he says. Soon after I moved in he brought me a broom with the bristles chopped off. "See, it fits perfectly," he said, laying the long, slender wooden handle in the metal track. "Unless an intruder breaks the glass, there's no way anyone is getting through this door. Promise me you'll put this in whenever you're home."

I promised, and have used the broom handle precisely zero times since. I insert the rod and tell myself that I'm doing so because Jake will most surely drop by later and give me hell if the door is not secured, but in actuality I'm spooked.

Once I'm sure that the dead bolt on the front door and each window is locked I sit down at my C-shaped kitchen counter that serves as my dining table and office area. Sitting on the Formica — a dated beige with a pale blue and brown boomerang pattern smattered throughout — is my laptop and phone. The captioned phone, a gift from my dad, allows me to have real-time phone conversations with others even though I can't really hear a word they are saying. The system scrolls the caller's words across the screen so I can see what is being said and I can answer as I always have when using a phone. It even translates into text any voice mail messages left when I'm away. Most of the time the phone sits idle except for my conversations with Nora, and my weekly calls with my dad and brother.

I have two pressing phone calls that I need

to make. The first to the center in hopes of rescheduling my interview, and then I need to call David. I'm not sure which call I dread the most. I find the number for the center, and after a few seconds the screen on the tabletop phone display reads "Five Mines Regional Cancer Center, this is Lori, how may I assist you?"

I take a deep breath. Though it's hard to explain, the anxiousness I feel when I speak into the receiver rivals that of having to sleep in a dark room. "Yes, hello," I begin, concentrating on modulating the volume of my voice and the enunciation of my words. "May I speak with Dr. Huntley?" Because I can't hear myself I don't know how loudly or softly I'm speaking. Usually I rely on clues from the facial expressions of the listener — like if they lean in to hear me better or if they cringe because I'm too loud for the situation. Talking by phone takes away those physical cues, making it impossible for me to know how I'm doing.

"Dr. Huntley isn't available right now. May I direct you to his voice mail?" the receptionist asks. My shoulders sag. I was hoping to speak to him in person. I want him to know just how much I want this job — how much I need this job. I agree and thank the receptionist, and after a minute the phone display invites me to leave a message for Dr. Huntley.

"Dr. Huntley, this is Amelia Winn. I'm so sorry about missing this morning's interview. I promise you it was for a very good reason and I'd really appreciate the opportunity to explain everything to you and hopefully reschedule our visit. Thank you. I look forward to hearing from you."

I leave my phone number, hang up and stare at the phone for several moments before I pick up the receiver again. I dial the number I know by heart. The number that once belonged to me too. This is the phone call I'm hoping will go straight to voice mail. There's a good chance that David is at the hospital but it could also be a day off for him. I'm not privy to his schedule anymore.

"Hello," the display reads and my stomach flip-flops.

"David?" I ask because the phone isn't able to identify who's speaking.

"It's me." Of course I can't gauge the emotion in his response but I imagine he's put on his clinical, slightly patronizing tone that he reserves for interns and people who have pissed him off.

"I can explain," I begin, but then stop. Will it even matter? Every move I've made, every word I've uttered in the last two years has been wrong. The display remains idle. I was once able to talk to David about anything. He's the smartest, most capable man I've ever met. He's an excellent ob-gyn, loved by his patients for his gentle bedside manner and well respected by his peers. But beyond that, what I love most about David is that at his core he's a good man. He would do anything to protect those he loves and there was a time when I was counted among that very small group.

"I was out paddle boarding this morning and something . . ." I hesitate. I know I'm not supposed to say anything but it's hard. David knew Gwen. She was my friend, a floater nurse at both hospitals who surely assisted David one time or another in the delivery room. The tragic irony, given Gwen's job and the fact that I found her floating in Five Mines, is not lost on me. "Something very bad happened. I couldn't get away in time for my interview with Dr. Huntley. I promise. I've already called the center and left him a message."

I pause, waiting for David to ask me if I'm okay, if I've been injured but no words appear on the screen. He is probably just relieved that I messed up before I even got the job — saves the trouble of Dr. Huntley having to fire me later and saves David some embarrassment. I ignore the twinge of hurt and plunge forward, determined to at least get my side of the story out. "I can't say anymore right now, David. It's a police matter."

"Fine, then." The words finally appear on the display. "I hope you get a second chance."

"Me too," I answer, and I think we both know I'm talking about much more than a chance at a clerical job. "How's Nora?" I ask.

"She's great." I imagine his voice rising with pride. "Parent-teacher conferences are next week. She can't wait to show off her classroom," he goes on to say. I want so badly to ask if I can come too. After all, for most of Nora's almost eight years, I was the one who organized and coordinated nearly every single event of her young life. I was the one who took Nora to her first day of kindergarten when David was stuck in a difficult delivery. I was the one who organized her birthday celebrations, baked each cake, wrapped each gift. I read her books before bed each night, put cartoon Band-Aids on her cuts and scrapes, held her when she woke up shaking from bad dreams. Of course I did. I'm her mother.

David doesn't invite me to teacher conferences any longer and I don't dare push it. I don't have any rights when it comes to Nora. Her birth mother, selfish, flighty and indifferent to her daughter, refused to give up parental rights even though David begged her to so that I could adopt her as my own and give Nora a real mother. But that's just how Trista is. She doesn't want the inconvenience of having a daughter but to be spiteful she says no to the one person who was thrilled to step into that role.

David, to his credit, after I promised him I had stopped drinking, has grudgingly allowed me to spend some time with Nora. Always in his presence, always in public.

"Can I call her later?" I ask. "I want to hear all about trick-or-treating and her costume."

"Yeah. How about around eight? We'll be back home by then."

"Thank you," I say, and then as an afterthought, add, "Watch the news tonight, David. It will explain a lot."

He doesn't say that he will or won't, but simply says goodbye and disconnects.

As I heat the kettle for tea, I toss a few pieces of kindling into the wood-burning stove. I have electric heat, but rarely have to turn it on. Twice a year I call an old friend of my dad's and he brings me enough wood to warm my home through the longest of winters. He stacks it behind the house and even covers it with a tarp to keep it dry. I settle into my mink-brown wide-wale corduroy–covered love seat and without invitation, Stitch squeezes in next to me and lays his whiskered chin on my lap. I leave my steaming mug of tea untouched on the side table next to me. I don't want to take the chance of spilling the scalding liquid on Stitch's head. Instead, I run my hand across his flank, my fingers catching on the burrs that have entwined themselves in his coat. Later, I will gently remove each, being extra careful not to yank the hair in the sensitive area around his scar. It wasn't until Stitch lived with me for a full year before he would fully expose his belly to me.

To the left of me, through another of my many windows, I have a clear line of sight to the four-wheeler I parked outside Evan Okada's outfitters. He must not have returned yet and I wonder if the officer has found any more articles of clothing that could possibly belong to Gwen.

I don't worry about missing the phone call from Dr. Huntley. I know the moment it rings, Stitch will alert me, as he has been trained to do. There is a narrow crack in the clouds that I know won't last long. I close my eyes, and the sun floods through the window so that instead of darkness behind my eyelids I see a warm amber glow and I can sleep.

4

Stitch wakes me with a poke and I immediately sit up and look to the telephone, but see no red flashing light to let me know it's ringing. Disoriented, I try to get my bearings. In the time I've been sleeping the sky has cleared and the sun has lowered but not quite dipped below the horizon, turning the sky a melancholy shade of blue. It must be nearing five o'clock. I've been asleep for hours. From the floor Stitch watches expectantly and when he's sure he has my attention he moves to the back door, and I startle when I see the hulking figure of a man standing there, hands shoved in his pockets. Right away I recognize that it is Jake, still dressed in his suit, and I blush, wondering how long he's been standing there watching me sleep.

I switch on a lamp, and he smiles smugly at me through the glass as I bend down to remove the wooden rod, then slide open the door. He steps inside, pauses to pet Stitch and slips off his dress shoes, thick with mud.

With a grin, Jake points to me and makes the sign for *tired* and I self-consciously fluff up my sleep-flattened hair. I don't know what it is about Jake but somehow I always revert back to that goofy kid who wants to impress her brother's best friend. He cuffs me on the shoulder and looks me in the eye. "How are you doing, Earhart?" he says, using the nickname he gave me back when I was eight and he was twelve and making the sign for *plane crash.* A gesture that is strikingly similar to the sign for *I love you.* I dressed up one Halloween as Amelia Earhart, the famed and ill-fated pilot, and the nickname stuck.

"I'm fine," I say. "I'm a nurse, Jake, I've seen dead people before."

"Yeah, but they usually don't pop up when you're casually paddling by."

"True," I admit. "But I really am okay. Were you able to get ahold of Gwen's husband?" I ask.

Jake's face sobers and he shakes his head.

"Do you think he did it?" I ask.

"It's usually the husband. So, yeah, chances are he did it, but we need to gather a hell of a lot more evidence before we settle on him."

I pick up my now room-temperature cup of tea and move to the sink to dump it out. "Want some coffee or tea?" I ask.

"Anything with caffeine would be great," he says when I turn back to face him. "I have a feeling I'm going to be up all night with this one." He follows me to the kitchen area and leans against the counter while I make the coffee.

"Do you think the shoe Stitch found belongs to Gwen?" I ask. I start the coffeemaker, hoping that the answer is no. It's bad enough knowing that Gwen died just a few miles away from me, but the thought that she might have been on the very trail that runs right up to my front door sends a chill through me. "It's an odd place to find a shoe," I say.

"It's an odd place to find a body," Jake says.

I tell him about seeing the beer bottle.

"Yeah, we saw that. We'll see if we can find any fingerprints, but it was probably just left there by some kids."

"What about footprints?" I ask. "I saw four sets. Mine, the DNR guy's, Stitch's paw prints and one more."

Jake taps the countertop with his fingers. "It was a muddy mess up there. But we tried to get casts of the prints. We'll see what comes of it. It could mean nothing. I guess whoever did this could have come by a different route."

I shake my head. "I've been through that area a thousand times. It'd be tough to force someone or carry them a different way. It's pretty rocky and woodsy."

"What are you thinking?" Jake asks, giving me his full attention. This is another thing I think is both great and confusing about Jake. Every once in a while he forgets that I'm his best friend's little sister and actually talks to me like I'm an intelligent human being. Other times he dismisses me as if I'm still an annoying kid.

"A motorboat was nearby just before Stitch found Gwen. The wake nearly knocked me off my board. Maybe he brought her there by boat and pushed her overboard there." This is a terrifying thought. Probably 75 percent of the households in Mathias own some kind of boat, including Jake, David and my neighbor Evan Okada. I rummage through my cupboard in hopes of finding something to offer Jake to eat. I pull down a box of crackers and then go to the refrigerator and find a block of cheddar cheese. "I guess he could have dumped her anywhere and the current brought her to where I found her. Do you have an idea of how she died yet?"

He shakes his head. "We'll have to wait for the autopsy." I pull a knife from a drawer and begin to slice the cheese into bite-size pieces. He pops one into his mouth and chews and swallows before speaking again. "I have my suspicions. It wasn't a peaceful death, that much I know."

"Does the press know yet?" I think about how I told David to watch the news tonight.

"Yeah, vultures," Jake says. I think of the turkey vultures flying overhead this morning. Had they already zeroed in on Gwen, ready to swoop in to pick away at her remains? "They must have heard it come over the scanner. By the time we transported the body to Mathias, the reporters were already at the dock waiting there with the ambulance."

"You moved her by boat?" I ask in surprise. "I thought you were moving her by OHV."

"Well, yeah," he says. "It was the fastest way. Took her in the DNR boat. Once we got to the public dock we transferred her to the ambulance. She's on her way to Des Moines for an autopsy as we speak. We should know more tomorrow afternoon." Stitch sits at my feet and I know he's waiting for me to toss him a cracker. I do, and he swallows it whole and waits for more.

"You shouldn't feed him that crap," Jake admonishes me. "It's not good for him."

"What? You never give Rookie treats?" I ask in mock disbelief. Rookie is Jake's former partner, a ferocious-looking German shepherd that would tear your throat out if Jake gave him the command. Rookie retired two years ago at the ripe old age of seven and now spends his days in full-fledged pet mode.

Jake doesn't bother answering. We both know that he only feeds Rookie the best. If a dog could be like a child to a person, Rookie's that dog. Jake's told me several times that Rookie saved his life more than once. The first was on the job when a suspect who had just robbed a pawnshop decided it was a good idea to start shooting. Jake, the second officer on the scene, arrived to find a veteran cop — Jake's mentor — lying in the street with a gunshot wound to the abdomen and the suspect holding a gun to the shop owner's head. Jake ducked behind his car, and was trying his damnedest to talk the man into giving up his weapon so he could get help to the injured cop. Instead, he started firing at Jake. Knowing that the officer was bleeding to death before his eyes, he ordered Rookie to *stellen* — to bite. Without hesitation, Rookie lunged toward the gunman, leaped through the air and latched onto the shooter's arm and didn't release until Jake commanded him to *pust* — let go.

The second time Rookie saved his life, Jake said, was after his wife, Sadie, committed suicide four years ago by leaping from the old train bridge into Five Mines. Though there was a witness who saw her jump they never found her body, just a splattering of blood from what was believed to be where she struck her head on the concrete piling below. She did leave a suicide note that Jake found lying on the kitchen counter later that night.

I'm sorry, Jake. I'm just so sad. Your life will be better without me. Love ~ Sadie

I've never seen Jake so distraught. My brother called and told me to go as fast as I could over to Jake's, that he was afraid Jake was going to hurt himself and that he'd be on the first plane from Denver. When I arrived at Jake's house I found him sitting on his back deck with his service revolver lying in his lap, Rookie at his feet. I remember the terror I felt when I saw the despondent look on his face — it was the face of someone who wanted to die. So different from the Jake I knew growing up. Jake was always the funny one who never let things get to him, could laugh at himself, defuse any tense situation.

I sat down in the chair next to him and put my hand over his. "Please don't," I whispered. He cried then. Great heaving sobs that I could never have imagined coming from the boy I once thought of as invincible. Rookie and I sat with him all night as he intermittently cried for, then raged against, the woman he loved. When he finally fell asleep, I eased the gun from his lap and hid it on a high shelf of the linen closet behind a stack of blankets. When I came back out to the deck, Rookie had squeezed into the spot next to Jake and nestled his head where the gun once lay.

Rookie gave Jake a reason to get up each morning and though it took a long time, about six months ago, glimmers of the Jake I used to know reappeared. He's smiling more and thinking of something else besides work. I've started to wonder if he might have met someone, may actually be dating again. I have to admit I'm not sure how I feel about this. What is happiness for someone mixed with a little jealousy called?

"Well, I'd better go feed Stitch his real

dinner," I say. "Help yourself to the coffee."

I go into the laundry room with Stitch at my heels and pull the bag of bargain brand dog food from a cupboard. I can't afford the good stuff for Stitch but he doesn't seem to mind and wags his tail while I scoop the kibble into his bowl. I can't bring myself to take any money from David right now. So for the last eighteen months that I've been living on my own, I've been living off my savings. My lawyer thinks I'm an idiot. Though I'm not too proud to take advantage of David's health insurance.

When I stand upright Jake is in the doorway, a serious look on his face, and for a moment I think it's because of my choice in dog food. "I have to go," he says, holding up his cell phone. "I just got the call. Someone was able to find Marty Locke."

"So it really is Gwen?" I ask. A part of me was hoping I was mistaken, that the woman in the river just looked like my old friend.

Jake points to himself, makes a fist against his chest and rotates it in a clockwise motion. "I'm sorry, Earhart," Jake says, coming to me and pulling me into a hug. And though I know it's completely platonic, another human being hasn't touched me this way in such a long time and the sensation seems foreign to me. His arms are strong and solid and all I want to do is to sink into his embrace but I know he has a job to do that could include telling a man that his wife isn't ever coming home. Jake takes a step back so I can see his face. "I'll call you when I can," he promises. "And remember you need to come to the station for a follow-up interview. How about tomorrow morning around ten?"

I agree and return to the kitchen where I pour his coffee into a stainless steel travel mug and walk him to the door.

Evening has fully descended and the world outside is buried in shadows. There are no stars shining, no moon, no light from Evan Okada's home. I wonder where he could be.

"Make sure you lock the door behind me," Jake says, taking the mug from my hand.

"I will," I assure him and watch as he strides purposefully to his car, unlocks the door, climbs in and turns the ignition. He lets the car idle for a moment and I realize he's waiting for me to shut and lock the door before he'll leave. I step back inside and slide the door shut. I make a point to waggle the broomstick in front of me and with great flourish place it in the door's track. Jake waves and drives away.

Before Evan Okada moved in, I never worried about anyone being able to see inside my house at night. I had no problem wearing my pajamas or less because my house was the last one on this section of the river and the house on the bluff stood empty for so long. Now I have to be conscious of the kayakers and hikers that have since discovered this little known part of Five Mines. I make the rounds, pulling each curtain shut and lowering each blind until the outside world disappears. Stitch has finished eating and follows me around as I tidy up the kitchen. I hand wash the dishes, put away the cheese and crackers. I sweep the cracker crumbs littered across the counter into my hand and let Stitch lick them away.

I can't stop thinking about Gwen.

I turn on the television and find a local channel. I rarely watch TV and when I do, it's mainly to catch up on what's happening beyond the walls of my house and practice my speech reading. I pull a pillow from the love seat, set it on the hardwood floor and sit as close to the television screen as I can. Stitch realizes that he gets the entire sofa to himself and climbs up and stretches his limbs across the cushions.

The bland sitcom I'm watching goes to a commercial and a breaking news banner fills the screen. The newscasters' faces are serious and I'm sure the story is going to be about Gwen. The closed caption ribbon scrolls across the bottom of the screen. Though I try to focus on the speakers' faces I still have to rely heavily on the captioning.

"A woman paddle boarding on the Five Mines River with her dog made a grisly discovery this Halloween morning," the newscaster begins. "We take you now to KFMI reporter Mallory Richmond at the Five Mines Marina for a live update on this very disturbing situation."

"That's right," the reporter says as she looks intently into the camera, "early this morning, a deaf woman and her service dog were paddle boarding just a few miles south of this very location when they stumbled upon the dead body of a yet to be identified woman floating in Five Mines." Behind her an American flag, illuminated by floodlights, whips wildly in the wind but somehow her perfectly straight blond hair remains in place. The screen flips to a video of an ambulance parked as close to the dock as possible, its back doors open wide.

Eagerly, I read the words crawling across the television screen. "Police spent the better part of the day at the actual crime scene collecting evidence. Officials aren't saying much but did confirm that the woman's remains were transported by a Department of Natural Resources boat and transferred to this awaiting ambulance, as you can see in the video." I watch as the DNR boat appears on screen and slowly makes its way to the dock.

As the boat comes closer I immediately recognize Jake with his broad shoulders and sandy hair. The DNR officer who was the first to arrive on the scene is steering the boat. His eyes widen when he realizes that a television camera is pointing directly at them. Jake, as calm as ever, simply ignores the reporters and busies himself with grabbing onto the dock to help guide the boat as close to the shore and ambulance as possible. Two EMTs dressed in their navy blue uniforms emerge from the ambulance, pull a stretcher from the rear, unfold the wheels and roll it down the dock.

The camera switches back to the reporter, who nods grimly into the camera, and I focus on her lips. "Police Detective Jake Schroeder, whom you saw in this video, had no comment, but sources close to the investigation have told me that the police department is looking at all missing person's cases."

The reporter signed off and the newscaster in the studio was speaking again. "Join us tonight for the ten o'clock news with more updates on this story along with the disturbing 9-1-1 call made by the woman who discovered the victim's body."

I groan, causing Stitch to heave himself from the couch and come and investigate. Even if they bleep out my name, if the news station plays the recording of the 9-1-1 tape all my friends and former colleagues will know it was me who made the call. I think it's safe to say that I'm the only deaf woman who owns a dog, paddle boards and lives on the banks of Five Mines. Stitch's ears perk up and he nudges my leg with his nose. I turn to look at what has caught his attention. The light on the phone is flashing and I hope it's Jake to tell me they caught the person who killed Gwen.

I reach for the receiver. "Hello," I say and watch the telephone display in anticipation.

"I just saw the news."

"Jake?" I ask.

"No, it's David. I just saw the news. You found her? The dead woman? Jesus, Amelia. Do they know who she is?"

I hesitate. I know I'm not supposed to say anything just yet. "I can't . . ." But this is

David I'm talking to. How can I keep this from him? David knew Gwen too — she worked at the same hospital, she filled in on the ob-gyn floor from time to time. "It's Gwen Locke, David, she was just identified, but it's not released to the public yet."

The screen is still for a moment. "That's horrible. Are they sure it's Gwen?"

"Yeah, I found her. It was awful." Tears creep into the corners of my eyes and I angrily swipe them away. I've cried too many times to David, begging him to forgive me, to take me back, only to be rejected over and over. I hate appearing weak in front of him.

"Jesus, Amelia, are you okay?"

"I'm fine." I'm surprised, touched even, that David would think to ask how I'm doing. He hasn't done that in a very long time. I try to remember his voice, the warm timbre that greeted me each day when he came home from the hospital, his soft laugh that made me laugh too. Suddenly I'm almost unbearably homesick for the old house. So much so that I almost tell David that I'm terrified of staying here in this house by myself even though that's not exactly the truth.

I miss the sunny kitchen where Nora and I would make cinnamon rolls and monkey bread for Sunday morning breakfasts. I miss the front porch where on summer afternoons I would sit on the wooden swing reading books and drinking iced tea while Nora colored and sipped lemonade. I miss waking up in my old bed, my limbs entwined with my husband's. "I'm fine," I repeat, more for my benefit than for David's.

"Do they know who did it?" he asks.

"No, not yet. But there was a boat, right around the time I found her."

"You saw it?" David asks. "Amelia, what if they saw you?"

"No, no," I hurry to explain. "I didn't see it, I just felt it. The wake knocked me down."

"Thank God for that," David says, and again I'm pleasantly surprised with David's concern for me but there's no way I'm going to let him know I care.

"Is Nora around?" I change the subject. "Can I talk to her?"

"She's here. You can talk to her. Just don't say anything about . . . you know. She doesn't know about any of this and I don't want to upset her."

“Of course I won’t say anything.” I’m indignant. Why in the world would I tell a seven-year-old about a corpse that I discovered? I wait impatiently for Nora to get on the line. Talking to her is the highlight of my days. Our conversations are never frequent or long enough.

“Hello?”

“Hi, Nora,” I say. “How was trick-or-treating?”

Nora goes on to tell me about her Frida Kahlo costume. “Daddy helped me find the perfect outfit and his friend helped me put real flowers in my hair.”

I feel like someone has sucker punched me in the gut. “What friend?” I try to ask casually but I can barely choke out the words.

“Helen,” Nora says but rushes on. “But I had to tell everyone who I was, except some old lady. She knew exactly who I was dressed up as. She said my unibrow looked real.” Nora loves art and would check out piles of books about artists from the library. That, and she had a magnificent art teacher in school who made sure that even the youngest of students were exposed to the great artists.

"Did Helen go trick-or-treating with you?" I ask.

"No, she had to go to work. She's a nurse like you." *Way to mix things up, David,* I think. David could date any woman in Mathias and he has to pick another nurse. I scan my memory for any nurses named Helen that I might know, but come up blank.

Nora goes on to describe her day at school. How she loves her homeroom teacher but that her music teacher is kind of grouchy. She talks about the new boy in her class that makes fun of her freckles and she mentions the math test that she missed four questions on.

Sometimes I hate this phone and wonder if I'd be better off not having it at all. All I have are the printed words of the conversation — I can't hear the emotion in her voice. I have no context. I don't know if Nora is pleased that the new boy teases her — maybe he likes her. I don't know if missing four questions on the math test is a good or bad thing. So I have to ask her and pretty soon the conversation has stalled and Nora is ready to hang up because, I think to myself, shouldn't a mom *know* these things — just be able to know how her daughter is feeling?

"Bye, Mom. Love you."

My eyes fill with tears again. "I love you too, Nora. I'll call you tomorrow."

I wait for a moment before hanging up in case David wants to speak to me again but no new words sweep across the screen so I replace the receiver. I think about what Nora said about David's friend Helen. Could he really have a girlfriend? We've been apart for a long time. It still shocks me that David hasn't had divorce papers delivered to my house for me to sign.

For the next two hours I sit in front of the television and watch some old movie but all the while I keep thinking of Gwen. We were good friends once. But that was before I got hit by the car, before I lost my hearing and abandoned my family and friends for alcohol. Gwen and I both grew up in Mathias, though I'm several years older. Our paths didn't cross until we were both nurses at Queen of Peace. She's what is called a floater nurse. She goes to wherever the action is in the hospital. If the emergency room is overflowing or maternity is bursting at the seams, she's there to assist. She was bubbly and a bit irreverent in the break room but the minute she stepped out on to the floor she became no-nonsense and unflappable.

We went through the sexual assault nurse examiner training together. During the workshops we learned how to assess and evaluate the injuries of sexual assault. We were also trained in the collection and packaging of forensic evidence from the crimes.

We bonded during the breaks and chatted about our lives. We had daughters the same age — Nora and Lane. We talked about our husbands and how challenging it could be balancing home life and nursing. During the first domestic violence case that we worked together, I was the on-call SANE nurse and was summoned to the Queen of Peace to collect the evidence. Gwen was also there, covering a shift in the emergency room. The victim, a thirty-year-old mother of two, was so distraught, striking and lashing out at the EMTs who brought her in that she managed to kick one of them squarely in the face, causing a fountain of blood to erupt from his nose. Gwen somehow managed to calm the badly beaten woman with her low, soothing voice while I collected the evidence.

Our friendship was sealed that night. Though after the fact the injured woman insisted that she fell down the steps, the evidence I was able to gather clearly showed that she was beaten with a leather belt, sending the husband to jail at least for a few days. Gwen and I talked every day after that. We met for coffee once a week, set up playdates for our girls. Then I was injured, started drinking and lost touch with just about everybody. About six months ago, though, Gwen had left me a phone message. When I read the transcript I found it to be just a regular, run-of-the-mill, "how're you doing, we haven't talked in a while" message. I hadn't bothered to call her back.

I have so many regrets. If only I hadn't taken that first drink to deaden the pain of being plunged into sudden silence. Which sounds so selfish now. It wasn't just losing my hearing, it was the loneliness that came with it, the sense of always being separate, apart from everyone I loved. What I wouldn't give to go back in time and make different choices.

Once the movie credits start, Stitch moves to the door and looks at me expectantly. My cue that he needs to go outside. I go through the whole rigmarole of opening the curtains, removing the wooden stick and sliding open the glass door. Stitch dashes outside and spends an inordinately long time doing his business. The air is heavy with the scent of oncoming rain. Rainstorms in the fall have a scent that is uniquely their own. A fetid, moldy, earthen smell. As if their sole purpose is to urge the remaining flora and fauna that it's time to rest, covering them in a soggy blanket and tamping them down close to the earth, which is ready to claim them for the winter.

I consider staying up to watch the ten o'clock news and see if they actually air my 9-1-1 call, but I really don't want to see my frantic words emblazoned across the screen. I turn off the television and toss a few more pieces of wood into the stove before I call Stitch back in. Despite my long nap and even though it's only a little bit after eight, I'm exhausted. I switch off the main floor lights, and Stitch and I head upstairs. I slip under the covers and Stitch takes his usual spot at the foot of the bed.

As conflicted as I am about how I feel about David, I miss turning over at night and finding his solid, comforting form right next to me. When David and Nora came into my life, I was the one who willingly, without question, opened my arms to them when they were at their lowest point. I was more of a mom to Nora in the last six years than her biological mother ever was and though legally David doesn't have to, he still lets me see her. Supervised of course. I miss, no matter how late we'd get home from the hospital, how David and I always made sure to kiss the other good-night and say I love you. Our little ritual.

I try to shake away the past. It does no good to mourn what was. All I have is the here and now, no matter how meager. But in the here and now, I hate nighttime. The absence of sound combined with the absence of light is terrifying. Now, just like I do every night before I go to sleep, I make sure my flashlight is in my bedside table drawer where it should be and I make sure my cell phone is fully charged and within hand's reach. My little ritual. Only now, with lights blazing and Stitch nearby am I able to close my eyes and rest.

5

I wake to Stitch's paw raking down my back. I roll over to my side. My bedside lamp is still burning and the clock reads twelve thirty. The sliver of black sky that I see between a gap in the blinds lets me know it's still the middle of the night. I squint up at Stitch who, for good measure, paws at me one more time, leaps from the bed and waits for me in the doorway.

Based on Stitch's training, I'm pretty confident that one of four things could have caused him to rouse me from a dead sleep: the phone is ringing, someone is at the door, the house is on fire or Stitch *really* has to go to the bathroom. I rarely get visitors or phone calls during the day, let alone at night, and I don't smell smoke, so I'm guessing that Stitch needs to go outside.

I groan and blearily follow Stitch down the steps, turning on lights as I go. Stitch makes a beeline for the sliding glass door and takes a seat. This small action causes me to freeze in place.

Communication between a person and their service dog is built on the ability to interpret the thousands of different nuances in each other's movements. If Stitch needed to go outside he would have simply stood by the door. When he sits I know that someone is standing on the other side.

My pulse quickens. Who would be knocking at twelve thirty in the middle of the night? Maybe it's Jake and he has some news about Gwen's murder or maybe someone is here to tell me that something bad has happened to Nora or my brother or dad. My stomach clenches at the thought, and then I notice the way the hair on Stitch's scruff is standing at attention and that he is warily eyeing the slight sway of the drapes moving back and forth.

In his excitement has Stitch bumped the curtains, causing the movement? My eyes slide to where the broomstick stands in the corner where I left it earlier. I must have forgotten to return it to the metal track when I was getting ready for bed.

Stitch's jaws are opening and closing wildly. Something is out there. Or someone. Cautiously, I push aside the drapes and peek out into the darkened yard. I can't see a thing. I unlock the door and slowly slide it open. Stitch wriggles through the small gap and dashes out into the rainy night.

"Stitch," I call. *"Ke mne!"* He doesn't comply. *"Ke mne!"* I yell again. I'm torn. I should go after him but the night is all encompassing and it's so dark that the weak light from above the door only spills a few feet into the yard, but I'd feel a hell of a lot safer if Stitch was back inside the house with me.

I step outside. The concrete steps are rough and cold beneath my feet. A soft mist dampens my skin. "Stitch," I call into the blackness. I have no idea which direction he's run off to and if I'm going to go find him I'm going to need to get dressed and put some shoes on.

I go back inside and set the wooden stick into its place. How could I have forgotten to do this before I went to bed? I'm disgusted with myself. I press my face against the glass and strain my eyes for any sign of Stitch. Nothing. I should call the police, but the thought of my home being overrun by officers probing and prying makes my stomach roil. *A woman was murdered,* a small voice in my head chastises me — as if I could forget. What if the killer figured out that I was the one to find Gwen? What if he thinks that I know more than I do? What if he saw the news report of my call to 9-1-1 and figured out who I was? Again, how many deaf women live along Five Mines? It wouldn't take much for someone to figure out it was me. What if he crept through my yard and was going to try to break in and Stitch scared him off?

Keeping my eye on the door, I move slowly backward toward the telephone. I don't want to turn around to pick up the phone and dial but I have to be able to see the display in order to communicate. Reluctantly, I turn and with shaking hands dial. It seems to take forever but finally a string of letters appears across the telephone display. "Dtrenkltve Shrader, this butter begud."

My transcribing service is pretty reliable, but not even the best could easily translate the mumblings of a man wakened from a dead sleep. "Jake, it's Amelia," I say. "I think someone tried to break into my house."

My words startle Jake fully awake and the display is easy to read. "Jesus, Amelia. Are you okay? Did you call 9-1-1?"

"I'm fine. And no, I called you first. I didn't want to make a big deal out of it. It's probably nothing."

"You should have called, they'd probably be

at your house by now," he says, and though I can't actually hear him I imagine he's more than a little irritated.

"I thought maybe you could come over? Not make a big deal out of it. It's probably nothing."

"You found a woman's body, there's nothing crazy about being freaked out about it. I'll be right there, but I'm going to call a car to meet me at your house. So don't be surprised when a squad car shows up. You got your doors locked?"

"Stitch got out and ran after something and hasn't come back yet. But the doors are locked now," I say, knowing that sooner or later I am going to have to tell him how I had forgotten to properly secure the door. "See you soon. And thanks, Jake."

"No problem, Earhart. You sure know how to keep things interesting around here. And don't even think about going out and looking for Stitch. Stay in the house."

I hang up, go to the laundry room and slip on my neoprene shoes, then go back to the glass door. Still no Stitch. Jake's order to stay in the house echoes in my head and I decide to go upstairs to my bedroom, open a window and holler for him from the safety of the second floor. Unless the possible intruder is some evil comic book villain, I don't think he would scale the roof to get to me.

I hurry up the stairs, unlatch and open the window that overlooks my front yard. Cold air instantly fills the room and a wet, loamy smell fills my nose. The higher vantage point doesn't help. If anything the horizon seems blacker, as if the earth and sky have become one.

"Stitch," I call, somewhat hesitantly at first as if I'm afraid to wake someone. But Evan Okada is my only neighbor for miles and frankly, I don't give a damn if I wake him up. *"Ke mne,"* I shout so loudly this time that I feel the words vibrating in my throat. *"Pojd sem!" Go inside.* I search the yard, hoping for a glimpse of Stitch's silvery coat. Nothing.

But in the distance, atop the bluff, a light appears in a second-floor window of Evan's house. I keep shouting and another light pops on, this one in a downstairs room. I'm hoping that I will cause such a ruckus that Evan will turn on his floodlights. The more light the better.

"Stitch, here! *Ke mne!*" I yell over and over until at last the outdoor security lights illuminate Evan's yard and the naked trees stripped bare of leaves from the wind and rain. There's still no sign of Stitch, which means he's either out of hearing range or purposely ignoring me. Though he's been trained to stick to my side, to follow my commands, he is still a bit flighty and stubborn. During our training, I asked Vilem how long it normally takes for him to work with a client and their new service dog. He hesitated and because I couldn't understand what he was saying through his thick Slovakian accent, he wrote it down. "Usually placement training is three to five days." I looked over at Stitch who was stalking a cottontail placidly chewing on clover. We were on day seventeen. "Don't worry," Vilem wrote in his spidery scrawl, "you two were made for each other."

Right now I'm not so sure about that.

My house is about a twenty-five minute drive from Mathias and it feels like an eternity for the police car to arrive. Futilely, I keep calling out and scanning the bluff for Stitch. The soft rain has turned into a drizzle, lightly splashing through the window screen and dampening my cheeks.

From the direction of the woods I see a light slowly bobbing through the tree trunks. A flashlight. I first think that it must be

Evan Okada coming down the bluff to see what all my yelling is about but I quickly discard that idea when his floodlights are extinguished. My stomach drops. Evan must have realized the sounds he heard are just from his crazy next-door neighbor and decided to go back to bed. I fight the urge to holler again in hopes that he'll come back outside.

The light is coming closer and closer. It has to be someone else. The murderer? Did whoever kill Gwen think I saw more than I actually did? Fear pounds a steady beat in my temple. I'm just about to yell out the window that the police are coming, that they will be here any second but stop myself. I don't want him disappearing into the woods. I want the police to catch this guy.

I settle on calling Jake again, but before I can go back down the stairs, cherry-colored flashing lights announce the arrival of the police cruiser. My eyes swing to the ever brightening cone of light from the flashlight now at the border of the woods. I can see the shadowy figure of the person holding the light but I can't tell if the owner is male or female, young or old. The light goes still and then disappears.

The police car pulls up to the house and

idles. Could the person in the woods be getting ready to ambush the officers? More likely than not, the arrival of the police scared him off and that's when I realize that whoever is there can see me too. I'm standing in my bedroom window with my lights blazing. I step away from the window and switch off the light.

By the time I get downstairs the officers are at my door, shoulders hunched, rapping on the glass window. The officer knocking on the door is tall and slim. His department-issued jacket stretched tight against his shoulders has the name *Bennett* embroidered in the fabric. His partner, with a jacket that says *Cole,* is two heads shorter and a hundred pounds lighter. They are both wearing waterproof jackets and hats to shield them from the rain. Both have a bored, "we got called out to the middle of nowhere for nothing" look on their faces. I remove the wooden pole from the track, unlock the door and slide it open.

"My dog started barking. Took off after someone," I explain. "He's still out there," I say, pointing in the direction of where I last saw the beam from the flashlight. "He has a flashlight and when he saw you, he turned it off." The officers turn away from me and look to the woods. "I'm the one who found the woman in the river," I say, and Cole's face shifts as if keen interest takes over. Bennett, if possible, looks even more skeptical. His lips slide into a dismissive smirk. I'm sure he's telling his partner that I'm just overreacting, jumping at every little sound. Cole shakes her head and gestures excitedly toward the trees. Because they aren't directly facing me I really have no idea what they are saying but I'm guessing she's telling Bennett that this might be their chance to nab a murderer. I wish Jake would get here.

"Please," I say, "I can't hear you. You have to look at me when you talk."

Cole turns back to face me. "Stay here, ma'am. Lock your door. We're going to check things out." I watch as they walk to their cruiser where Cole reports something over the radio and Bennett grabs a high-powered flashlight before they head off toward the woods. Soon they have melted into the trees and are completely out of sight. I slide the door shut. Instead of laying down the wooden rod, I hold on to it while I wait for Jake to arrive. I figure I can always use it as a weapon if I have to.

I try to call Jake again but there is no answer. I pace the floor, pausing periodically to look out the window to see if Stitch has returned. It's pouring now and I can't help but think of Stitch outside in the wet and cold. Even at his most mischievous, he's never been away from me this long.

Finally, the glow of headlights appears and an SUV pulls up next to the police car. Jake has arrived and he's brought along Rookie. If I didn't already know Rookie pretty well I'd be scared shitless. He's a beast with sharp eyes and even sharper teeth. I slide open the door, and Jake and Rookie step inside, drenched from the short trip from the car.

"You okay?" he asks me again for the second time in just a few hours.

I nod. "Hold on," I say and go to the laundry room where I grab two towels from the dryer. When I return I hand Jake the towels and he rubs his head dry. "Where're Cole and Bennett?" he asks, then bends down to wipe the mud from Rookie's paws.

"I saw someone in the woods with a flashlight. They went after him."

Jake shakes his head. "They shouldn't have left you here all by yourself. They should have waited until I got here." A muscle twitches in Jake's jaw and I know he's angry. The two officers are in for an earful when they return. I almost feel sorry for them. Jake looks around the room. "Did

Stitch come back yet?"

"No, he's still out there," I say and another wave of worry washes over me.

"You opened the door?" Jake signs. Rookie lifts his head, suddenly alert, his amber eyes wary.

We both glance at the broomstick I'm still holding. To his credit, Jake doesn't say anything. The last thing I need is a lecture.

"Did Bennett and Cole check the house?" Jake asks.

"No one got in." I shake my head. "Stitch just heard or saw something outside."

"Jesus," he says. He begins to move through the cabin, checking each room, looking for any sign of an intruder. He flings aside drapes, looks in closets and behind the shower curtain. I follow him up the steps and into my bedroom.

He gets down on his hands and knees and checks beneath my bed. When he's sure no one is lying in wait, he gets up and sits on the edge of the mattress and looks at me grimly. It's strange having him in the room where I'm at my most vulnerable. The one place I seem to be able to rest. He's never been in this room before. Not since we were kids anyway. And then we were young and innocent and the only thing Jake was interested in was getting out on the river to fish.

"I'm calling for more backup," he says when we reach the bottom of the steps. As he digs into his pocket for his cell phone, I grab his arm. Three figures stand outside my door. Flanked on either side by Officers Cole and Bennett is my neighbor Evan Okada. All three are soaking wet and covered with mud. Evan's hands are cuffed behind his back, there's a deep cut above his eyebrow and his right eye is nearly swollen shut. It didn't appear that my neighbor surrendered willingly.

Through the glass door, Cole says something. I look to Jake to translate for me. "She wants to know if this is the intruder."

"I never saw anyone," I explain. "But this is Evan Okada, my neighbor. He's the one who lent you his four-wheelers today. Why would he try and break into my house?"

"I'm going to open the door," Jake signs. "He's cuffed, so you don't have anything to be scared of."

Of all the emotions that could be scrambling through my brain right now, fear isn't one of them. Confusion is at the top of my list.

"Go ahead," I say, crossing my arms in front of my chest, conscious of the fact I'm not wearing a bra. Jake slides the door open and an arctic blast of air rushes in. If anyone is looking scared at the moment it's Evan Okada. His black hair is plastered to his head and his uninjured eye is wide with alarm. Water intermingled with blood is running down his face in pink rivulets. He looks at me pleadingly and begins to speak, his mouth moving so rapidly that I have no idea what he's saying. Bennett elbows him in the ribs, and Evan's mouth shuts into a tight grimace. Cole begins to speak and I turn to Jake, who does his best to translate for me.

"They found him at the edge of the woods over there moving away from your house. He didn't stop when they ordered him to so they grabbed him."

"You're not going to arrest him, are you?" I ask in alarm.

I watch as Jake says something to Cole and Bennett. With a hand on each of Evan's elbows they lead him to the squad car and unceremoniously insert him in the backseat. Whoever ends up having to clean the mud off the interior of their car has quite the job in front of them.

"I don't believe it," I say as they drive away.

"How well do you know this guy?" Jake asks, his brow furrowing with concern.

"We just met the other day," I explain. "I

really don't think . . ." Just then a silver flash darts through the open door and skids across the linoleum floor, leaving a streak of mud in his wake. Stitch has come back. Rookie stands and begins barking, teeth flashing, his tail tucked and his ears pressed flat against his head. I'm certain that Rookie is about to tear Stitch's throat out. I'm transfixed by the ferocity of the dog that just a moment ago was dozing languidly by the fire.

Jake turns toward the frenzied dog and suddenly Rookie's posture completely changes. His jaws close and he drops to the floor, his tail waving lazily back and forth. For his part, Stitch, whose wet, silver coat clings to his bony frame, is shaking uncontrollably. I kneel down at his side.

"Where were you?" I murmur into his ear. "Bad dog, bad." I scold him, but tenderly, tears pricking at my eyes.

Jake turns his back to me and gives me a moment to compose myself. That's one of the great things about Jake, he knows when to leave well enough alone. He knows how attached to Stitch I've become, how much I rely on him not only as a service dog but as a companion. After all, he can relate. After Sadie leaped from Five Mines Bridge, Rookie did the same for him.

He hands me the damp towel he used to dry his own head and I begin to softly rub Stitch's fur dry. Fine-spun scratches line his already scarred belly as if he had been running through thorny thickets. Had he been chasing Evan Okada through the woods? Or someone else? The thought that Evan really could have been lurking outside my house makes no sense to me.

When Stitch's fur is somewhat dry and his tremors cease, I stand. Another pair of officers arrives and we watch while they dust the sliding glass door for fingerprints. For some reason this makes everything seem too real to me, and tears burn my eyes. If Jake notices, he thankfully doesn't say anything. He knows I hate to cry. Once when we were kids I fell off my bike while trying to keep up with Jake and my brother and ended up dislocating my elbow. As if put out, Jake and Andrew stopped to help me and though I was in excruciating pain I didn't cry, but simply climbed back up on my bike and on wobbly legs, holding my injured arm close, pedaled home. Jake's expression of admiration when he saw my cast and his exclamation of, *That had to hurt like hell, Earhart. Why didn't you tell us?* made it all worthwhile.

"I should get to the station and see what's

going on with your neighbor," Jake says. "You sure know how to attract the crazies, don't you?" I respond with a sour smile. His face grows serious and his blue eyes bore into mine. "You get some rest, okay, Earhart? I'll call you tomorrow and give you an update." He turns to go and Rookie gets to his feet. Stitch eyes him warily, keeping his distance. Jake pauses and turns back to me. "You want to come back to my place? Just for the night? I won't even be there, but if you'd feel safer, you can crash in my guest room." I'm pretty good at figuring out facial expressions but I can't quite figure out what I see on Jake's face. Hope? Maybe pity.

I shake my head, caught off guard at how much I really want to say yes, but instead say, "No thanks. We're good here. But, Jake, I really don't think it was my neighbor." I tell him about how I saw the light go on in Evan's second-floor window after I found my door open. "I don't even know if anyone was really out there. Stitch just freaked out and I got scared. I think maybe I made a lot of fuss over nothing."

"We'll check it out. In the very least, he shouldn't have tried to run from Bennett and Cole." Jake signs. "I'm still going to have a patrol car park outside your house the rest of the night."

"That's really not necessary," I protest, but Jake gives me a look that says it isn't up for discussion.

Stitch and I watch Jake and Rookie leave, one happily, the other reluctantly. I slide the broomstick into its place on the metal track at the base of the door and close the curtains. I spend a few minutes rubbing Stitch's still-damp coat and when I realize that it will take me all night to dry his fur this way I give up and go grab my hair dryer. I sit on the couch with Stitch on the floor between my legs as I blow-dry his coat. Stitch is in heaven. He closes his eyes and revels in the warm stream of air washing over him.

The glare of headlights filters through the drapes, and I peek out to see a patrol car parked in front of the house. Confident that we're safe for the night, Stitch and I climb the steps to the bedroom. This time, instead of settling himself at the foot of my bed like he usually does, Stitch noses his way beneath the covers and curls up into a tight ball right next to me. Gradually, he relaxes and I can feel the gentle rise and fall of his chest as he drifts off to sleep.

For me, sleep doesn't come so easily. Why was Evan skulking around my house in the pouring rain? Was he just trying to be a good neighbor and checking up on me, or was he up to something? If it was all just a mix-up I will swallow my pride and tell him I'm sorry. Hell, maybe I'll even bake him some lemon squares. Despite the heat from Stitch tucked up right next to me, I can't get comfortable and I know that sleep will be a long time coming.

6

I awaken with a fragment of restless dreams still swirling around my head. A familiar anxiety has wrapped itself around my chest and I'm reluctant to leave the warmth of my bed, but Stitch is looking at me expectantly.

The chaos of the day before must have worn the two of us out because neither Stitch nor I stir until nearly nine o'clock. I go to the window to see if the police officer that Jake posted outside my house is still here. He's not. Either the police think that I was jumping at shadows or Evan Okada was the perpetrator. Though I only met Evan briefly, I have a hard time believing that he could be a killer, let alone my intruder.

We are both moving extra slow this All Soul's Day morning. My muscles are achy, I think, due to my tumble to the ground after finding Gwen in the river. I'm hesitant to let Stitch outside, afraid that he might take off into the woods again. So I do something I have rarely done and only in public places since Stitch first came into my life. I clip a leash to his collar. His silver eyes look up at me in reproach. "I'm sorry," I tell him, but he seems deflated as I lead him out into the yard.

When we come back inside my phone is flashing and I rush to answer it. "We had to let your neighbor go," Jake says by way of greeting. "We didn't have enough evidence to hold him. He swears up and down that he heard barking and yelling coming from your house and just came down the bluff to see what was going on."

"Do you believe him?" I ask.

"Yeah, I believe him. There was no sign of an attempted break-in, no footprints. And Okada wasn't exactly dressed for breaking and entering when Bennett and Cole nabbed him. He was wearing flannel pajama bottoms and a white sweatshirt. Not what I'd call cat burglar attire. Not that his sweatshirt is white anymore. When he didn't respond to the order to stop right away, Cole and Bennett tackled him in the mud. Okada said once he saw that the police arrived, he figured things were under control and he was heading back up to his house. Said he couldn't hear the order because of the noise from the heavy rain."

"That's kind of what I figured," I say. "So you don't think I have anything to worry about with him right next door to me? What about his outdoor lights? Why did they go off when he was coming down the bluff?"

"They're motion sensitive lights. They go off after a few minutes and that's what he says happened," Jake explains. "It looks like he's exactly who he says he is. A former dot-com guy who wanted to start his own canoe rental business. I don't think you have a thing to worry about, but just in case, I gave him a good talking-to. I think it is safe to say that he won't dare look sideways at you anytime soon."

Great. Welcome to the neighborhood, I think. "So you don't think anyone was out there? You think I overreacted?" I ask, heat rising to my cheeks.

"You've been through a lot," Jakes says. "It's understandable that you'd be a little jumpy. Stitch probably just heard an animal outside and took off after it."

I groan. "Don't worry about it, Earhart, it's our job. Just make sure to keep your doors locked." Jake and I say our goodbyes.

The temperature is warmer than fore-casted and for a moment I consider taking my board out on the river again, but then dismiss the idea. The journey would be too unnerving and I wonder if Five Mines will always conjure this same fear and uneasiness and cease to be the lifesaving respite it has come to be for me. I'm a trauma nurse. *Was* a trauma nurse. And I always prided myself in handling the most stressful, unpredictable of scenarios and now my dog chases a squirrel in the woods and I freak out.

My tongue suddenly tingles for a drink. I miss the first frosty bite of liquid and the slow burn as the alcohol slides down my throat. Normally, I take Stitch out onto the river or into the woods when I get these cravings but I may have to come up with a different means of distraction for a while.

I let Stitch outside and double-check the answering machine. I know the clinic is open six days a week and I'm hoping there will be a message from Dr. Huntley about rescheduling our interview. Nothing. The urge to retrieve the bottle from beneath the bathroom sink is overwhelming and I know what I have to do and it can't wait until Monday.

I scoop dog food into Stitch's dish and fill the other one with fresh water before jumping into the shower. I manage to wash and rinse my hair before the hot water runs out.

I blow-dry my hair and try to smooth it into submission. Stitch has finished eating and watches me curiously as I dig out my makeup case. For the first time in months, I rub foundation over my skin, swirl blush on my cheeks, line my eyelids with liner, sweep mascara across my lashes and dab on red lipstick. I stare at my reflection in the mirror. I look clownish and in frustration wash my face. I start over, this time adding only the mascara and lip gloss. Much better, I decide.

Back upstairs I dress in my interview outfit — a gray skirt that hits me just above the knees, a white silk shell and a gray jacket that matches the skirt. I slide on panty hose, remembering how much I hate wearing them, and step into the only pair of high heels I own. On the floor of my closet is a colorful pair of running shoes that makes me think of the shoe that Stitch found in the woods yesterday. My stomach rumbles and I know I should eat something before I leave. Unaccustomed to walking in heels, I carefully walk down the steps and grab a granola bar from the kitchen, tossing it into my purse. At the door I bend down so I'm at eye level with Stitch, not an easy task in these shoes. "I'm sorry, you'll have to stay here," I tell him. Stitch doesn't believe me.

His tail wags happily and he crowds more closely to the door. I rarely go anywhere without Stitch, but this outing is the exception. I need Dr. Huntley to focus on me and me only. I need to convince him I'm ready to return to work. "No, Stitch," I say more firmly. *"Kotec." Kennel.*

Stitch's tail sags but he complies and slowly goes to his kennel that sits beneath one of the living room windows. "I'm sorry," I say. He goes in the kennel headfirst, turns around and flops down on the quilt that lines the bottom, and then lays his head on his paws. I never shut and lock the kennel door. Once I leave, Stitch will emerge from the kennel and lie down in a sunbeam, rising occasionally to follow it as it slowly makes its way across the floor.

I exit the back door, taking the time to lock it securely behind me. I feel exposed, being outside without Stitch. He is my ears and a second set of eyes for me. I'm afraid even though it's unlikely that Gwen's killer is nearby. I swivel my head from side to side, trying to take in the entirety of my surroundings. Each sway of a branch, each leaf skittering across the yard briefly snags my attention and by the time I climb into my Jeep and lock the door I'm sweating. As predicted, Stitch has already left his kennel and is watching me from a window. I give him a wave, start the car and pull onto the road that will eventually take me to Mathias.

From my gravel road I turn right onto Highway 51, a pretty length of thoroughfare lined with sugar maples on one side, the last of their crimson leaves hanging on for dear life, and cornfields on the other. Soon the fields and trees turn to an industrial strip lined with gas stations, a furniture store and a smattering of fast-food restaurants. I travel through four sets of traffic lights before taking a left into a sparse residential neighborhood filled with once stately colonials that when I was growing up were populated by Mathias's elite. Now most of the colonials have been sectioned off into apartments rented out by young families just starting out or by college students who attend Dewey, a small, private university. I pass an elementary school, take a right onto Clover Street and head up a steep hill that is hell to maneuver in the winter. At the very end of the dead-end street overlooking a breathtaking view of the city and the river is Five Mines Regional Cancer Center. Made of native limestone, it's an unassuming one-story building that could be mistaken for an insurance office or a dentist's office.

This is it, I tell myself. My chance to finally return to the world of the living. I need this job. I need to prove to David and Nora that the woman and mother they once knew is back. I need to prove it to myself.

With a deep breath I walk up the path, slippery from the night's rain and push my way through the double glass doors to an entryway and through another set of doors that takes me into a large reception area currently empty of patients. The walls are painted a soothing taupe, and matted and framed black-and-white photos of the river hang on the walls. Whoever designed the room was going for living room chic and actually succeeded quite well. Comfortable-looking chairs are clustered around coffee tables stacked with magazines and vases filled with fresh flowers. Instead of harsh fluorescent overhead lights, table lamps glow softly atop side tables. At one end of the room is a station where patients can pour themselves a cup of coffee or water from a pitcher filled with ice cubes and sliced lemons.

I approach the woman behind the main desk. She is sixtyish with a severely angled bob dyed an unnatural shade of black. She is slim and capable-looking. "Good morning," she says as I read her brightly painted lips. "May I help you?"

I try to push away the anxiety that always comes when I have to interact with new people, with people who don't know me, who aren't aware of my hearing loss. "I'm Amelia Winn," I say, and the woman's eyebrows rise in recognition. "I wasn't able to make it to my appointment with Dr. Huntley yesterday but I'm hoping to be able to visit with him this morning. Is he in?"

"Oh, yes," she says. "I'm Barb, Dr. Huntley's office manager. I'll go see if he's willing to meet with you."

Ouch. I can tell Barb runs a tight ship here and has a long memory. If I get the job I think it's going to take a long time for Barb to forgive me for missing my first interview. She returns after a moment. "This way," she says. I have to walk fast to keep up with her.

I follow her down a long hallway.

She pauses at a door that is slightly ajar and knocks. The person on the other side of the door must have told us to come in because Barb gives me a tight smile and pushes the door open wide for me.

I've only met Joe Huntley in passing before but I know that he and David are friends, both on staff at Queen of Peace. David and Dr. Huntley went to medical school together. David specializing in gynecology and obstetrics and Dr. Huntley in oncology, so I figure that he is in his late forties or early fifties. He looks more like a rugby player than a doctor. He's about my height and solidly built. His nose is slightly off center as if it has been broken more than once and his gray, thinning hair is cropped short. He regards me curiously from behind a pair of half-moon reading glasses but when Barb introduces us he smiles kindly and immediately I'm put at ease.

"Thank you for taking the time to visit with me, Dr. Huntley. I'm sorry I missed our interview yesterday," I say, hoping that he won't change his mind and send me on my way.

I fix my eyes on his lips, intent on deciphering his every word. If I'm lucky, I'll be able to figure out about every other word. I'll have to use his body language and context to figure out the rest. "Please call me Joseph. We're glad to have you join us. David speaks highly of you."

This surprises me. It's no secret that David and I have been separated for the better part of two years and I haven't been the most stellar of wives but it's good to know that he can still find a few nice things to say about me.

"You're deaf," Dr. Huntley says without preamble. "Or should I say hearing impaired? What is the politically correct term one should use these days?"

"*Deaf* or *hard of hearing* seem to be the going labels," I say. Before I lost my ability to hear, I too thought that hearing impaired was the thing to say, but after emerging from my miasma of alcohol I decided to educate myself. After a little research I learned that you can be deaf with a lowercase *d* or Deaf with a capital *D.* To be *deaf* means that you physically cannot hear and to be *Deaf* means that culturally, you identify with the Deaf community. Since I'm the only deaf person I know, I consider myself deaf with a little *d.*

"You missed our interview yesterday," Dr. Huntley says, propping his reading glasses atop his head.

I take a breath, eager to explain. "I had every intention of coming in for the interview, but I had to assist with a police matter. As a witness," I add. "I couldn't get away."

"The woman in the river," Dr. Huntley states. "I saw the news. Heard your 9-1-1 call on the news this morning." My heart sinks. Not one of my finer moments I'm sure. He extends his hand, inviting me to take a seat. I sit, wanting so badly to examine every inch of his office, curious to learn more about my husband's medical school friend. I'm afraid that I will miss what he is saying so I keep my eyes locked on his thin lips. "You were remarkably composed under the circumstances," he says. "Not too many people would respond so calmly when unexpectedly faced with a dead body."

I'm surprised but pleased with Dr. Huntley's interpretation of the 9-1-1 call. While speaking with the dispatcher, I felt anything but calm and composed.

"Thank you," I say.

"The woman you found. The woman in the river — did the police identify her yet?" he asks. I know there is a good chance that Dr. Huntley knows Gwen too, but if the police haven't made an official announcement as to who the victim is, I'm sure not going to.

"As far as I know they haven't identified her yet."

"So very sad," he says. "I can't imagine." Dr. Huntley lifts a mug, leaving a damp ring behind. He says something else from behind the rim of his coffee cup and upon seeing my confusion, lowers it. "I'm sorry. I asked how you learned to read lips. You do very well."

"Mostly by necessity, I guess. You learn the basics pretty quickly, but to have a true conversation with someone I needed to learn much more. I started by taking an online course."

Dr. Huntley raises his eyebrows. "I never knew there was such a thing."

"Yes, it was very helpful," I explain. "I watched a series of videos, practiced, took quizzes. But that wasn't enough. I work with a speech pathologist, as well."

"David says you were an exceptional nurse," Dr. Huntley says, leaning back in his chair.

"I still am," I say, bristling at the past tense description of my abilities. "My licensing is up-to-date. I'm knowledgeable, reliable and good with my patients. For the past three months I have been working with my speech pathologist on my enunciation, medical terminology and scenarios that relate to patient care. I'm hoping to go back to nursing soon."

"David's a good judge of character," Dr. Huntley says. "We graduated from med school together. Kept in touch ever since. Did he ever tell you how he came to practice medicine in Mathias?"

I figure it was because his ex-wife, Trista, was from here but I wasn't about to say that to Dr. Huntley so I just shake my head.

"I grew up here and David came home with me one weekend from the University of Iowa. He fell in love with the town." And Trista, I think, but he doesn't mention her. "Said he was going to set up shop here one day and he did. Man of his word," Dr. Huntley says.

"Yes," I say out loud. To myself I add, except when it comes to sickness and health.

I know I'm not being fair. I put David and Nora through hell. And though I know our marriage is over, I want us to get along. I want to play a part in Nora's life.

"We offer a variety of cancer treatments here, including chemotherapy, and we're the only provider of radiation therapy in the tristate area — over twenty-five thousand procedures per year," Dr. Huntley says, getting back to our interview. "We battle cancer aggressively." My eyes are locked on his face. His passion is mesmerizing. "Patients have to be willing to trust me, trust my staff. That's the only way they will get through the battle. They come here desperate for answers, desperate for help. They want someone to tell them what needs to be done to save their lives. My staff must be able to handle the most challenging and heartbreaking of cases and must be able to wake up each morning and do it all over again," he says, his face filled with pride. I wonder if he's married and has children. I look around his office for any photos or hand-drawn pictures. Nothing. It seems to me that his entire world is probably this clinic.

"I understand," I say. "I'm reliable. Nothing will get in the way of my professional responsibilities. Nothing," I add just in case any tales of my earlier public drinking displays have reached his ears.

"As a nurse you know how important it is to be a reassuring, soothing presence for patients."

"I do know. I worked for fifteen years as an emergency room nurse and for three years as a sexual assault nurse examiner." I feel my confidence grow. I can talk for hours about the cases I've seen in the ER, about the women and, while less common but no less violent, the men brutalized by domestic abuse.

Dr. Huntley tilts his head and regards me thoughtfully. "You can start on Monday. Right now I can offer you twenty hours of work per week. Eight to noon. You will do clerical work, filing, word processing and the like. Unfortunately, no patient care. But maybe one day. We'll see." He stands and smiles down at me and I realize that I have a job. Not a nursing position, but at least I'll be working in a medical setting. A step in the right direction.

"Thank you, Dr. Huntley . . . Joseph," I say gratefully as he walks me to his office door.

"Congratulations, Amelia. Glad to have you aboard."

I stop by Barb's office and she has me fill out the needed paperwork and hands me a piece of paper with an overview of my hours and the duties that I'll be responsible for. A surge of anxiety rushes through me. Except for the time I spend with Nora and Jake I've become pretty adept at avoiding all people and social situations. Now I'll have to interact with an office full of people I don't know and for a moment I'm sure this is all a huge mistake.

"What about dogs?" I ask, thinking of Stitch. "I have a service dog that helps me with day-to-day tasks. He's well-behaved and good with people. Do you think Dr. Huntley will be opposed to me bringing him to work?"

Barb hesitates, not sure how to respond. I've seen the same look on others when I bring Stitch into a place of business. Some people don't think that dogs belong in the workplace or just don't understand how important service pets are to their handlers. Stitch isn't only my ears but a calming presence in a hearing world that I don't belong to anymore.

I feel a hand on my elbow and I turn to find Dr. Huntley at my side. "Of course you can bring your dog. The more the merrier," I read on his lips. "Just bring the paperwork in with you and I'll see you on Monday." He hands Barb a file folder and pats me on the arm before taking his leave. I can see why Dr. Huntley has such a good reputation in town for his bedside manner. I haven't even started the job and already I feel like a part of the team. I push away the doubts that David has planted in my head. Maybe this will work out, after all. Maybe this really is a new beginning for me.

7

Whenever I had good news to share I'd call David. When I finished my training and got the job as a sexual assault nurse examiner with the county I called David. When I testified in my first court case that resulted in the conviction of a rapist, I called David. When I was named Health Care Worker of the Month at Queen of Peace I called David. I want to call him now, but he's been clear that he isn't thrilled about me working at the center. Instead, I decide to go to police headquarters to share my good news with Jake and to go over my story about finding Gwen's body again.

The Mathias Police Department is like most of the buildings located in the downtown area. Old. Built in the 1850s, the Old Jail as it's fondly called is on its last leg. An addition to the structure was erected in the 1940s, but crime in the area grew with the population of Mathias and the building will officially close in a few months when the newly constructed police department, located three blocks away, is scheduled to open. The Mathias Historical Society already has plans to transform the jail into a museum. I find a parking spot on the street in front of the jail and push through the front door. I forgo the elevator and take the steps up to the second floor where official police duties are conducted.

The temperature inside the building is as cold as the air outside despite the steam rising from the cast-iron radiators that punctuate the hallway. A receptionist talking on the telephone sits behind a glass partition. Scuffed gray tiles lie beneath a charcoal industrial rug, and ash-colored walls add to the gloomy feel of the space. The receptionist, dressed in a thick woolen sweater, her nose tipped red and looking miserable, hangs up the phone and starts tapping on her computer. I know the office Jake shares with two other detectives is down the hallway and I can probably just walk right past her without her noticing me but I also know that is frowned upon.

Finally she looks up from the computer. "May I help you?"

"I'm here to see Detective Jake Schroeder," I say.

"Your name, please?"

"Amelia Winn," I answer, and this gets me a double take.

"You found the woman in the river," she says.

"Yes," I say, trying to sound patient. "Detective Schroeder wanted me to stop by to answer a few more questions." She picks up her phone, speaks into it and within a minute, Jake pokes his head outside his office door and waves me toward him.

"Earhart," he signs, "come on back." He waves me into his office, a small cramped room that houses three desks, a coffeemaker, a portable whiteboard and a wall lined with mismatched file cabinets. The room is empty except for the two of us. Jake swipes a rolling chair from behind his neighbor's desk and pulls it up to his.

"Is there any more news about Gwen?" I ask as I take a seat.

"Actually, a lot has happened. Marty Locke officially identified his wife's body yesterday, just before she was sent to Des Moines for the autopsy. There's going to be a press conference in about an hour to announce it."

It's still surreal. "I can't believe it's her. Do you know how she died yet?"

"She has a nasty wound on the back of

her head," Jake signs. "And from the mark around her neck that I saw when we pulled her from the river, my guess is she was strangled."

I hadn't noticed any injuries to Gwen's neck when I found her and though I suspect she hadn't died from natural causes, it's disturbing to learn. "Who would do that?" I ask in disbelief. "Do you have any suspects?" I have no plans to stop hiking in the woods or walking along the river's edge, but I'd sure feel a lot better knowing whoever killed Gwen was safely behind bars.

"The murderer — my bet is on the husband. It's always the husband. We have some more work to do before we can make an arrest, though, but don't even think about going out on the river alone until we arrest him, you hear me?" Jake says. I don't like being told what to do, so I pretend I don't know what he's saying and I peel off my coat.

"What about the shoe Stitch found?" I ask. "Did it belong to Gwen?"

"We don't think so. That's one of the first things we checked out. Gwen wore a size seven and the shoe was a size nine." Jake eyes me curiously. "Hey, why are you so dressed up?"

"Oh, just this little thing called a job

interview," I say coyly.

"At the cancer center? That was today? How'd it go?"

"I got the job," I say with a smile.

"Of course you did. I didn't doubt it for a second." Jake stands and takes my hand and twirls me around on the chair's casters. He spins me around faster like he did when we were kids playing on the merry-go-round, except back then his goal was to get me to tumble off and onto the ground.

When he stops we're both laughing and I'm dizzy. It takes a few seconds for me to steady myself and the muscles in my cheeks ache. I haven't smiled like this in months. When we emerge from his office the secretary raises her eyebrows knowingly and I begin to correct her misunderstanding but then stop. Let her think what she wants.

Jake walks me down the hall to the conference room for my follow-up interview with the certified interpreter and I spend the next hour going over everything I remember about yesterday morning. It's no less heartbreaking the second time. When we're finished, I sign my statement and Jake and I walk together out to my car.

"Let's go celebrate tonight," he signs once I'm in the driver's seat and just about to shut the car door.

"Celebrate?" I repeat to give me time to process what Jake's saying.

"Yeah, celebrate your new job. We could go out, get something to eat. Somewhere nice." Jake looks down at me hopefully. Jake and I are friends: we go to sign language classes, go to an afternoon hockey game or two, even grab lunch once in a while, usually a burger at some dive bar near the police station. What we don't do is go somewhere nice. I know much of the time Jake spends with me is out of a sense of duty. Jake and my brother, Andrew, are as close as brothers and my parents had always been like surrogate parents when his own couldn't quite pull it together. I know because of this he feels obligated to keep an eye on me.

When I don't respond right away, Jake backpedals. "Hey, another time." He taps the top of my Jeep with a closed fist. "Talk to you later, Earhart." He clasps his hands together and gives them one firm shake, the sign for congratulations.

I watch as Jake looks both ways for traffic before trotting across the street back to the police station. Is he just being a good friend offering to take me out to celebrate my new job? He knows that the majority of my friends ditched me when David did. Maybe he felt sorry for me having only Stitch to go home to, having no one else to share my good news with. But I think I might have seen a flash of disappointment in his eyes when I didn't respond. For years I had hoped that Jake Schroeder would show some interest in me beyond friendship, but I was always Andrew's little sister, then there was Sadie and then there was David.

Now there's no Sadie, no David.

I drive away from the curb and travel three blocks before taking a detour in the parking lot of a pharmacy. I pull into a parking spot and take out my phone and before I change my mind I begin texting.

How about Lo Schiavio's at six thirty? I'll meet you there.

I wait for what feels like an eternity, staring at my screen. Finally, I give up and begin the twenty-five-minute drive back home. He is probably in the middle of questioning Gwen's husband or is out on another call. It's ridiculous for me to expect him to immediately respond to my text. Or, I think glumly, I had my chance and he thought better of the whole "going out to dinner on a grown-up date" thing. Or I'm insane and reading way too much into the invitation. I settle on the latter and decide that Stitch and I will celebrate on our own this evening with a pizza, hot chocolate minus the Baileys and a good mystery novel.

No pizza place will deliver to my house out in the boonies so I stop at a local restaurant and order a medium taco pizza buried in seasoned beef, lettuce, tomatoes, sour cream, taco chips and jalapeño peppers that make your eyes water. It takes a good twenty minutes for them to fix the pizza, so I sit in a dark corner of the restaurant and sip on a Diet Coke and pick up an abandoned newspaper, the *Mathias Daily Miner.* Though they don't include her name, on the front page is a photograph of Gwen Locke's body being loaded into the ambulance by the EMTs. The headline screams in big black letters: Murder on Five Mines. The story takes up the entire front page and continues on to page three. In a smaller inset box is the transcript of my call to 9-1-1. Just as in the television news story, I'm not mentioned by name but I have a feeling that it won't be long before the press figures out who I am and comes knocking at my door.

Jake is quoted as saying that due to the ongoing nature of the investigation, he's not at liberty to discuss specific details of the case, but can say that they are following a number of leads. In an hour his chief will announce to the world that Gwen has been murdered and the husband is the primary person of interest.

I think back to what Jake said in his office. It's always the husband. I only met Marty a few times but he always seemed easygoing and affable. I know Gwen's mother lives in town and that she will likely be the one to take care of Lane if Marty is arrested. The article goes on to list a variety of theories as to who the murderer might be: a husband, a boyfriend, a drifter, an unknown man or woman who had been linked to two similar homicides in northern Wisconsin.

A waitress approaches with a cardboard pizza box and the spicy scent of peppers and onion fills my nose and my stomach rumbles. I return to my Jeep and set the box on the passenger seat next to me, start the engine and begin the drive home. I don't last two blocks before I lift a corner of the box and pinch off a slice of pizza when my phone vibrates in my pocket. I pull it free and smile at the text message waiting for me.

Lo Schiavio's it is.

8

I stand in front of my closet trying to figure out what to wear to dinner. I refuse to label this as a date — even in my own mind. Nothing seems to fit the occasion. Jeans and a sweater are too casual and a dress seems like I'm trying too hard. I settle on a simple tunic, leggings and flats.

Stitch is not pleased when at six o'clock he realizes I'm planning on leaving the house without him again. Twice in one day is a record for me. Stitch turns up his nose at the slice of taco pizza I cut up and put into his food dish as a peace offering and doesn't even look at me when I rub his ears and say goodbye.

Jake is waiting for me at the front entrance when I arrive, and my stomach does a not-so-unpleasant flutter when he smiles. "You look nice," he signs when I reach him.

"Well, I guess this is what an employed person is supposed to look like," I say. "Or so I'm told."

Housed inside a tall building, Lo Schiavio's has the best atmosphere and food in town. It's an authentic Italian restaurant owned and operated by a family that immigrated to the United States just before World War II. Claudio and Serafina Lo Schiavio opened the restaurant in the late 1950s and it's been a Mathias institution ever since. Though Serafina died a few years ago, the Lo Schiavio daughters have taken over. Claudio can often be found sitting at the bar chatting with the regulars but I don't see him there right now. The exposed brick walls are covered with framed black-and-white photos from Claudio and Serafina's early life on the Amalfi Coast, and the wooden beams that crisscross the ceiling are wrapped with twinkling fairy lights. The tables are covered in heavy linens and illuminated by small candles. Efficient waitstaff dressed in black pants and white shirts move gracefully between tables, filling water and wineglasses.

Though I can't hear music anymore, I know that soft music always plays in the background: Italian operas like *La Bohème* and *Aida* and tenors like Pavarotti and Bocelli. In better days, when David, Nora and I would go to Lo Schiavio's, Nora would always entertain us with her lip-synched rendition of "That's Amore." These days, my sense of sound is limited to its echoes as it travels through air, water, solids. I can feel the clap of thunder, the thrum of loud music, the slam of a door as it vibrates through my bones. Once in a while, I'll sit in my car, turn up the radio as loud as it will go and lay my hands on the dash and feel the throbbing pulse of music against my skin.

I try to push away the ghosts that somehow always come to me in the memory of sound as the host leads Jake and me up two flights of stairs past casks of wines and shelves filled with olive oil and seats us in a dim corner. Already I know this could be a problem. It's hard to eat and sign at the same time and if I can't clearly see Jake's lips there will be no way we are going to be able to carry on a conversation. As always, he seems to be able to read the stricken look on my face, rises and proceeds to gather up a half dozen of the small votive candles from the unoccupied tables and sets them strategically on ours. It does the trick and the collection of flames is enough for me to decipher Jake's words.

"Brilliant," I say as he settles back into his chair. Jake waves away the compliment and opens his menu.

"Remember we're here to celebrate your new job and not my obvious and incomparable intelligence."

"Noted," I laugh.

When our server returns she glances curiously at all the candles illuminating our table.

"Mood lighting," Jake says, looking straight at me, a huge grin on his face. Like always I can't tell if he's serious or just joking. I've known Jake forever and he's still the same handsome boy with the impish smile. He was a four-sport kid in high school: football, basketball, track and baseball. Tall and solid, he's still exceptionally fit for a forty-five-year-old, though I would never tell him that.

The waitress asks if we'd like a sample of the house wine. I feel the heat rise in my cheeks. I don't know why I'm embarrassed. Jake knows all about my drinking problem, was the one who gave me a kick in the ass to deal with it. "Just water for me," Jake requests. And I do the same.

"You didn't have to do that," I say once the waitress is out of earshot.

"I know." Jake unfolds his napkin and lays it on his lap. "I did it for me. Until this homicide is closed I have to be stone-cold sober."

"I read in the paper that you said you may be making an arrest soon." I change the subject. Jake nods. "Gwen Locke's husband?" I ask, and the look on his face confirms it.

The waitress returns with our water and then leaves us to peruse the menu for a few minutes. I'm not particularly hungry, but the food here is amazing. "The sky's the limit, Earhart," Jake says. "You're gainfully employed now — you can afford it." Well, there goes any inkling that this is a date. I guess we're paying for our own meals tonight. I can't tell if I'm relieved or disappointed. "Besides —" Jake gives my hand a friendly squeeze "— you deserve it."

"I do," I agree with feeling. "Dammit, I do." Jake signals the waitress over and she takes our orders.

As we nibble on the garlic bread and salad that the waitress brings I say, "I bet you're relieved to have this murder solved already. I know I'll sleep a lot better knowing that the person responsible is behind bars." I see a slight misgiving cross Jake's face. It's nearly imperceptible but I've known Jake long enough to know when something isn't quite right. "What?" I ask. "You said you're going to go arrest Marty Locke tonight. Don't you think he did it?"

Jake takes another bite of bread, chews and swallows before answering. "Just bringing him in for questioning again. He says he was on the road for work the night Gwen went missing. The kid spent the night with a babysitter because Gwen worked a double at Q & P. According to Gwen's mother, the two of them have been going through a rough patch. That Gwen talked about a trial separation. Plus, we found her abandoned car. Only prints inside belong to Gwen and Marty."

"Anywhere near the marina?" I ask, thinking about my theory that whoever killed Gwen transported her by boat.

"Not even close. A highway patrol officer found it on the side of the road north of town."

"But . . ." I say, knowing that there's something not sitting right with Jake.

"But I just have a feeling that there's more to it. In my experience, a guy who's royally pissed at his wife — I mean mad enough to kill her — doesn't do it so . . . so methodically. There was barely a mark on her."

"What about the gash on the back of her head?" I ask.

"ME said that would have only stunned

her," Jake explains. "The official cause of death is asphyxia due to ligature strangulation."

"So you think that if Marty killed his wife he would have beat her or stabbed her? It seems to me that strangling someone is pretty personal — pretty ugly," I counter.

"Yes, but it's more than that. This can't leave this room." Jake pulls his chair more closely to me. "A guy who strangles his wife or girlfriend uses his hands or maybe an object he finds within reach — a belt, a scarf. But this guy used something else." He touches his neck. "The marks around her throat . . . We haven't figured it out just yet."

"Lots of husbands are guilty of premeditated murder. What makes you think Gwen's husband might be innocent? What does your chief say?"

"The chief wants the right guy arrested and all the evidence right now points to the husband. I don't know if he's innocent or guilty. I'm just saying that from the initial findings from the autopsy Gwen Locke wasn't just strangled. She was strangled, revived, then strangled again. And again."

My stomach churns. "She was tortured? Why?"

"Yeah, she was tortured," Jake signs.

"Maybe she had some info that the murderer was trying to get out of her? I don't know." The light from the candles on the table casts dappled shadows across Jake's face. He looks worn-out and I can tell how heavily this murder weighs on him. I look around the room. The waitress ascends the steps, her tray laden down with our plates of food, and sets them down in front of us. I wait until she leaves before I speak again.

I hate to ask the next question, but I've worked as a nurse too long to not. "Was she sexually assaulted?"

"The initial report was inconclusive. It's tough to tell at first glance. She was found naked. That does indicate a sexual aspect but there wasn't any noticeable bruising or trauma. They're running more tests and swabbing for DNA. It will take some time to get those results back."

In my experience DNA results can never come fast enough and even if the high-profile nature of a case comes into play it could still take well over a week to receive any kind of report. "If it wasn't sexually motivated why do you suppose she was killed in that way?"

Jake thinks for a moment and then makes the signs for four of the most chilling words in any language let alone ASL. *Greed. Hate.*

Revenge. Evil.

"So you think whoever killed Gwen didn't necessarily want to rape her but wanted her to suffer, wanted to punish her for something she might have done?" I think of what I know about my old friend. She could be headstrong when it came to advocating for a patient, rubbed some people the wrong way, but she always had the victims' interests at heart. I couldn't imagine someone wanting to hurt her so brutally.

"I'm keeping an open mind but if the final autopsy results show no evidence of sexual assault, my guess is that Gwen Locke did something to royally piss someone off and just killing her once wasn't enough. He . . . or she, incapacitated her by hitting her in the head and then brought her to the brink of death over and over again by strangling her." Jake picks up his fork and pokes at the food on his plate. I think we've both lost our appetites.

I let this scenario sink in. The terror of staring into the eyes of someone intent on squeezing the air from your lungs is bad enough. But why would someone loosen the rope, let you catch your breath and then pull it tight over and over again? It's nearly unimaginable. But so is seeing a car barreling toward you and knowing there's nowhere to run.

Images of bright headlights and a full moon flash through my brain. Just out of my reach is the sound of katydids, tires squealing and Stacey Barnes's screams. I can almost remember what they sound like, although I would do anything to forget.

Across from me Jake is waving his hand in front of my face, trying to get my attention. "Sorry," I say.

"Spit it out, Earhart," he signs. And I can't help but smile. Jake always seems to know when I want to say something even before I do.

"I know it's going to sound crazy, but I just can't help thinking that maybe there might be a connection between my hit-and-run and Gwen's murder." Jake doesn't tell me I'm nuts so I go on. "For one, we are both sexual assault nurse examiners and we both helped to put some very bad men away because of the evidence we collected."

"I don't know." Jake shakes his head. "You and the other victim . . ."

"Stacey Barnes," I remind him. I don't want anyone to forget her name. I know I never will.

"You and Stacey Barnes were hit by a car and Gwen was beaten and strangled. Two very different MOs." Jake looks skeptical.

"I know it's far-fetched but the point is, based on the skid marks at the scene of the hit-and-run, your friends in blue determined that the car sped up before it intentionally ran into us. I'm not saying that it's the same person, maybe just the same kind of person — a rapist or an abusive boyfriend or husband looking for revenge."

"Or it could be some freak who has a thing for beautiful nurses," Jake says, making the sign for *beautiful* with a flourish.

"Yeah right," I say, laughing it off. "They probably have nothing to do with each other. It was just a thought." But I can't help thinking that maybe there could be some kind of connection. Maybe an old case, maybe Jake's tasteless comment about a crazy person out there targeting nurses isn't so far off.

"Try not to worry," Jake says. "It's probably the husband — it's always the husband. We'll find out who did this."

I want to believe him, but the police still haven't figured out who was driving the car that mowed Stacey and me down and whenever I cross a street I can't help but look twice.

The candles on the table begin to flicker and burn out one by one and our conversation turns to lighter topics. I ask him if he has talked to Andrew lately and if he could please tell him that it was his turn to come and visit me this time. Actually, it was my turn to go out to Denver, but I haven't been able to bring myself to travel since I lost my hearing. We talk about Stitch and Rookie as if they are our children and by the time dessert arrives the tension has faded and we're both more relaxed.

We argue over the bill but Jake wins. "Next time it's my treat," I declare, pleasantly surprised that Jake foots the bill. Usually we go Dutch. And Jake doesn't balk so maybe there will be a next time.

We gather up our doggie bags and walk outside. The moon is a frosty orb against a navy blue sky. The air is crisp and still, as if it is listening for what might come next. It smells like it could snow and a childlike excitement fills my chest. I've always loved the first snow of the year. We stop at my car and Jake holds my take-out bag while I unlock my door.

"Thanks for a great night," I say. "I really needed this." Jake's face is only inches from mine and he gives me that half smile that has had the capability of making me go weak in the knees ever since I was a kid.

"I had fun too," he signs, pulling open the driver's-side door. "Text me when you get home so I know you're safe and sound, okay?"

"Aye, aye." I give him a two-fingered salute. "Good luck tonight," I say, my tone growing serious.

"Thanks. Justice always prevails, right?" he asks as I settle into my seat.

I don't respond because we both know that life isn't always just or fair. Sadie dying wasn't fair, the way I lost my hearing and then lost my marriage wasn't fair. And Gwen Locke being murdered sure as hell wasn't fair.

It's nine o'clock by the time I get home and I sit in the driver's seat with the engine idling for ten minutes before I get up the nerve to get out of my car. I hate that I'm scared of my own yard. I hate that someone has this power over me. I count to three and throw open the car door and scramble across the driveway and up the steps like a child who leaps under the covers before the boogeyman reaches out from beneath the bed to grab her. With shaking hands I unlock the door and find Stitch lying in the same spot where he was when I left. He ignores me for about twenty seconds before curiosity about what's in the doggie bag gets the better of him. "Hold on," I say, "you need to go outside first."

I'm not so afraid of being outside with Stitch at my side but I keep him in my sights. I remember I promised Jake that I would let him know I made it home okay, so I shoot him a text, and then Stitch and I go back inside.

In the kitchen Stitch watches as I slice my leftover steak into bite-size pieces. "What?" I ask as I fish the piece of pizza from his bowl and replace it with the steak. "Taco pizza isn't good enough for you?" The steak barely hits the bottom of his dish before Stitch gobbles it up. "Slow down, you'll choke," I scold.

I settle in front of my computer and spend the next hour practicing my speech reading by watching episodes of *Nurse Jackie* online. Multisyllabic, medical terminology is a killer when it comes to reading lips.

I'm still having trouble believing that Monday morning I'll be working at the clinic. Not as a nurse, just yet, but it's just a matter of time. I'll get there. I know I should call David and tell him I got the job but I'm still a little irked about his comment that I was *once* a good nurse. I guess I can't blame him. As much as I hate admitting it, I had a problem with drinking. Have a problem with drinking. It interfered with all aspects of my life, especially my marriage.

David may not love me the way he used to but he knows I'm a damn good nurse. I couldn't imagine a world where I could be profoundly deaf and a nurse and so instead I drank. A lot. At first I did a pretty decent job of only drinking after Nora and David went to bed. For a while David slept with me but each night I struggled to fall asleep. The silence and the dark filled me with paralyzing anxiety and I would break into a clammy sweat, my heart pounded until I became dizzy and would have to turn on a light. With David's grueling schedule at the hospital he needed every minute of sleep he could get so he would go downstairs to the guest bedroom, leaving me alone with lights blazing and a bottle of wine.

I look at the phone. It's probably too late to call David anyway but I dial before I change my mind.

"Hello?" the display reads.

"Hi, David, it's Amelia. Am I calling too late?"

"No, no. Nora is spending the night with a friend tonight. I'm just getting caught up on some work."

Nora is a quirky little girl who sometimes isn't sure how to act around her peers so I'm so glad to hear that she is spending time with a friend.

"Yes, apparently they're going to order pizza and have a movie marathon. Nora was very excited."

"That sounds like fun," I say, wishing I was there to see the two girls snuggled into their sleeping bags, stuffed animals tucked in their arms, giggling over whatever movie they were watching, a bowl of popcorn between them. "Hey, I wanted to let you know that I met with Dr. Huntley today. I start on Monday."

"That's great, Amelia," David says. "Good for you."

I wish I could hear his voice. I wonder if there is warmth and pride there or if he's just going through the motions, being polite. He's made it quite clear that he doesn't think it's a good idea that I'll be working in the clinic.

"I won't be working with patients, but who knows, I've got my foot in the door. I . . . I just wanted to thank you. I know that you could have told Dr. Huntley not to hire me and you didn't do that. I really appreciate that."

"You're welcome," he responds, and I wait for him to say more but he doesn't. I don't know what I expected. Maybe an "I knew you could do it" or "They're lucky to have you." But I'll take what I can get.

"Okay, well," I finally say. "When Nora gets home tell her I said hi and I'll give her a call."

We disconnect and I find that my hands are sweating. Am I going to be anxious every single time I have a conversation with David? But I feel something else too. I'm excited. I have a job. And who knows, maybe I'll be able to start working with patients again. There have to be some deaf nurses out there. I'll prove to David and Dr. Huntley and everyone else that nursing is what I should be doing. It is what I was born to do.

9

Sunday morning dawns bright and sunny and the craziness of the past few days seems like a bad dream but I know it's not. I look forward to the quiet and solitude of the weekend that stretches out before me. But I've got a little unfinished business to take care of. I need to go make amends with my neighbor.

Instead of making Evan lemon squares I find a package of preportioned chocolate chip cookie dough in the back of the freezer behind some frozen peas and a bottle of vodka I had forgotten about. I pop the cookies into the oven and pour the vodka down the drain.

Twenty minutes later, carrying a plastic container of still-warm cookies with a thank-you note taped to the lid, Stitch and I step out into the November sunshine. The sky is a gauzy blue behind trees that are stripped bare, their discarded foliage spongy beneath my feet. I'm dressed in a medium-weight parka that I can tell, even though my breath comes out in white puffs, will be too warm to wear by noon.

Actually, this would be a beautiful morning to take the kayak out on Five Mines. I've found that as long as I'm dressed for it, the river is my perfect playground in all kinds of weather. If Jake can prove it, and Gwen's husband is the culprit, then I'll have my river back. I know that sounds callous, but after losing so much, mostly due to my own stupid choices, sometimes I feel like Five Mines is the only sure thing I have anymore.

"I'm trusting you not to run off," I say to Stitch who, for the moment, is obediently at my side. As we approach, I can see that Evan's storage building is shut up tight. Either he doesn't have any appointments scheduled for this Sunday morning or everyone has canceled. Based on the brisk business that Evan has done up until now, I figure that all his clients, spooked by the discovery of Gwen's body, have canceled.

Stitch and I climb the stone steps to Evan's house. By the time we reach the top of the bluff I'm out of breath and sweating. No wonder Evan transports his customers up and down by four-wheeler. It's a workout all on its own by foot. The house is beautiful. Two stories tall and made from hewn logs the color of honey, stone and glass, the home is at once obnoxiously large and oddly homey-looking.

I knock on the double door, painted a deep mallard green. There's no answer. I move back and look up at the second-story windows. Evan steps into view and stares down at us. The remnants of his scuffle with Bennett and Cole are evident on his face. There's an ugly gash above his eyebrow, his cheek scraped and one eye is swollen and discolored. I grimace and wave. He moves away from the windows and I wait a few more minutes for him to come to the door. He doesn't. I can't really blame him. I wouldn't want to talk to me, either. I leave the container of cookies by his front door and Stitch and I walk down the bluff back to the house.

Just as I predicted the day has warmed considerably and I decide that I'm not letting anything keep me away from Five Mines. It is a beautiful day for a ride in the kayak and I'm going. I've wasted too much time hiding away from the world, from myself. Well, no more. I have Stitch and he'll look out for me.

After lunch I put on my waterproof paddling pants and jacket and pull my two-person kayak out of the shed. With Stitch right beside me, I haul it down to the river's edge. I strap a life jacket expressly made for dogs on Stitch since we'll be going into much deeper water today. I have no intention of going back to the crime scene. Instead, we'll take a different back channel and work our way north.

The current is moving swiftly and I really only have to use my paddle to keep the kayak facing forward. Stitch, oddly enough, is content just sitting in the front seat of the kayak. He must still be worn-out from his midnight run. Silver flashes appear just below the surface of the water. Carp or bluegill. I think about all the other critters that swim below my kayak. Otter, channel catfish and gizzard shad. Another world, and I wonder if it is as silent as my own.

It doesn't take long and we're approaching Bishop's Island, an expanse of wooded land about two miles long and three-quarters of a mile wide. If I go left I'll end up in the spot where I found Gwen; if I go right I won't. I go right. This is a more well-traveled circuit of the river than I usually take and I see several fishing boats and a few other kayakers. After twenty minutes of paddling I pull off onto a sandy beach and let Stitch stretch his legs and run.

I'm almost afraid at what he'll find, but all he brings back to me is an algae-covered stick that I toss a dozen times or so for him to retrieve. I wonder how Jake did with questioning Marty Locke last night and wonder if an arrest was made.

I check my phone but don't have a text from him. I'm a little disappointed. I've replayed our dinner over and over in my mind and as much as I've told myself that it wasn't one, it kind of felt like a real date. Stupid, I know. We're just friends. We've always been just friends. But it felt comfortable, it felt, I don't know, easy. I hate this limbo that I'm in. Married but separated. Sometimes I just wish that David would make up his mind. That I'd make up my mind. That I'd just say fuck it, it's over. But then I take the risk of not ever seeing Nora again.

I shouldn't be shocked that Jake hasn't texted. Even though it's Sunday, I know detectives don't work Monday through Friday, nine to five. He's in the middle of a murder investigation. He's busy. He's probably been up all night and is exhausted.

I call to Stitch, who has been digging a hole in the sand. He bounds back to me and shakes himself, pelting me with the coarse grains of sand that his coat collected in his play. I corral him back into the kayak and push it off into the brackish water before climbing in myself. Heading upstream in the kayak is much more difficult than downstream, which is why I only traveled a short distance. That's why outfitters like Evan's do so well. He provides the kayaks and then meets his clients down river in a large vehicle, straps the kayaks to the roof and then hauls them back up to their cars.

My muscles are straining against the push of the current, but the exertion feels good. By the time I reach the island my arms are burning and I still have a long way to go before I'm back at my dock. I may have underestimated the current and overestimated my kayaking abilities today. The last thing I want to do is travel to the same spot where we found Gwen, but at this rate it will take me twice as long if I take the alternate route.

"I must be nuts," I say to Stitch as I pull my paddle through the water and head up the back channel that I will forever, at least in my own mind, refer to as Gwen's. I mean to get us home as quickly as possible but as we near the spot where Stitch first spotted Gwen I stop paddling. I'm not sure what I think I might find. Certainly the police and the forensics team have searched the entire area meticulously, have collected each scrap of paper, each tin can, each out-of-the-ordinary item as possible evidence.

I'm no better than the horde of media that met Gwen's remains at the marina, but I don't come back here out of morbid curiosity, this I'm sure of. I don't know why I'm drawn to this spot.

The online obituary said that Gwen's funeral service was going to be held on Tuesday morning. The photo accompanying the obit could be Gwen's ID photo from Queen of Peace. It's a head shot of a smiling Gwen wearing hospital scrubs. She looks healthy and happy.

I haven't decided if I'm going to attend the funeral or not. Part of me wants the opportunity to see that Gwen is laid to rest surrounded by her friends and family, not discarded like a piece of trash in Five Mines. Part of me doesn't believe that I have the right to attend the funeral.

I vaguely remember Gwen coming to see me in the hospital. David told me she had called several times to come see me when I was convalescing at home, but I refused. She sent a card begging me to call her, to talk to her. I remember reading it and tossing it in the trash with all the others. I didn't want anyone's sympathy, didn't want people to pity me.

The last remaining leaves on the trees quiver tremulously above me as if one good scare will send them tumbling down. Upriver, my old friend the great blue heron is wading, belly deep, her plumed black-and-white-striped crown regally scanning the water for fish. I look up and notice her bulky stick nest in the tree above me. She could be the only witness to what exactly transpired here a few days earlier. Did she see someone toss Gwen into the river, or perhaps she observed the actual murder?

My breath quickens as the kayak draws closer to the jumble of fallen branches that tethered Gwen to the land rather than releasing her fully to the river. Stitch, sensing my anxiousness, stands. His body tenses, and I reach forward to rub his head to let him know that it's okay but he ignores me. I follow Stitch's line of vision and lock eyes with a man standing on the muddy bank near where Gwen's body once lay. He's nearly bald, slightly built and wearing a button-down shirt and khakis. He's definitely not dressed for hiking.

The expression on his face mirrors my own. First surprise, then fear. He's just as shocked to find me there as I am to find him. Like a magnet, my kayak is drawn toward him on the current. His expression shifts once more. His eyes harden and narrow into an icy glare. With a gentle bump, my kayak strikes the copse of fallen tree limbs that separates me from the man on the bank by less than fifty feet. Obscured by tangled clusters of deep brown fox sedge, something glints in his right hand and he tosses it to the ground. A knife? A gun?

Stitch begins barking, his jaws snapping wildly. He clambers from his seat, his front paws on the spray deck. The kayak rocks and the motion spurs me into action. Using my oar, I push against the fallen limbs, sending my kayak propelling backward and into a spin. When I finally get the kayak under control and once again facing the bank, the man has disappeared.

I sit there for a full five minutes, trying to catch my breath and scanning the shore for any sign of the man. How did he get there? Did he hike the trail or come by boat? I think of the near break-in at my house and can't help but wonder if maybe it wasn't a false alarm. If this man was involved. Stitch has returned to his usual docile self so I know the man is long gone. I know I should just paddle home but curiosity gets the better of me and I cautiously make my way to shore. Keeping Stitch close to my side, I pick my way toward the spot where I think the man dropped what he was holding.

I smell it first. A heady, fragrant smell that reminds me of my grandmother's perfume. There it lies, pale, white and delicate. Not a knife or gun. A spray of white flowers, long stemmed and wrapped in silver metallic tissue paper. Calla lilies.

I text Jake to let him know that I saw a man and what I've found. He responds immediately asking me what the hell I'm doing at the crime scene.

Kayaking with Stitch, I respond. I thought it would be okay. You said her husband probably did it.

I can imagine Jake shaking his head in exasperation. I didn't say that. I said we were questioning him. Besides, we had to let him go.

I glance around nervously. Would the murderer really come back to the scene of the crime and leave flowers? Who do you think would leave flowers? How would they know exactly where to put them?

My screen is still for a moment and then Jake's response fills my screen. Could be anyone. A friend, a family member. Soon the place will probably be filled with flowers and stuffed animals and photos of Gwen.

Aren't you going to at least come look at them? They could mean something.

It means someone cared about her. GO HOME!

I expel a breath of frustration. Is it so odd that a man who isn't Gwen's husband would come all the way out here to lay flowers at the spot where a loved one died? Jake didn't think so, but I'm a little more skeptical. Even though the media gave the approximate location where Gwen was found, it is no easy feat getting here. Whoever came here must have cared about Gwen very much. I snap a quick picture of the bouquet before shoving my phone back into my pocket and then summon Stitch to join me back at the kayak.

I know Gwen has siblings who live out of state and I wonder if they have arrived in town yet. And if they have, would the first place they go be the spot where her body was found? I don't think so, but maybe I'd feel differently if it had been Andrew or my dad who had been killed. I know that I bring flowers to my mother's grave on Mother's Day and her birthday each year. Maybe if a loved one of mine was murdered I'd be the first person there at the site of their death with a bouquet of snow-white lilies.

By the time we reach my dock I'm sweating, my muscles are burning and I'm out of breath. So much for the impending snow I smelled in the air. Another false alarm. Typical Iowa weather.

Stitch leaps to the wooden platform and tears off toward the house while I pull myself out of the kayak. With difficulty I lug the kayak from the water and as I was taught, so as not to strain my back, I bend my knees and grab the far side rim of the kayak with one hand and lift it to my shoulder. Placing my arm inside the cockpit, I support the kayak along my back without actually allowing the full weight to rest on my shoulder.

The exodus of autumn makes me sad. For years I dreamed of one day taking a long-distance trek down the Mississippi with whatever I could pack into my kayak. David and I used to talk about it. He and Nora would be my travel crew, driving the support car, providing me with food and water and moral support. We even tossed around the idea of beginning at the headwaters in Minnesota and traveling the twenty-three hundred miles down to the Gulf of Mexico.

Now it looks like it will be just me and Stitch making the trip. I've been training all summer and fall but I know I have a long way to go in order to be strong and skilled enough to make the journey. The impending winter will make it difficult for me to be prepared and I will have to train in other ways: on the rowing machine at the YMCA, lifting weights, cross-country skiing. Doable, but not quite the same.

By the time I reach the shed, a brusque breeze has cooled the salty layer of perspiration on my skin and I'm eager to go inside and take a hot shower. But first I grab a boar bristle brush that I keep in an old milk crate along with grubby, tooth-marked tennis balls, a nearly bald squeaky toy disguised as a squirrel and a cracked Frisbee. I sit with Stitch on the front steps and slide the brush through his coat and comb away the remaining sand that clings to his fur.

The image of the flowers lying starkly white against the muddy riverbank keeps invading my thoughts. Unlike the lilies that I've seen in funeral arrangements, the calla lilies left behind were more appropriate for a wedding bouquet. I'm sure there is significance to this flower choice. It wasn't her husband, so it had to be someone else. Was Gwen seeing another man? Had Marty found out that she had been cheating on him and in a rage killed her?

I rub a hand over Stitch's back, now smooth and free of the gritty sand and prickly burrs. He looks up at me with his assessing gray eyes, the color of a gathering storm, as if he knows that I'm just about to stick my nose where it doesn't belong.

"I'm just curious," I say. Stitch yawns, revealing his pearl-colored teeth, a gesture I know that in dog speak doesn't mean he's sleepy but that he's a bit stressed. "Don't worry," I assure him and rub the soft fold behind his ear. "It's no big deal."

I return the brush to the milk crate, lock the shed, and Stitch and I head into the house. I make a point to secure the door behind me, broomstick and all, refill Stitch's water bowl, grab my own water glass and fill it to the rim. I take a seat at the kitchen counter, my hot shower forgotten for the moment, and bring up my long-neglected Facebook page.

After the hit-and-run I was in no shape to keep up with social media. I had lost my hearing, had a severe concussion that made any kind of screen time migraine inducing. Plus, I wasn't feeling particularly social. The happy, carefree images that my friends posted of themselves with their families made me sad and more than a little jealous. Later, it just pissed me off and I would leave alcohol-fueled, snarky, mean-spirited comments on posts. One by one I was unfriended.

I enter Gwen's name in the search bar and immediately her profile picture pops up. It's the same picture that was used in her obituary. I spend a few minutes scrolling through her page. Hundreds of friends have posted condolences to Marty and Lane on the page. There are several pictures of Gwen with Lane, gap-toothed and smiling, but there are only a handful of photographs of Marty. In each he appears to be distracted, as if his mind is somewhere else or he wants to be someplace else. I think of Jake's early prediction that Marty is the one who killed Gwen. Maybe he's right.

But then who was the man by the river? A relative? A family friend? And if his being at the crime scene was only to lay down flowers in memoriam why did he look so scared and then so angry when he saw me? Why did he run away?

I click on Gwen's friends list and about two dozen friends' names that we have in common appear. I don't think I know or have ever seen the man who dropped the flowers at the river before, but I quickly look through the profile pics just in case. Not there.

Next I start clicking on the comments left behind by those who posted on her wall. One by one I go through each. None of the accompanying pictures looks like the man I saw. I sigh. This could take hours. I click on comment after comment until the room begins to darken. I stand, stretch my arms over my head and consider logging off. Instead, I turn on the kitchen light and sit back down.

A flash of irritation at Jake goes through me. I can't believe he dismissed me so easily. I'm not sure if stalking Gwen's Facebook page is going to help me find the man, but I'm sure going to keep trying.

I go back to the top of Gwen's page and begin clicking on the comments again. This time I go deeper. I read a comment and then read each reply listed beneath and one name and profile picture consistently appears. He gives his name as P. McNaughton.

McNaughton is a common last name in Mathias. Just about everyone I know is related to a McNaughton in some way. By birth, by marriage, or three-times removed.

The person's name is accompanied by a picture of a man, half his face hidden by a professional grade camera held up to his eye. All of his comments are a refrain on the same theme: Gwen will be missed, such a tragedy, she was an angel on earth. What is most remarkable about his comments is the sheer number of them. I make a quick count and come up with thirty-six. All in response to another's comment.

I click on P. McNaughton's image and it takes me to his page. I scrutinize the photo carefully. I can't tell for sure if he and the man I saw dropping the flowers at the river are one and the same. I scroll through his photos in hopes of finding a picture that fully reveals his face. P. McNaughton is at the very least an amateur photographer. I skim past pictures of sunsets and clouds and I pause when I come to a series of photos that look suspiciously like they could have been taken in the area of Five Mines near my home. Interesting.

Finally, I come across a photo of the man and it's clear that it is the person I saw earlier today. Same slight build, same receding hairline, same intense gaze. I return to the top of his page and see that he lists Mathias as his hometown. No profession is listed.

So what have I learned? Not much. Maybe Jake was right, that he's just a friend of

Gwen's who marked his condolences with a bouquet of flowers. Or maybe there's more to it.

I read through P.'s comments one more time and, again, nothing really jumps out at me except that there are so many of them and he obviously really cared about Gwen. I'm just about to call it a night when another comment from McNaughton appears on Gwen's page. I'll miss her terribly — a light has gone from the world. My fingers itch to respond but someone does it for me. A woman named Chris, who I know as a skilled care nurse at Mathias Regional, replies to him, Amen.

I hesitate and type, How do you know Gwen? I watch the screen, waiting for his response but none comes. He's gone.

Strange. I click on the woman's profile and send her a friend request and a message asking her what the deal is with P. McNaughton. I consider sending McNaughton a friend request too, but think better of it. He acted so suspiciously at the river and I don't want him to know my name in case he had something to do with Gwen's murder.

I decide that I can at least be somewhat productive while I wait around for Chris to reply to my message so I spend the rest of the evening researching more about Five Mines Regional Cancer Center and Dr. Huntley just so I'm clear as to what I am to expect in working there. He has nearly a five-star rating on MedicalReportCard.com. Dozens of patients rave about his bedside manner and the time and dedication he gives to those under his care. One woman describes how Dr. Huntley is always available at any hour of the day and how he patiently answers all of her questions.

There are only a few negative reviews. One from a woman with the user name of LWinthrop who says that Dr. Huntley became belligerent whenever she questioned him about the treatment protocol he prescribed for her husband. He asked me if I graduated from medical school and when I said I didn't he responded, "Then let me do my job."

The other reviewers skewered her. How dare you criticize Dr. Huntley! He's the most dedicated doctor I know. I've been to two other doctors and Dr. Huntley is the only one who listens to me. And on and on.

By the time I read through all the reviews and check out a few other sites I'm convinced that Dr. Huntley is a highly qualified, well-loved physician. Compared to the reviews of many of the other doctors, Dr. Huntley is top-notch.

I get ready for bed with a sense of possibility and excitement that I haven't felt in a very long time. This is the beginning, I think to myself. My first step back into nursing.

Guiltily, my thoughts shift once again to Gwen. I check my Facebook page for a message from Chris and to see if P. McNaughton posted any more comments on Gwen's page but find nothing. It doesn't seem right. Just as a new life is starting for me, just as I'm getting a second chance, Gwen's life has been brutally ended.

10

The morning of my first day at the center can't have started any worse. I oversleep. Last night I couldn't get the man I saw by the river out of my head and I kept checking my Facebook page to see if P. McNaughton had left any more comments but found none and Chris didn't send me a message. When I finally fell asleep it was around 1:00 a.m.

I haven't needed to wake up at a certain time in more than a year and I manage to fail miserably when it comes to my brand-new, no-fail, flashing-light, bed-vibrating alarm clock expressly made for the hard of hearing. Stitch nudges me awake at seven twenty-five and I need to arrive at the center by eight. In lieu of showering, I get dressed, comb my hair, feed Stitch and make it out the door by seven forty. That leaves me twenty minutes for the twenty-five-minute drive to Mathias.

Breathlessly, I step through the center's front door at 7:58. So much for arriving early to make a good impression. There is a plump, freckle-faced woman seated behind a tall counter speaking on the phone. When she sees me she smiles and holds up a finger to let me know she will just be a moment longer. Already the waiting room is filling up. A couple sits shoulder to shoulder, holding hands. An elderly man connected to an oxygen tank works a crossword puzzle while his wife shuffles through a thick stack of what looks like insurance forms. A young woman, her smooth head covered with a bright pink head scarf, is sitting in a far corner of the room, flicking through a magazine with unseeing eyes. Though her face is expressionless, her bouncing leg gives away her agitation. A toddler plays happily at her feet.

I sit on the opposite side of the room and wait for the receptionist to finish with her phone call. A minute or two later, a nurse in yellow scrubs opens a door and summons the young woman who rises from her seat, bends down and picks up the small child and follows the nurse from the room on unsteady feet. It wasn't so long ago that I was the nurse in the scrubs. I was the one who gently guided patients to an examination room. I wonder what is coming next for the woman. Is she nearing the end of her treatment? Is she getting good news or bad? Part of being a nurse is sitting with the patients when they receive the best news of their lives. Or the worst.

The receptionist steps out from behind her barrier and greets us with a toothy smile. "You must be Amelia and this must be Stitch. I'm Lori."

This brief introduction is all I really catch. I shake her hand and futilely try to follow what she is saying. Lori's mouth is moving too fast and she's not used to communicating with a deaf person. I was offered a sign language interpreter to help with today's training, but I declined. Now I'm wishing I hadn't. I've been so independent my whole life and even more so since David and I separated. It's hard for me to accept help, even harder to ask for it.

Combined with Lori's rapid description and last night's online research, I learn that Dr. Huntley is the medical director for this location and three other satellite clinics dotted across the county. Oncologists from eleven counties from the tristate area utilize the state-of-the art technology provided by the center.

I also learn that the clinic has another

oncologist, a Dr. Sabet, four nurses, a nurse practitioner, Barb (the office manager) and an additional receptionist. Inpatient care is done at Queen of Peace and all other treatments and procedures are done on-site at the clinic.

Lori leads me down a long hallway to a door that's marked Infusion Center. Inside is a surprisingly cheerful room filled with individual infusion areas separated by curtains. Each area holds an infusion chair that looks much like a comfortable recliner, a television and an additional chair for a companion. All the infusion chairs face a wall of windows providing a stunning view of Mathias and the river. Lori also points out a door labeled Radiation Therapies, though we don't go inside.

We return to the front of the office, and Lori pauses in front of a closed unmarked door. She opens it and flips on a light to reveal a large, windowless room filled with a maze of battered gray metal file cabinets. Taking up most of a wall is an empty, but brand-new open shelving unit that nearly reaches the ceiling. Against another wall is a top-of-the-line scanner and a long, narrow desk that holds a computer and a telephone.

"We're working on digitizing all our files. It's not glamorous work, but you'll be scanning and transferring all patient information into the computer. Don't worry about the files in this cabinet." She points to a six-drawer cabinet in the corner of the room. "Those are our inactive files. We're in the process of shredding them." The room is dim and depressing. I knew the job consisted of clerical work but I'd hoped that I'd have more interaction with the nurses and even with patients.

"Don't worry," Lori says, reading the expression on my face. "We won't keep you locked in here all by yourself if you don't want to. If you get lonely you can bring your computer out to the reception area and you can move back and forth between the two rooms to do your work."

"Thank you," I say with relief. If I had to be stuck by myself in that grim, dark room all day long I may just start drinking again.

"What do you think?" Lori asks. "You ready to get started?"

"I am," I say, and I spend the next three hours tediously transferring names, birth dates, family histories, immunizations and other information from the paper files into the computerized system. I'm a little unprepared for the disarray I find the files in. Many are out of alphabetical order and several times I find a doctor's note or lab result in the wrong patient's file. I set these wayward documents aside until I can refile them in the correct spots.

The work may be monotonous but Lori checks in on me every so often to see if I need anything, and after an hour of work Lori urges me from the file room for a break. I've been around so many people who can't be bothered to engage in conversation with me. So I appreciate Lori's efforts.

We sit behind the main desk and she shows me a picture of her sixteen-year-old daughter and asks me if I have any kids.

"A stepdaughter," I say, pulling out my own phone and showing her a picture of Nora. "She's seven, almost eight."

"Cute. What's your husband do?" she asks innocently.

"He's a doctor," I say. "David Winn. He's an ob-gyn with Queen of Peace."

"I know of him," she says. "He's my sister's doc. She says he's a nice guy."

"He is," I agree. I don't mention that we're separated. If the clinic is like all the other health care facilities I've worked for, it won't be long until everyone knows my business.

An older gentleman with black hair salted with gray and wearing a white lab coat approaches the main desk. Lori stands and I set my phone aside and also get to my feet.

"This is Dr. Sabet, Dr. Huntley's partner," Lori says, introducing us.

"It's nice to meet you," I say.

"And this is Amelia Winn," Lori continues. "She's working on scanning all the patient records into the new system."

"Welcome, and it's my pleasure," Dr. Sabet says, and we shake hands. I have to really concentrate on the movement of his lips. I wonder if Dr. Sabet speaks with an accent, something that always throws me off when I'm trying to speech read. "Have you seen Dr. Huntley?" he asks, looking harried.

"He's with a patient right now," Lori explains. "Exam room three."

"Please tell him I'd like to speak with him when he gets a moment," Dr. Sabet says. He pauses, scanning the crowded waiting room. Another patient comes through the entrance and Dr. Sabet shakes his head and picks up a file from Lori's desk, then retreats down the hallway. I wonder if the clinic is always this busy.

The young woman and child that I saw in the waiting room when I first arrived come out of the examination room. If she looked scared and bewildered before, she is even more so now. I want so badly to go to her and tell her that everything will be okay. But I know that there is nothing okay about having cancer. There are no guarantees. I give her an encouraging smile but she looks right through me. I wonder who is at home waiting for her.

I watch the woman leave and Lori, noticing my worry, lays a hand on my arm and I read her lips. "Breast cancer. Stage four. She's only twenty-five. But Dr. Huntley is her doctor. He's the best."

I return to my files and out of curiosity, I search for the file for LWinthrop's husband, the woman who left such harsh comments about Dr. Huntley and the center on the website I found last night. I type the last name Winthrop into the center's patient database and come up with John R. Winthrop and a listing of basic information: address, phone number, age of thirty-nine, wife's name, Linda, but nothing else.

I decide to take a look in the paper files. I go to the file drawer labeled *W* and riffle through the folders but I can't find it. I think a moment. This could be an example of the inactive files to be shredded that Lori told me not to worry about. I go to the corner and pull open the bottom drawer in the hopes that it will be filed under *W.* No such luck. It looks like the inactive files were just tossed in here randomly and one drawer is half-filled with what looks like patient and insurance company billing statements. It takes me about fifteen minutes but I find what I'm looking for. John R. Winthrop. It's a thick one and it takes two hands to pull it free.

I open the file and pick through the pages until I think I find reference to what appears to be his last visit to the clinic, when he was given an infusion of Rituximab. It's dated eight months ago, not long before Linda Winthrop left the review. I return to the beginning of the file. John Winthrop was diagnosed with a condition called idiopathic thrombocytopenic purpura or ITP. Not cancer, but a bleeding disorder where the immune system destroys its own platelets, making it difficult for blood to clot. ITP falls under the umbrella of illnesses that Dr. Huntley would treat as an oncologist/hematologist. The file gives me no sense as to why Linda Winthrop would be disillusioned with her husband's treatment. But in my experience this isn't all that uncommon. Choosing a doctor is very personal, not unlike choosing a mate, and finding the perfect physician can take a few tries. I return the file to its spot and get back to work.

I scan and upload three more files, each taking about thirty minutes to complete and when I look at my watch again it's after noon. Time to go. I tidy up my work area, round up Stitch who wandered off to visit the staff lounge.

When Stitch and I step out into the cool air I'm at once exhausted and exhilarated. My first day of work in two years. I want to talk to someone, to tell someone about Lori and that maybe someday I'll actually be working as a nurse again. My brother will still be at work, my dad out on the golf course. I will call them this evening. I think of Jake. I pull my phone from my pocket and find a text already waiting for me. It's not from Jake but from David.

How was your first day?

I'm not sure how to respond. Almost every conversation that I've had with David, in person or by text, has been loaded. I can't tell if he's genuinely interested or just wants to know if I screwed things up.

I decide to presume positive intentions and reply, Great! I have my own desk.

Impressive, David replies with what I'm

sure is sarcasm and then adds, Are you going to Gwen's funeral tomorrow?

I have mixed feelings about attending the services. Tomorrow is only my second day of work and I'm hesitant to ask for time off already. But Gwen and I were once friends and I was the one who found her. I feel like I need to be there but don't know if I can bring myself to attend.

I'm not sure, I text back, and it surprises me when he quickly responds I'll be there. I know that David and Gwen were acquainted, that she occasionally worked on the maternity floor and surely helped David deliver a few babies, but did he know her well enough to attend her funeral?

Another text comes through and I look at it for a few beats waiting for the punch line. Come over for dinner on Friday. Nora and I will cook.

Well, this is an interesting turn of events. Is my estranged husband really inviting me back into his house? He's just trying to be supportive, I tell myself. After all, the sooner I get my act together, the sooner he can cut me loose with a clear conscience. Not that I've been a burden on him, financially speaking. Once I moved out, I refused to take any money from him, surviving on my meager savings and cashing in my 401(k) plan twenty-five years too early.

Sounds good, I finally type. What can I bring?

Dessert and Stitch. Come around six.

I smile. See you Friday.

11

When I arrive at the Lutheran church where Gwen's funeral is being held I park beneath the shade of several towering pine trees. I've brought Stitch with me and the morning air is cool enough that I can leave him in the Jeep with the windows cracked and a brand-new bone and he'll be just fine.

I find a spot to sit in the rear of the church and watch as the mourners file in. Many I know by name, even more by sight. There are nurses and doctors, aides and custodial workers from the hospitals. I recognize the CEO of Mathias Regional Hospital and several of the board members from Queen of Peace. I can't help but notice the curious looks that I get. Most of these people haven't seen me out in public in nearly two years.

The hush of church has always left me conflicted. When I was young and would attend Mass with my parents and brother, it was as if the moment we stepped inside church the outside world would slip away. So different from our gregarious life at home filled with laughter and fun. I didn't like it. During the long spans of silence I would covertly make noise as I sat next to my mother, drumming on the wooden bench with my fingers, rustling the pages of the missalette, swinging my legs so that the tips of my shiny black patent leather shoes tapped the seat in front of us. My mother would try to still me with a hand on the knee or a stern look. It would work for a while but then I would click my tongue against the roof of my mouth or press my lips together and hum until the fusty old woman in front of us would turn around and glare at me and my father would have to take me outside. What I wouldn't give to hear even the slightest of murmurs, the scuff of feet across the tiled floor, the sonorous timbre of the priest's voice.

David comes up the aisle, and I slide over a spot so he can join me. "You came," he says.

"We were friends, I found her," I say, and by the way he flinches I know that I'm speaking too loudly for the occasion. It's difficult for me to regulate my volume.

"I know," David says. "I just didn't think

church was your thing."

He's right. Church isn't my thing. After the accident I stopped attending weekly Mass with David and Nora. At first, I was just trying to regain my strength after being injured so badly, and then it seemed a little silly when I couldn't actually hear what the priest was preaching about. And then that hour at home while the two of them were away was a convenient time to get appropriately sloshed to face the day ahead of me.

"I thought I should come," I say, leaving it at that. David's wearing a suit and tie but he looks worn-out, his face heavy with fatigue. Probably lots of midnight baby deliveries. I remember him staggering into bed after busy nights at the hospital.

I see Jake out of the corner of my eye as he sits in the pew just across from us on the other side of the aisle. He doesn't even glance our way. I know he's here in an official capacity. I've read enough mystery novels, seen enough crime dramas to know that the police always attend the funeral of a murder victim. Jake will mentally take note of the mourners, focusing primarily on the main suspect, who in this case is the husband, Marty Locke.

I'm still a little stung that Jake dismissed

my sighting of the strange man with the bouquet of flowers down by the river. Sure, it could have been a friend or family member honoring her passing, but I'm positive it was more than that. I stare at Jake, willing him to look my way, but he looks everywhere but at me, his face inscrutable.

David leans in close to me as if to murmur in my ear, then catches himself and pulls back. Whispering doesn't work for me. David never learned sign language. Not that I blame him. I didn't even learn it until well after he threw my drunken ass out of the house. But I know his facial expressions and mannerisms as well as I know my own and can figure out about 80 percent of what he says.

I turn my head so that I can see his lips and our noses are only inches apart. It's at once disconcerting and so familiar. "Do you have to go into work after this?"

I nod. "Joseph just told me to come in after the services." A look that I can't quite name crosses David's face when I use Dr. Huntley's first name. Disapproval? Jealousy? David lays a hand on the small of my back and to my dismay a rush of electricity courses through me.

"You're still coming over on Friday for dinner, right?" David asks, and I nod. I don't know what to make of this. Is David just being the friendly, supportive ex or is it something more? I don't know if I want to find out. I've spent a long time trying to get over David and every time I see him I realize I haven't come as far as I thought.

The funeral service begins, and I resign myself to following the cues of David and those around me about when to sit and stand. The minister is much too far away for me to see his face. Instead, I watch the faces of those who knew and loved Gwen. There are lots of tears.

At the front of the church sits Marty with their daughter, Lane, who looks slightly dazed. The reality of losing her mother hasn't struck just yet. But it will. I know. My mom died of a brain aneurysm when I was thirteen. She was in our kitchen pouring coffee into a mug and then she was on the floor. I miss her every single day.

An elderly woman who looks like an older version of Gwen sits on the other side of Lane. Does Gwen's mother believe that her daughter's husband killed her? If so, how could she bear to sit next to him, let alone be in the same church?

I try to see who Jake is focusing his attention on. For the most part it looks like he is interested in Marty and his behavior.

Marty's reactions look entirely appropriate under the circumstances — intermittent tears, hand firmly clutching on to his daughter's. Jake catches me staring at him and glowers briefly at me before allowing a slight smile to reach his lips. He's still mad at me for being nosy, but not very. We're going to be okay.

I glance around the church, looking for more people I know. In front of me and off to the right I spot my dentist and a few more nurses that I've worked with in the past. The reality is that of all the people in this church the only two that I've had any meaningful interaction with in the last few years are Jake and David. And David is probably pushing it.

Suddenly, my eyes land on a familiar profile. Standing in a pew one aisle over is P. McNaughton. He's dressed in clean but shabby khakis and his sport jacket stretches tautly across his narrow shoulders. Maybe he simply is a friend of Gwen's who stopped by the river to mourn her passing. He turns his face and our eyes lock. I must make some kind of sound, because David looks at me with concern. McNaughton's intense gaze is unflinching and it's all I can do to keep from looking away. I've had much scarier people stare me down in the ER, but something in his dark eyes gives me pause. Again, just like at the river, in addition to anger I find what can only be described as fear on his face. But not a timid, reticent kind of fear. More of a backed-into-a-corner, fight rather than flight agitation.

When he finally pulls his eyes from mine, I look to the front of the church and feel like I can breathe again. Why is my presence so unsettling to him? When I glance back at McNaughton he's sidling from the pew and, head down, is moving toward the exit.

If what he was doing down by the river was so innocent, why would he run from me again? I have no idea what I'm going to do or say if I catch up with him, but before I can stop myself, I elbow past David to follow McNaughton from the church.

When I step outside it takes a moment for my eyes to adjust to the bright sunlight after the cool dimness of the church. I scurry down the steps and to the sidewalk that lines the busy street in front of the church. Looking both left and right I see no sign of McNaughton. He's gone.

I turn back toward the church trying to figure out what I'm going to do next. There's no way that after my sudden exit I'm going back inside for the remainder of the funeral. I'm sure David thinks I've lost my mind again and I don't even want to know what Jake is thinking.

I have a feeling I'm going to find out sooner than I'd like. Jake pushes through the church doors and squints into the sunshine. When he sees me he wastes no time jogging down the steps and to my side.

"What the hell, Earhart?" he signs. "What are you doing?"

I could tell him the truth, that I figured out who the man at the river was. I could tell him about the odd messages P. McNaughton posted on Facebook. I could tell him that when McNaughton recognized me, he took off. But what's the use? Jake will just tell me I'm overreacting, that I'm reading too much into a simple gesture of grief. Instead, I give him a weak smile and lay a hand over my stomach. "I'm not feeling great," I say. "I just needed some fresh air. I'm feeling better now."

Jake regards me skeptically but doesn't press further.

"Nice funeral," he signs instead. "Good turnout."

"Yeah," I agree. "Right now, I don't think I could even fill up two pews if it was mine." I think of the way that Gwen's daughter, Lane, kept looking around as if searching for her mother. Would Nora miss me that way if I were to die? Would David even allow her to come to my funeral?

"Aww, come on," Jake says, poking me in the shoulder. "You'd fill up at least three pews, I'd make sure of it."

"Gee, thanks," I say. "You're a gem." I pull out my keys and we begin walking toward the parking lot. "Aren't you going to the cemetery?"

"No, another detective is already there. The burial is just for the immediate family, but I still want someone to be there to keep an eye out. See if Marty acts oddly."

"So he's still the main suspect?" I ask.

"He says he was in Waterloo for work. We're checking out his alibi. So, until we know for sure where he was, yes, he's our main suspect."

Again, I debate whether to tell him about McNaughton. If I say anything I'm sure to get my ass chewed for interfering in police business. But if I stay quiet and Jake finds out that I was withholding information he'd be just as pissed. I can't win.

"I think Gwen might have had a stalker," I say as we finally reach my Jeep.

"The flower guy?" he asks, and from the look on his face I know he's not impressed. Jake crosses his arms in front of his chest and waits for me to say more but he's pissing me off so I keep quiet.

"Well," Jake prods.

"His name is P. McNaughton and he was here, at the funeral. When he saw me, he panicked and ran out of the church. He left weird messages on Facebook."

"Amelia," Jake says.

"Maybe he had something to do —"

"Amelia," Jake says again, rubbing his forehead. "You have to stop." Jake grabs hold of the open car door between us while Stitch squirms between the seats trying to get Jake's attention but Jake is focused on me. "You need to stop. Let me do my job."

"Then do it," I say in frustration. "I found her body, someone tried to break into my house. Have you found out who did that yet? No, you haven't." Jake's face reddens in anger but he doesn't answer. "I find this weird guy, who is not Gwen's husband by the way, laying flowers at the murder site and now he's at her funeral. Plus, he left dozens of posts online about Gwen. Did you even know about that?"

"Are you done?" Jake signs. "You have no idea what we know. And that's the way it's supposed to be. We're the cops, you're . . ." He hesitates, as if not sure what to say.

"What, Jake?" I sputter. "What am I?

Deaf? A lowly office worker with too much time on her hands? A drunk? Is that what I am?"

"That's not what I mean, and you know it. Maybe you're right about this guy, but let us do the work and we'll find out what he's all about. Maybe he did murder Gwen. Maybe he is dangerous. So stay away from him and let us find out. I can't work this case and worry about you too."

As much as I hate to admit it, he's right, I'm getting in the way of the investigation. Maybe McNaughton has been stalking Gwen and she rejected him and he ended up killing her in a fit of rage. But maybe he had nothing at all to do with this and I'm muddying the investigation.

"I'm sorry," I finally manage to say. "I thought I was helping."

"Well, you're not." The clipped movement of his hands lets me know how frustrated he is with me.

"Fine," I say as I slide into the driver's seat and try to yank the car door from his grasp. He holds on tight.

"Don't worry, we got this, Earhart," he says, bending down so I can see his face, his hard features softening. "You focus on your new job, let me focus on mine. Okay? Let the flower guy go."

"Fine," I say again as I start the engine. "I'll let it go." He looks at me for a moment longer and I hold his gaze. We both know I'm lying.

He stands upright, shuts the door and then takes a step back from the car. I pull away and when I look back in my rearview mirror he's still watching me, hands stuffed in his pockets, shaking his head.

12

I drive to the clinic and sit in the parking lot for a few minutes absentmindedly rubbing Stitch's head and thinking about what Jake told me about leaving the investigation to the police. He's right, I should, but I don't think I can let this go. It isn't just that I was the one to find Gwen — that alone would be enough — but she was my friend and she reached out to me more than once and I dismissed her like our friendship meant nothing.

I use my cell phone to look up P. McNaughton's address. No less than twenty McNaughtons pop up, but only two with the first initial *P.* Penny McNaughton on Wildwood Drive and Peter McNaughton on Mercer Street.

I'm tempted to drive over there right now, but to do what? Knock on the door and if Peter answers ask him what he was doing at the river and at the funeral? He probably had more of a right to be there than I did. No, I need to think about this a little more.

Even if I wanted to go to Peter's house, I can't. I have to get to work. Jake is probably right, I should focus my energies on my new job. How much trouble can I get into there?

When I walk into the clinic with Stitch I find Dr. Huntley standing at the front desk talking with a woman of about fifty. She supports her emaciated frame by leaning against the counter. Her eyes are haunted and sunk deeply into her skull. Just peeking out from the neckline of her shirt is the raised outline of her port. Dr. Huntley appears to be speaking intently, and the woman looks up at him, hanging on to his every word.

I see that the television monitors placed throughout the waiting area are turned to a local news station and of course the topic of conversation is Gwen Locke's murder. The closed captioning running across the screen tells me they are revisiting and recycling every scant piece of information about Gwen's death that they can. I'm about to slink away when snippets of my 9-1-1 call appear on the monitor. They still don't mention me by name but by now it's common knowledge that I'm the caller. The newscaster brings up a bit of information that I didn't realize was going to be released to the public. The presence of a boat around the area of Five Mines where I found Gwen.

I'm a bit surprised it's even getting mentioned. I never actually saw the boat, I simply felt the wake it churned up. The boat could have been in the area and speeding about for any number of different reasons: a joyrider, an early-morning fisherman late for a day job, a murderer dumping a body. At any rate, the newscaster is advising viewers to contact the Mathias Police Department with any information regarding a boat and its driver no matter how inconsequential it seems.

I want to get back to the file room as unobtrusively as possible but I feel Lori's hand on my arm. I look away from the television to find Lori, along with Dr. Huntley and a few patients standing at the front desk, looking at me. "You saw a boat? Did you see who was driving it?" she asks.

I shake my head. "I'm not supposed to discuss the case," I say apologetically, hoping that will be enough to quiet any questions. I don't know anything and I don't want to be known as the lady at the clinic who found the body in the river. I just want to go about my business.

I excuse myself and retreat to the file room

where someone has set a new stack of files and a pile of unopened mail next to the scanner. I toss my keys onto my desk and decide to tackle the files first.

I've gotten through two when Dr. Huntley pokes his head into the room. "Amelia," he says. "How are you? I wasn't expecting you back from the funeral services so early. There was no need to rush back."

"I decided not to go to the grave site," I explain, leaving out the bit about how I chased Peter McNaughton out of the church. "The services ended a bit sooner than I thought, so I came over here."

"Good enough," Dr. Huntley says, pulling a pen from his white coat and spinning it in his fingers. "Sad about that woman, though."

"It is sad," I agree. "Did you know her?" I ask. "Gwen Locke? She was a floater nurse at Q & P."

Dr. Huntley leans against my desk, thinking for a moment and then shakes his head. He fumbles with his pen, dropping it to the floor. I bend over to pick it up and hand it back to him. "Her name sounds familiar, but I don't remember ever working with her. Are you getting settled in all right?" he asks and I nod. "Great," he adds. "Just let me know if you need anything."

After he leaves I return to my scanning and filing. Each piece of paper is an education in pain and suffering. Cancer does not discriminate. It doesn't care if you are young or old, rich or poor. It doesn't care about your race, color or creed. The drugs and treatments that are wielded to destroy the cancer can be just as devastating as the disease. After all, to battle a beast like cancer, you need to use something as equally cunning and toxic. I scan documents that refer to PET scans, maintenance therapy and IV treatments, I enter words like *Zometa* and *Methotrexate* and *Doxorubicin* into the computer system.

The last folder in my pile is especially thick. Though I'm only supposed to scan documents and then enter basic demographic information into the computer, I can't help but become immersed in the sad story of forty-nine-year-old Arlene Roberts of Broken Branch, a small town an hour from Mathias. She was referred to the clinic after visiting her regular doctor complaining of a fever, general malaise and an odd lump beneath her armpit. After taking a biopsy of the lump and sending it off to a lab for review, Dr. Huntley diagnosed Arlene with non-Hodgkin's lymphoma. Six months and upward of thirty chemo treatments later,

Arlene Roberts was dead. Each visit and every symptom and complication was meticulously chronicled by Dr. Huntley.

I frown and flip back through the pages. Despite the comprehensive paperwork, I can't seem to find the report that outlines the biopsy results. I'm sure it's simply misplaced and I jot a reminder on a sticky note and affix it to the front of the file and then scan and upload the files I do have.

Several files later I look up at the clock. It's well after four and I log off my computer and make a note of where I've left off in my filing. I close the file room door behind me. Down the long hallway I see Dr. Huntley pushing a man in a wheelchair toward an examining room. He leans over and says something into the man's ear and both break into wide smiles. Again, I'm struck by the rapport Dr. Huntley has with his patients. Lori is busy on the phone so I give her a quick goodbye wave and head out to the parking lot with Stitch.

I get into my Jeep and contemplate my next move. I should go home. Stitch is restless from being cooped up in the car and at the clinic all day and I should take him for a run, but I keep thinking about Peter McNaughton and his strange behavior at Gwen's funeral. Why would he take off in the middle of the services? What was it about seeing me that made him run? Could he have been up to something more nefarious than putting flowers where Gwen was found? Maybe searching for evidence that he left behind?

I pull out my phone and quickly check Gwen's Facebook page for any additional posts from Peter. There are dozens more comments on what a lovely funeral it was though none are from Peter, but I see I have a message from Chris, my old nursing friend.

Hi, Amelia. It's good to hear from you. I can't believe Gwen is gone! I saw you at the funeral but I couldn't find you after the service. Poor Marty and Lane. Have they arrested anyone? As for Peter McNaughton, Gwen and I went to high school with him. You were off to college by then. Peter went to a fancy private boarding school until his family's finances tanked and he had to come back to Mathias and attend public school like the rest of us regular folks. From what I remember, Peter came in the middle of our junior year. Once all the money was gone, Peter's mom refused to leave the house and Peter's father dealt with it by drinking bottle after bottle of fancy wine from his own private reserve.

I can relate except I could only afford the cheap stuff.

Peter was (is!) definitely weird. He was made fun of a lot at school. Kids weren't very nice to him, but I have to say he wasn't easy to like. Always hanging around uninvited, creepy.

I'm still on the skilled care floor at Mathias Regional. How about you? Don't be a stranger.

Chris

Well, this explains a lot. Before I can change my mind, I put the Jeep into gear and start driving toward Mercer Street. Everyone in Mathias is well acquainted with Mercer Street and the beautiful three-story, mid-Victorians there. The McNaughton house is constructed out of finely cut ashlar and was erected by descendants of the family during the Civil War. The front and side porches with their Tudor-style wooden arches must have once given it a genteel charm. Large double windows with broad cornice stone lintels and stone sills are dressed with heavy drapes making it impossible to see inside, but I can't help but get the sense that someone is watching me from within. The crowning glory of the structure, an octagonal belvedere with windows on each side, sits atop a hipped roof made of slate. Now it's just a run-down old house with a sagging porch and peeling paint where a formerly wealthy old man lives with his creepy son.

I park my Jeep down the street and wait. Growing up, there were all manner of ghost stories surrounding this house, the most chilling being that a young woman, a great-great-aunt of the McNaughtons, sat staring out the windows of the belvedere waiting for her true love, a soldier in the Civil War, to return home to her. He did come back, but too late. Despondent from being separated from her soldier and believing that he would never come back, she climbed through a window and threw herself from the peak.

Whenever I think of this story, I can't help thinking about Jake's wife, Sadie. Right up until the moment she leaped from Five Mines Bridge they had seemed so much in love. Always laughing, always touching each other as if one of them might suddenly drift away.

A few cars drive by and I pretend to be talking on my cell phone. If a concerned neighbor knocks on my window and wants to talk to me, I will have a difficult time explaining why I can't hear them but appear to be having an intense conversation with someone on my phone.

Thankfully, no one gives me a second glance and after about an hour I'm about ready to call it a day and head back home when a battered silver BMW circa 1970s passes me with Peter McNaughton behind the wheel. He pulls into the long driveway, parks and steps from the car, clutching a paper grocery sack to his chest. Without looking around Peter makes a beeline toward the detached garage. He steps out of my line of vision, and I scoot the Jeep forward a few feet, hoping that Peter won't notice.

He's unlocking the walk-in door to the garage when he pauses. He cocks his head as if hearing a far-off sound. He looks around, his eyes darting from side to side. He pushes the door open and then freezes. I follow his gaze as he turns toward the house, a look of grim resignation on his face. Standing on the porch is a frail old man with the pinched look of someone who has never been content. The elder McNaughton, I conclude. The two exchange words and though I have no idea what they are saying, it's clear that neither of them is happy.

Peter holds up his finger as if telling his father that he'll be just a moment and the old man's expression becomes mutinous and his mouth opens and closes in what I'm sure is a venomous tirade. Peter's slim frame quivers in agitation as he sets the sack just inside the door and then shuts it quickly behind him. With his head down, he scurries through the front yard and up the porch steps to where his father waits. Peter goes into the house and after a brief moment returns carrying a heavy jacket and what I think is a black-and-gray knit scarf. Peter helps his father into the coat and begins to wind the scarf around his neck. I think of what Jake said about Gwen having been strangled and I shake away the grotesque image of Peter looming over Gwen's nude body, scarf in hand.

Leaning heavily on his son, the old man continues his diatribe as they cautiously make their way down the rickety front steps. Peter keeps his mouth firmly shut, but I can tell his silence comes at a cost. Matching his father's shuffling gait, he guides the old man to the passenger seat of the BMW.

Once his father is inside and the door is shut, Peter pauses and looks around. He looks desperate, as if he wants to run, to disappear, and for a second I think he's going to spot me watching him but he doesn't. He's too absorbed in his own thoughts, his own personal prison, and briefly I feel sorry for him, but then I remember his strange behavior and I remember Gwen. What was in the paper sack that he placed in the garage? Why did he look so secretive? Peter moves to the driver's side of the BMW, gets inside and backs down the driveway and disappears down the street.

It's beginning to get dark and almost as if on cue, lights are turned on within the homes and curtains are being drawn. A car with a pizza delivery sign strapped to the roof drives past and pulls into a driveway two houses down. Stitch lifts his nose, suddenly alert. It's his suppertime.

What would Jake say if he knew I was sitting here waiting for a man I don't even know because he bought flowers for a woman I haven't talked to in two years? He'd shake his head in exasperation and tell me to leave the police work to the police. What would David say? He'd think I was crazy. He would think twice before letting Nora spend more time with me.

I start the car, determined to drop this whole thing. It's none of my business, I lost touch with Gwen a long time ago, had shut her completely out of my life, like I had so many others. I need to focus on the here, the now. I can't rejoin the living when I'm spending so much time thinking about the dead.

But something stops me from pulling away from the curb. Instead, I put the Jeep back into Park, grab Stitch's leash and we both get out of the car.

The street appears deserted but I have no way of knowing if someone is peeking out from behind a curtain. I bend down as if to clip the leash to Stitch's collar and whisper in his ear, *"Volno." Go ahead.* Stitch trots ahead of me and up the McNaughton driveway. *"Volno,"* I call again, hoping that none of the neighbors speak Czech. As long as I keep moving toward the garage and giving Stitch the command he'll keep heading that way. I stop and as if exasperated, put my hands on my hips. "Stitch, *volno,*" I call. Stitch, excited about his newfound freedom, scurries even farther away from me and begins sniffing at the scraggly holly bushes that edge the side of the garage.

I catch up to him and make a quick scan of the street as I stretch the sleeve of my coat over my hand to avoid leaving any fingerprints and then twist the doorknob. It swings open easily. I call to Stitch and we both slip inside, and I shut the door.

The garage is windowless, pitch-black and is creepy as hell. For me, the only thing worse than not being able to hear is not being able to see. A wave of vertigo nearly knocks me on my face and I grab the doorjamb to steady myself. The dizziness hits me sometimes, when I least expect it. In the early days, alcohol helped. Well, not really helped, but there is something infinitely more pleasant about a room spinning from the effects of wine than of my damaged vestibular system.

I fumble for my phone and use it as a flashlight so I can at least see a few inches in front of me. I slowly move the beam chest high around the perimeter of the wall in search of a light switch and find one just to the left of the door. I flip it on, and light floods the building.

To my surprise the interior of the garage is in absolute pristine condition. It certainly isn't the torture chamber that I envisioned but almost as disconcerting there are none of the usual functional items associated with a garage. There are no rakes or shovels propped up against the walls. No garbage cans or recycling bins. No dusty or cobwebbed corners. There is no telltale oil stain blooming across the concrete floor. In fact, it doesn't look like a vehicle has been stored in here for years.

"Sedni," I tell Stitch, and he sits directly in front of the door. *"Pozor."* Suddenly, Stitch is alert and fully focused on the door. Vigilantly, he will guard this spot and let me know if anyone is approaching. Unless something else catches his attention, of course.

A large mahogany desk sits in a corner along with a matching chair. They look like antiques, valuable. Beneath the desk and chair, covering the concrete is an old Persian rug. Just to the right of the desk is a tall bookshelf lined with books and photo albums. Next to the bookshelf is a compact minirefrigerator and sitting at an angle toward the desk is a space heater. Weird. It looks like Peter made the garage into his home office. Really weird, especially given the size of his house. Surely there must be space for Peter to have his own office there. Unless he wants to be assured privacy.

I have no idea how long Peter and his father will be away so I have to hurry. Stitch is already on his feet and distracted, sniffing at the paper bag Peter set on the floor before he left. I squat down and cautiously peer inside to find four bottles of a locally brewed beer, a few Granny Smith apples, a banana, three rolled-up newspapers and a bag of chips. Groceries. Okay, I'm an idiot. Of course a grown man who still lives with his cantankerous father would like a little privacy once in a while. It makes sense that Peter would come out to his man cave, sit at his desk, drink his beer, eat his Doritos and read the newspaper.

I should just leave but my curiosity gets the best of me and I once again tell Stitch to sit and watch and he complies with what I think might be a roll of the eyes.

I leave the sack where it sits and cross the garage to Peter's makeshift office. The top of the desk is bare except for a desktop computer and a small table lamp with a brightly colored stained glass shade. To my untrained eye my bet is on Tiffany. I pull open one of the desk drawers and find what one would expect: pens, pencils, scissors, a glue stick, tape, a stapler. The difference being that instead of a tangled jumble of office supplies found in most drawers, Peter has a spot for each in a custom-made desk organizer. Each compartment labeled with a sticker in case one would forget just where the paper clips might go.

I turn to check on Stitch and he's where I left him guarding the door. I open the next drawer. Peter appears to use this one for his personal files. Each is labeled and organized alphabetically. I tell myself that I'll just take a peek inside the final drawer and then I'm out of here.

I open the drawer and find newspaper articles. I pick up the stack. There are dozens of them all held together with a paper clip. The one on top is Gwen's obituary from our local paper. Not odd in itself, people cut obituaries out of the paper all the time. It's the accompanying articles that cause my heart to skip a beat. Most are from the Mathias paper but some are from newspapers as far away as Des Moines, Omaha and Chicago. They all refer to Gwen, her murder and the investigation. Some take up more than one page, some are only a few sentences long. Peter McNaughton, murderer or not, at the very least has an unhealthy obsession with Gwen.

The minutes are ticking by. Peter and his father may have run a quick errand and could be back at any moment. I try to arrange the clippings as neatly as I found them and return them to the drawer. I turn my attention to the bookshelf and from the titles I learn that Peter has an affinity for photography, string theory and true crime. Again, everything is organized alphabetically and by subject. The dust jacket of one of the books on the bottom shelf seems slightly off. I bend down for a better look. *Beautiful Symmetry — String Theory and the Universe* by Virgil Todd. It's subtle, but the dust jacket is too small for the book it covers. With difficulty, I pull the heavy book from the shelf and set it on Peter's desk. I peel away the jacket to find a large, worn, brown leather scrapbook. I peek over at Stitch again. He's still in his designated spot. Relaxed but watchful.

On the first page is a birth announcement proclaiming the arrival of a six-pound-three-ounce baby boy to Warren and Veronica McNaughton. It is accompanied by a photo of the young family. Veronica is sitting in a chair and holding Peter, and Warren is standing directly behind her, his eyes focused on a spot beyond the camera, one foot jutted out to the side as if already fleeing the frame. Veronica is a frail, birdlike woman with dark, serious eyes.

The following pages are much of the same. Family photographs highlighting birthdays and holidays. I frown, confused. Why would Peter feel the need to hide the scrapbook behind a physics book jacket? It doesn't make sense.

I flip to the middle of the book. There are

several photos of a group of about eight boys in their early teens. They are all dressed in pants and navy jackets with an insignia of some kind. Probably the crest of the fancy boarding school he attended before the family finances went belly-up. It takes me a moment to find Peter among the group. He looks happy, like he belongs.

Next comes a series of school pictures. Peter smiling from the page before is gone along with his school uniform. These must have been taken after he left the private school and had to attend public school like the rest of us. In his place is an awkward, scowling young man with his mother's serious dark eyes and his father's nervous energy sitting just below the surface of his skin.

I turn to the next page. Peter is older by a few years in this photo — sixteen or seventeen. His hair is longer and curls around his ears. A smattering of acne mars his forehead. He's dressed in a black tuxedo and stands stiffly next to a girl of about the same age.

It's the image of the girl that makes my heart skip a beat. It's Gwen. Younger by twenty-five years but it's definitely her. She's wearing a tea-length midnight blue taffeta prom dress and a wrist corsage made up of calla lilies and baby's breath. She is smiling brightly, completely at ease while Peter looks like he could throw up.

Had Peter and Gwen dated at one time? I couldn't quite picture it. Everything I knew about Gwen led me to believe that she was popular, outgoing, confident. I flip forward a few more pages and there is only one more picture of Gwen and Peter together. They are dressed in graduation robes and mortarboards and from the medals hanging from ribbons around their necks it looks like they were valedictorian and salutatorian of their graduating class. Again, Gwen is beaming but Peter looks ill at ease and casts a longing look toward Gwen. After all these years could Peter be obsessed with Gwen?

I answer my own question when I turn the page and find the first article about the murder when no victim had been named yet. Did he cut out this article after the public learned that Gwen was the woman killed or did he already know? The collection of news clippings and the flowers, calla lilies no less, left at the crime scene would surely point to this. Plus, I still couldn't quite reconcile why in the world Peter would run from the funeral after seeing me.

I look over at Stitch fully expecting him to be sprawled out across the floor fast asleep.

Instead, he's standing fully alert with ears perked up and twitching.

Someone is coming.

Though I'm tempted to take it with me, I replace the dust jacket on the scrapbook and return it to its spot on the shelf. Trying to move as lightly as possible I hurry over to the light switch and flip it to the off position. I find the garage doorknob and hesitate. Should I make a run for it or move slowly and creep back to my car? I take a deep breath as I turn the knob and open the door as little as possible, and letting Stitch go in front of me, squeeze through the opening and quickly shut the door behind me. The BMW is in the driveway, lights off and for a second I'm sure I'm caught but then I see Peter helping his father up the porch steps. If he looks left I'm caught and once McNaughton Sr. is through the front door, I'm sure Peter will come back out to the garage to finish whatever he started.

My best hope is to divert Peter's attention from the garage until I can slip away. "Stitch, *vpred,*" I whisper and point. Stitch tears off in a silver streak across the front yard and Peter and his father both swing their heads to the right. I don't even hesitate and take off running toward the back of the house. My plan is to go around the perimeter of the McNaughton house and meet up with Stitch on the other side. Just a lady whose dog got away. No big deal.

I move swiftly around the house, ducking low when I come to a window just in case someone inside happens to look out. I do catch a glimpse inside the home and am shocked by the stark contrast of the obsessively clean garage and the McNaughton house. It appears to be inhabited by hoarders. Stacks of newspapers, boxes and magazines are piled chest high. Black garbage sacks are strewn around the room haphazardly. Jesus, no wonder Peter hides out in the garage. I can't imagine living in such conditions.

I need to keep moving and just to be safe I cross over into a neighbor's backyard. Using the overgrown forsythia bushes as cover, I pause when an interior light pops on and someone looks out the window. I hold my breath, not daring to move. Even though I can't hear, I sometimes forget that I'm capable of making plenty of noise and clearly I've garnered some attention. The figure behind the window scans the yard and even comes out to the backyard to get a closer look.

Finally, after what feels like an eternity,

the homeowner goes back inside and the lights are extinguished. I scurry through the remainder of the yard, around the corner and onto the sidewalk. I try to steady my breathing as I pull the hood of my coat up around my ears as if to ward off the cold. I hold Stitch's leash loosely at my side.

Stitch trots toward me from the other direction just like I knew he would. I try to keep my attention on him and not look toward the McNaughton house. "Bad boy," I say in what I think is a loud, stern voice.

I try to keep my movements casual and measured but my hands are shaking as I try to clip the leash to his collar. It takes me three tries, but I finally succeed and load Stitch into the Jeep. Once inside, doors locked and engine started, I allow myself to look up at the house. Peter has come down to the bottom of his driveway, not fifty feet away, and is just standing there, watching me. His eyes flick toward the garage and then back, boring into me. He knows I was in his garage and he knows what I've found. I throw the Jeep into gear and with my heart slamming into my chest I speed away.

13

I crank up the heat in the Jeep but it's not until I reach the outskirts of Mathias that my hands stop shaking. What was I thinking? Now Peter McNaughton knows I've been snooping around his house and he obviously has something to hide. Why else would he try to conceal a scrapbook filled with pictures and news articles about a woman with whom he attended high school? Maybe Peter never fully got over Gwen. What if he tried to rekindle whatever it was he thought the two of them had together from high school and Gwen, married and with a child, told him to get lost? Maybe the rejection sent Peter over the edge and he killed her. People have murdered for less.

A deserted country road at night when there is no moon, no stars, is exceptionally dark. The only light comes from my headlights. I turn on my high beams but even that seems inadequate. I keep glancing in my rearview mirror expecting Peter's BMW to come barreling up behind me. I press down on the gas, urging the Jeep forward. I can't wait to get home. I want to lock myself inside with Stitch and build a fire. And if I'm honest with myself I want a drink. Badly.

I turn down my lane and when I reach the house I'm met with complete darkness. When I left this morning I didn't bother to turn on the porch lights. I park as close to the door as possible and look at Stitch to see if he is as nervous as I am. He's not. Though he paces the backseat, it's not out of any sense of danger, he's just anxious to get out of the car and to his supper. With phone and keys in hand, I slide from the Jeep, let Stitch out and hurry to the front door.

Stitch gets there first and is snuffling at the ground when I join him. He's found something.

I shine the light from my cell toward the front step and see an envelope lying there. I pause to look around the yard to see if whoever delivered the note is still around. I pick up the envelope, unlock and open the door, pull Stitch in with me and then quickly lock myself inside.

I turn on the lights, pull all the blinds and

then sit down at the kitchen counter and examine the envelope. My name is written in an unfamiliar scrawl across the front of the white envelope. There is no postage or postmark so the mail carrier didn't deliver it. What if it's from Peter McNaughton? What if it's a warning to back off and stay away from him? I know I'm being ridiculous. There's no way that Peter would know where I live. As far as I know he doesn't even know my name and besides, my address and phone number are unlisted.

Disgusted with my skittishness, I rip open the envelope. Inside is a thick piece of stationery with the letter *O* in large, ornate, script. I sigh. It's from Evan Okada thanking me for the cookies and accepting my apology for the misunderstanding. He goes on to say that I should feel free to call on him if I need anything at all. I peek out my window and up at Evan's house on the bluff. No lights shine from the windows. Now, that's a nice guy, I think. Someone who is able to let go of the fact that I got him arrested for simply coming down the bluff in a rainstorm to make sure that I was okay.

I set the note aside and look at my phone. I am all set to call Jake with all that I learned about Peter McNaughton, but what do I really know? He's a high school friend of Gwen's. He brought flowers to the place where she died. He clipped out a few news articles about her. He attended her funeral. Not one of these facts is alarming on its own. Jake is going to think I've been drinking again if I come to him with this. And what if I'm completely off base? What if I call the cops and an innocent man gets in trouble? No, I can't call Jake just yet. I need more proof.

I go to my computer and log on to Facebook and scan Gwen's page for any more comments from Peter. Nothing. In fact, all of his earlier posts to her page have been deleted. Peter's worried. He's starting to cover his tracks. Maybe at this moment he's finding a new hiding place for his scrapbook. Maybe he's destroying evidence and any other connections to Gwen. Instead of calling Jake and having to endure a lecture about leaving well enough alone, I decide to send him an email.

Jake, I know you think I'm overreacting but you really need to check out Peter McNaughton. I think he knows more than he's letting on. Please trust me on this. At least

look into where he was the night Gwen died.
Amelia

I reread what I've written. Great. That's not conspiracy theory-ish at all. I hit Send anyway. My inbox is overflowing with about two years' worth of neglected and unanswered emails. Most are junk mail or spam and I delete these without opening them. There are a few from old acquaintances that I haven't talked to since before the accident. I delete these also. There's one from a college friend that I haven't been in contact with since well before the accident. While she's someone I'd like to reconnect with, I don't have the energy to write some huge explanation of what has happened to me in the last two decades. I decide to come back to that one later.

Blindly, I hit Delete over and over again until an email catches my eye. It's from Gwen dated about a month ago with a subject line that reads Happy Birthday. Why would Gwen email me after so long? Why would she bother to offer me any good wishes after I completely cut her out of my life, refused to see her, refused to let her be my friend?

I open the email and see that along with

the lengthy letter Gwen has included an attachment. I click and a picture of Gwen and her daughter, Lane, appears. Lane is sitting on Gwen's lap and they are both smiling into the camera blissfully unaware of how terribly things are going to change in a matter of a few short weeks. Tears swell in my eyes and a wave of regret washes over me.

Dear Amelia,
Hello, old friend, and I do mean old — you are five years older than me. Happy birthday! I hope you are doing something special for yourself. Cake, ice cream, the works!

All is well in the Locke household. Marty really likes his new job at Deere and Lane has been busy all summer with swim lessons and day camp. Lane is loving second grade. She asks after Nora once in a while and asks when they can get together and play.

I ran into Terry from our nurse examiner training and she said she heard that you were doing really well. I'm glad to hear it. I would love to get together sometime and catch up. I miss our talks. In fact, I could really use your advice. I think something very strange is going on at work and I need to run it by someone so they can tell me I'm crazy. Just let me know what works for you and let's make it happen. It's been way too long, Amelia.

Hugs,
Gwen

I've been so self-absorbed, so selfish. How hard would it have been to send a response back to Gwen? A simple thank-you for thinking of me. Not only did I ruin my friendship, but I ended Lane's and Nora's, as well.

I also can't help thinking about what Gwen wrote about a problem at work and wonder if it may have had anything to do with her death. Most likely someone was stealing her lunch out of the refrigerator in the staff lounge, but what if it was something more serious? But then my entire theory about Peter McNaughton flies out the window.

I wonder if I should forward her email on to Jake but decide against it. I'll see what he has to say about Peter McNaughton first. I close my laptop.

I'm too keyed up to relax. This is when I'm my own worst enemy, when I can't keep my mind from spinning and I get the urge to drink. I go into the laundry room to change into running clothes and when I come back out Stitch is standing by the door. I don't want to go outside. An evil man may be out there waiting for me but it's even scarier to be in here alone with the devil sitting beneath my kitchen sink. Stitch does his little dance of excitement when he sees my running shoes. I open the door and together we step out into the cold, dark night, then start running.

Once we get to the main road I run facing traffic so I can see what might be coming. We only encounter two cars and neither of them appears to be an old BMW. Unless Peter decides to come up the old mud road to get to my house it doesn't look like I'll have to worry about him. At least tonight anyway. The cold air feels good against my face and once my muscles warm up I can feel the tension leach from my body, the need for a drink eases. After two and a half miles I feel like I'm going to be okay. I turn around to make the trek back home when my cell phone vibrates against my hip and I find a text message from Jake.

Marty Locke's alibi has checked out. He's in the clear.

I send him a quick thank-you for the info,

put my phone away, and Stitch and I start running again. Jake's text should make me feel better and it does in the sense that at least Gwen wasn't killed by the man who was supposed to love her most in the world. At least Lane won't lose her father too.

But too many questions still swirl around in my head. Peter knows that I've been snooping around his house. He clearly knew Gwen. What if he's the killer? What if he somehow found a way to get into my house? I scan the darkened countryside for any hint that someone might be lurking nearby, but the road is deserted. There are no houses, no cars and despite my need to get out of the house I understand just how foolish it is to be out here all by myself. If Peter came after me right now no one would hear me call for help. No one would hear me scream. I pick up my pace. Now I really have to fill Jake in on my suspicions about Peter. I just have to think of a way to tell him without letting on that I trespassed on the McNaughton property.

And then there's Gwen's email. It seems like such a small thing — a conflict at work — but when it comes to murder everything is important. I wonder if Gwen talked to Marty about any problems at work. Really it could range from a coworker not pulling their weight to sexual harassment. All possibilities. But enough to kill over? I doubt it.

By the time we reach the house I'm still thoroughly confused about Gwen's murder and am beginning to think that the most likely scenario is that she was in the wrong place at the wrong time and was randomly grabbed by a stranger. This makes my decision to go out for a late-night run all by myself all the more questionable. I pull my house key from my pocket and unlock the door and Stitch runs in search of his water dish while I unzip my jacket and head back to take a shower.

I step into the kitchen area and my blood runs cold. An open bottle of wine and a glass, half-filled with ruby-red liquid right next to it. I didn't pour that glass. I know I didn't.

I lunge for my phone, ready to dial 9-1-1 but then stop. If someone were in the house with me right now Stitch would be going berserk. But he's not. He's settled on the love seat and is scratching his ear with a back paw. Whoever was here is long gone. Just like the other night.

I check the other door and it's latched; the broomstick is in place. I look back at the wineglass. I've been on binges when I drank until I blacked out, woke up in places that I didn't remember going to, but that was when I consumed a hell of a lot of alcohol. I know I was tempted, but I haven't had a drink in eighteen months. I go from window to window and they're all locked up tight. I move through each room, looking for any other signs that someone was in the house. Nothing else seems out of the ordinary except that a framed picture of Nora and me that I have sitting next to my bed has been turned facedown. I could very easily have knocked the picture frame over, but I don't think so. Could someone have broken into the cabin, poured a glass of wine and then come up to my bedroom and moved the picture? I return the picture to the correct position and head back downstairs.

I'm just being paranoid. But how would someone have gotten in without breaking a window or a door? There's only one possibility. The extra key that I have hidden outside. But no one could know where it is. I don't keep it beneath a welcome mat — I don't even have one — and I don't keep it hidden beneath a flowerpot. I keep my extra key in a small magnetic box that I tuck behind my front license plate.

Taking Stitch with me, we go outside and I run my fingers behind the license plate.

The metal box is right where I left it. I pull it free and slide the cover open. The house key is there but that doesn't mean someone couldn't have used the key and then put it back. I should call the police, call Jake, but what am I going to say? Someone broke into my house and poured me a glass of wine? My credibility with Jake right now is shaky at best.

Besides, no one knows about my hidden key. But that's not exactly true. David knows I keep a house key hidden on my car. He's the one who gave me the idea for it years ago. But of all people, why in the world would David come into my house and drink a half a glass of wine? It's just crazy.

I look up at Evan's house on the bluff. But he doesn't make sense, either. I know for a fact I haven't had to use the extra key since I've moved in here so there's no way he could have seen me use it. I slide the cover back into place and clutch the case in my hand and bring it back inside with me.

I look at the nearly full bottle of wine still sitting on the counter and try to decide what to do. I could just pour the remaining liquid down the drain and throw the bottle in the garbage can. But what if whoever did this left fingerprints behind? Someone is messing with my head. I pull a clean dishrag from a drawer and use it as I gingerly pick up the wineglass and dump the contents into the sink and then transfer the glass and bottle to the cupboard beneath the sink, behind a bottle of dish soap and next to my own bottle of wine that I secreted away. If I don't have to look at it, maybe I won't be tempted to take a drink.

I stand upright and double-check the windows and doors one more time. Everything is locked up tight. Even still, first thing in the morning, I'm going to call and make an appointment to get my locks changed. Just to be safe.

14

I spend half the night thinking about the bottle of wine left on my counter. Maybe I should have called the police — but what would they do? I've already called them once to the house and it was a false alarm. They'd probably just chalk it up to the hysterical lady who's too spooked to stay at her house all alone. But I know someone is messing with my head and the only person I can think of who would do this is David. But why? He's actually been kind of nice to me as of late. Is it all an act? And what does he have to gain? I have no legal rights when it comes to Nora and I haven't asked him for any money. It doesn't make sense.

Before I leave for work in the morning I call the locksmith and they tell me they can't come out to change all the locks until Saturday morning. Still two days away but then there will be no way David or anyone else will be able to get into the house. I'll find a new hiding place for the extra key.

As I drive to the clinic I decide that I'm going to invest in a security camera so I can nail David for screwing with me. In the meantime, I've removed my extra key from its hiding place behind the bumper of my Jeep.

The minute Stitch and I walk into the waiting room I can tell I'm not going to get much filing done today. The patients are all instantly enthralled by Stitch. They take turns petting him and Stitch is basking in all the attention.

When I finally get to my desk and start my data entry it's nearly nine o'clock. Each file that I open tells a story and today I learn about a sixty-three-year-old woman named Sharon Quigley who has small cell lung cancer, and Mitchell Rivera, a forty-eight-year-old man from a nearby town who has a diagnosis of myelodysplastic syndrome. Simply explained, it's a type of cancer where the bone marrow doesn't make enough healthy blood cells.

Again, there appears to be missing paperwork in the file including initial lab work and the results of a bone marrow aspiration and biopsy. Because Barb is the office manager, I should probably go to her and tell her about the misplaced reports, but I don't want to get anyone in trouble. It's not that missing paperwork is an unusual occurrence. It happened when I was in the ER too. We tried to be very careful, but once in a while a report or two would go rogue.

I decide to just make a mental note of the missing information when Dr. Huntley peeks his head in the door. "How are you getting along?" he asks as Stitch gets up to greet him.

"Fine, thanks," I say and then decide to mention the documents. "I did notice that in some of the files it looks like there are some lab reports missing." I hand him Mitchell's file. "See, his initial CBC and biopsy paperwork aren't in here."

Dr. Huntley opens the file and his forehead creases as he flips through the pages. "That's odd," he says, handing the file back to me. "Maybe they were accidentally placed in another patient's file."

"I'll keep an eye out for them, but there are a few other files that seem incomplete too. I've been jotting down notes."

"Well, it's a good thing we're getting a handle on all these paper files now. Once we go to a fully digitized system, we won't have these errors. Thanks for catching them," he says and rubs Stitch's head. He pulls a small dog treat from his white coat pocket and looks for my permission before giving it to him. I nod. I know that Lori has a stash of treats in her desk drawer just for Stitch and several times a day someone stops by to give him one. I'm going to end up having a very spoiled dog on my hands from working here.

I watch through the doorway as one of the nurses leads a patient to one of the examining rooms. The pale, drawn face trudging forward hoping, praying for a little good news, a little relief. I remember this from when I worked with patients: the gratitude they felt when I was able to ease their pain or listened to them, or was just there for them. Of course there were also those patients who threw up on me or tried to grab my ass. I try not to focus on those patients so much.

I miss my old life and the hectic craziness of the ER. I can't imagine spending the next twenty years — let alone the next six months — sitting in this windowless room going through files. But here I am. I know that Lori offered to have me come and work in the reception area, but interacting with others is exhausting and this dark, little room is, in its own way, comforting. I pull another file from the cabinet and begin to read. Simon Burger. Sixty-nine years old. Testicular cancer.

After work, Stitch and I spend the afternoon killing time before heading over to my speech therapy appointment. We drive to the Mathias river walk and Stitch and I sit on a bench in the covered pavilion that looks over the choppy water that is the same color as the iron-gray sky. The biting, clean scent of snow is in the air. I wonder if this is another Iowa weather fake out. I've thought it was going to snow for days now.

Once again, I can't believe how much my hometown has transformed over the past twenty-odd years. Downtown Mathias, once grimy and neglected, is now a tourist attraction where people come to shop and dine. Today the cool weather has kept people away and Stitch and I are the only visitors. Stout herring gulls spiral above us in loops, scavenging for scraps of food.

The cold prods us onward and we start to walk again until we come upon the old train bridge where Sadie leaped into the water. Why, why, would she want so badly to die? To leave someone who loved her as much as Jake did? I'll never understand it. I wonder if Jake ever comes down here and walks this path thinking the same thing. Probably not. I still find it painful to drive past David's clinic, and he's still alive.

The forecasted snow finally begins to fall but still a fisherman braves the cold and slowly steers his small boat through the choppy water. I think of Gwen. How did her killer transport her to the curve of the river where I discovered her? Knowing Gwen, there was no possible way someone could have forced her to walk the trails to her own death. She would have fought, and according to Jake there didn't appear to be any defensive injuries on her body.

I'm convinced that the only way the killer could have gotten her to the river was to incapacitate her first, then take her by boat to the spot where I found her. But why would he strangle her, revive her, and strangle her again? Was her killer some sicko who got off on squeezing the breath out of her or was he trying to force her to tell him something he wanted to know? What could be so important?

I think of Gwen's email and the phone message she left me. What would possess her to reach out to me again after so much time? Maybe Marty will know. If I could talk to him for just a few minutes maybe, in the very least, he could tell me why Gwen was so eager to reconnect with me? Was it because she missed our friendship or because of something else?

I look at my watch. I still have an hour and a half before I have to be at my speech rehab appointment. Do I really stop over at Marty's house? Is it too soon? Too intrusive? But what if he holds the answers needed to bring her killer to justice? I know he would want to help.

The snow is falling more heavily now, so Stitch and I walk back to the car. Once back on the road, we stop off at a local take-and-bake shop and pick up a pan of lasagna and garlic bread to bring to Marty. After my accident, droves of people showed up at the house with meals for us. I know that David and Nora really appreciated it. As for me I didn't eat much, I was too busy drinking my meals.

Once back on the road I start second-guessing my impulsive decision to go see Marty. How would I feel if someone showed up on my doorstep without any notice soon after I lost someone I loved? In reality I know exactly how I would feel and what I would do. After I lost my hearing I didn't want to see anyone. I avoided others at all costs, including Gwen and Jake. It was worse after David ordered me to leave. All I wanted to do was curl up into a ball and die. It wasn't until Jake dragged me out of bed and practically forced me to go to an AA meeting did I begin to emerge from my self-imposed exile.

I almost hope that Marty won't be home as I turn down their street. Gwen and Marty's house is the same as a dozen others that line their quiet street. All the homes are split-levels with either tan or gray siding. All have the same hipped and half-hipped rooflines and black shutters. I pull into the Lockes' sloped driveway and before I even put the Jeep into Park the curtains that cover the front window sway open.

There's no going back now. The door opens and a haggard figure comes into view. Marty looks startlingly different than he did at the funeral. He is unshaven and his dark hair is greasy and lays in oily hanks around his face.

I step from the Jeep, release Stitch and grab the pan of lasagna and bread before heading up the walk. "Hi, Marty," I call, "it's Amelia Winn."

Marty looks at me through dull, blue eyes that seem to have sunken into his skull. His lips are chapped and he holds on to the door frame as if to steady himself. "I knew Gwen. We worked together at Queen of Peace, and we were friends. Lane and my daughter, Nora, used to play together."

Marty licks his lips and I wonder if he's been drinking. I take a step closer to try to see if I can smell any alcohol on his breath. I can't. He pulls a pair of glasses out of his wrinkled front shirt pocket and puts them on. "Of course, I remember you, Amelia," he says. "How are you? Please come in."

"I'm doing well, thanks. Do you mind if Stitch comes too?" I ask.

Marty ruffles Stitch's head. "No, the more the merrier." He steps aside to let us enter. A pile of shoes sits by the front door and a jacket has been tossed carelessly on the floor. Marty self-consciously runs a hand through his hair. "Lane's still at school. She wanted to stay home with me but her counselor at school thought it would be better for her to be with her classmates. Stick to a routine." He looks around the room. "I haven't had a chance to clean up yet today." A laundry basket filled with clothes waiting to be folded sits on the floor, a thin layer of dust covers the coffee table, and a pillow and a blanket lay in a tangle on the couch. The space has the forlorn look of a once well-tended room that takes too much energy to care for anymore.

Marty catches me looking at the pillow and blanket. "It's hard to sleep in my bedroom without her," he says. I want to tell him I understand. I still don't sleep well without David at my side. I want to tell him that I sleep with the lights on and with one hand on Stitch so I know I'm not alone. But all I can do is nod.

I follow him to the kitchen where a stack of unopened mail is scattered across the table, dirty dishes are piled in the sink and plastic bags half-filled with groceries sit on the counter as if forgotten. The smell of spoiled milk and fried eggs permeates the room. "I brought you a lasagna and some garlic bread. You can freeze it until you want to eat it. The baking directions are right on top there."

"Thanks," he says, accepting the pan from me and transferring it to the refrigerator. "Coffee?" he asks. I'm not thirsty, but I say yes just to be polite. He searches the cupboard for two mugs and pulls the carafe from the warming plate and pours. He hands me a cup and I take a sip.

"Gwen told me you were in an accident and lost your hearing," Marty says and takes a big gulp of his own coffee.

"I'm getting the hang of it," I say. "Most of the time I have to fill in the gaps to know what people are saying. I speech read and rely on gestures and facial expressions. If you use short sentences and I can see your face, I'll get the gist."

"Kind of like *Wheel of Fortune,* huh?" he says, smiling at his own joke.

"More like charades," I say, "but I get along okay." We busy ourselves with drinking coffee to fill the awkward silence that follows.

"Marty, I am so sorry," I finally say, my throat tight with tears. "Gwen and I lost touch over the past few years but she was always a good friend to me."

Marty scrapes his bottom teeth against his top lip as if trying to bite back the emotions threatening to spill over. "I saw you at the funeral. Thanks for coming."

"You're welcome," I say, absentmindedly brushing toast crumbs that sprinkle the surface of the kitchen island into my hand. A butter knife tacky with congealed jelly sticks to the countertop and I pry it loose. The place is a mess. Lane shouldn't be living in these conditions. I add the crumbs and the dirty knife to the overflowing sink.

"For a while the police thought I might have killed her," Marty says. "Can you believe it? Me kill Gwen." He shakes his head at the inanity of the thought.

"Do you have any idea who might have done it?" I ask.

"The police asked me that too." He rakes

his fingers through his hair and when he pulls his hand away it's standing in oily spikes. "I can't think of anyone who would want to hurt Gwen. All she ever did was try to help people."

"Gwen tried to reach out to me after my accident, tried to help me. But I shut her out. I feel so bad about that."

Marty nods his head as if remembering. "She was sad about that. But understood."

"I got an email from Gwen a while back, wishing me a happy birthday. She also said she was having some kind of work dilemma. Do you have any idea what that might have been about?"

Marty pauses, thinking before he speaks. His face slowly hardens, the dimming afternoon sunshine casting a harsh light on his features. "Once in a while she would get threats from some men."

"What men?" I prod when he doesn't continue.

"The rapists and men who beat their wives and girlfriends," he says bitterly. "They would call the house or show up at the hospital and tell her to stay away."

I think of my hit-and-run and it makes sense that these men, who were most likely facing criminal charges, would try to intimidate Gwen so she would back off. "Did you tell the police this?" I ask.

"Yeah, but I couldn't tell them who the guys were. I really have no idea. Everyone she worked with loved Gwen." Marty's eyes shine with admiration as he remembers.

"What about a Peter McNaughton?" I ask. "Did Gwen ever say anything about him?"

To my surprise, Marty smiles wryly and shakes his head. "Peter McNaughton is harmless. He and Gwen were friends from way back when. Peter is a bit odd but Gwen was never scared of him. Why? Did something happen with Peter? Did he do something?"

"No, no," I backtrack. "I just saw him at the funeral and wondered. So you can't think of anything work-related that worried Gwen?"

"The only other thing I can think of is Gwen mentioned a patient she met at the hospital who she was worried about."

"Do you remember the patient's name? What was wrong with her?"

"All I can remember is she had a name that was a kind of a bug or insect. It was an odd name. I'll think of it."

"Do you remember what department she was working in when she met the patient?" I ask. If Marty can tell me this, I might be able to narrow down what the problem could have been.

"I think she said the woman was going to have a baby or had a baby maybe." Marty shakes his head. "I'm not sure, but Gwen was pretty riled up."

"How long ago was this? Did you tell the police?"

"Maybe a month ago." He shakes his head. "I didn't say anything. Gwen didn't mention a hospital or doctor by name. Just said that she didn't like it when people played God." That sounded a lot like the Gwen I remembered. Feisty and looking out for the underdog. "All I could give them was her calendar where she kept track of all her appointments. Do you think I should call them back and tell them?"

"It wouldn't hurt," I say. "So the police have Gwen's calendar, then?" I ask, disappointed. How I would like to get a look at Gwen's schedule over the past year.

"They made a copy of it and gave it back." Marty points to a calendar still opened to October hanging on the wall next to the refrigerator. I go over to get a closer look. The month of October features a picture of the Great Wall of China. I remember Gwen talking of always wanting to visit it. I wonder if she ever got there.

I run my fingers over the small, tight script

that fills nearly every date box. Gwen's handwriting. I try to decipher the cryptic shorthand. *L~GrScouts* and *G~QP/ER* under October 5 must mean that Lane had Girl Scouts and that Gwen had a shift in the Queen of Peace emergency room. Under October 30, the night before I found her body, it reads *L~cost, G~MR/Onc, M~oil change.*

Marty comes up behind me. I can smell the sour odors of clothing worn too long and unwashed skin. I turn so I can see his lips. "Lane needed to bring a costume to school for Halloween," he says, translating the code for me. "Gwen had a shift at Mathias Regional and I had an appointment to take the car in for an oil change."

"It looks like she was working a lot," I observe.

"Yeah, she was trying to take on as many shifts as she could. We were trying to save a little extra money."

"Would you mind if I took the calendar for a few days?" I ask, expecting Marty to balk at such a strange request.

"Go ahead," he says, taking it down from the wall for me. "It makes me sad to look at the damn thing."

"I should probably get going," I say as he

hands me the calendar. "I'm so sorry about Gwen."

Marty glances around the room helplessly and takes in the brimming sink and sticky counters. "It's all so overwhelming," he says, rubbing his eyes with his thumb and index finger. "At least Gwen's mom is in town, that helps."

"You can call me if you need anything at all," I say. "Help with Lane or to run some errands. Just let me know." I write down my cell number on a scrap of paper, give Marty a quick hug and we say our goodbyes.

It's still snowing when I load Stitch into the Jeep and we drive along the slick roads to my speech rehab appointment and make it just in time. I spend the next forty-five minutes working with the therapist on correctly saying my *s, sh, r, f* and *th* sounds.

When we step back outside at least another inch of snow has already blanketed the ground and it's still coming down. Stitch leaps into the air, snapping at the spiraling filaments. I close my eyes, open my mouth and extend my tongue to catch a few flakes of my own, momentarily transported back in time to when I was a child wearing mismatched winter gloves and hand-me-down snow boots from my brother. This is the comforting hush that I remember from my childhood — the quiet that comes with snowfall, when the entire world is muffled beneath a downy quilt of snow. For the first time in a very long time, the silence and the dark do not frighten me.

I stand with my arms outstretched, face uplifted to the darkening sky until my skin is damp with moisture and my cheeks burn with the cold. I bend down and scoop up a handful of snow into a ball and throw it across the parking lot. Stitch sprints after it, his back legs slipping momentarily before gaining traction. He loses sight of the snowball and his eyes dart around in confusion. I pack another and toss the ball lightly into the air and Stitch, graceful as any ballerina, leaps through the air and catches the sphere in his teeth where it explodes into a thousand tiny bits.

Again and again I pat the snow into balls and throw them for Stitch to catch. He has worked himself into a frenzy, darting first toward me and then away, his tail wagging furiously. He tries his best to retrieve the slushy orbs I throw but much to his bewilderment they melt before he can bring it back to me. The streetlights pop on, giving the snowfall a fairy tale–like quality.

It takes me a moment to realize that I'm laughing. Not just smiling, not giggling or chuckling, I'm full-out laughing. Stitch pauses in his play, his chest rising and falling rapidly, his tongue lolling heavily from his mouth, to stare at me. I don't think Stitch has ever heard me laugh before. He's heard me give stern commands, he's heard me whisper softly in his ear. He's even heard me cry, but never laugh. Not like this.

Stitch doesn't quite know what to make of this; he steps tentatively closer and regards me with newfound interest. I scrape up another fistful of snow and launch it as far as I can. Stitch goes out long, his powerful legs churning up the snow, as he crosses the deserted parking lot. I try to remember what my laugh sounds like, but I can't. It's like trying to remember the face of a long-dead relative or a long-lost love — just out of reach.

When my fingers are red and raw and my shoes and socks are wet from the snow, I call Stitch back to me. It's time to go home. I brush the snow from the Jeep's windows, open the door, pull the lever that makes the front seat tilt forward and urge Stitch inside. *"Ke mne,"* I tell him, hoping that he and his wet paws will stay in the backseat. I shut Stitch inside and am just reaching for the door handle when I feel a presence behind me. I want it to be Corrine, my speech therapist, but I know it's not. I quickly turn around, heart pounding. Instead of Corrine I find Peter McNaughton not more than twenty feet away. He's bounding toward me.

I'm frozen to the spot and can't tear my eyes away from his face. His skin is pale, his mouth an angry red slash. His lips move rapidly but I have no idea what he's saying. Out of the corner of my eye I see that Stitch, sensing my distress, has started pawing at the window.

I reach behind me searching for the door handle. He continues his approach and without laying a hand on me forces me against the cold metal of the Jeep. My fingers find the handle and I lift it. I'm able to pull the door open a few inches and Stitch is over the seat in an instant trying to nose his way through the small opening. Peter moves quickly forward and shoves the door shut nearly catching Stitch's snout. He's so close that I can smell the stale stench of coffee on his breath. I search wildly for any sign of help but the parking lot is empty of people.

Peter's mouth continues to twist in anger and he's speaking so fast that I'm only able to untangle a few random words. *Garage, trespass, police.* With an open hand he strikes the Jeep just behind my left ear. Was this what happened to Gwen? Did Peter become so angry, so incensed that he lost control and killed her?

If I can just squeeze past him, I think I'll be able to outrun him and make it back to the speech therapy clinic. But what if the office is locked up tight for the night? What will I do then?

"Stop!" I shout. "Get back." I press the palms of my hands to his chest and shove. He stumbles a few steps backward and for a moment I think he's going to fall but he catches himself and staggers upright. "What do you want?" I ask.

Just as quickly as Peter's assault has started it's over. I don't know if he sees the terror in my eyes or if he's afraid that Stitch's barking will alert someone from inside one of the nearby businesses, but he holds his hands out as if placating me.

"What do I want?" he asks, his eyes widen in disbelief. "What do I want?" he repeats. "You need to leave me alone. Stay away from me. Stay away from my home."

"Why were you at the river?" I ask, knowing that I should just get into my car and get the hell out of there. "Why did you run from the church when you saw me?"

"Why were *you* at the river?" He shoots right back at me. "How do you know

Gwen?"

I'm taken off guard by his questions. This isn't how I would think a man guilty of murder would behave. "I found her," I find myself explaining. "We were friends once."

"You're the one who called 9-1-1?" He regards me suspiciously and then glances at Stitch who is still going crazy in the Jeep.

"Yes," I say. Slowly, I step backward knowing it's now time to take my leave. McNaughton might be calm for the moment but that can all change in a second.

"You think I hurt her, don't you? That's why you came to my house. It wasn't me. We've been friends for years." All the fight has gone out of him and I have no doubt that one solid punch to his stomach would send him to his knees. "I would never hurt Gwen," he says.

Suddenly, I feel sorry for him. There's nothing frightening or menacing about him and for some reason I believe what he is saying.

"Then who?" I ask. "Who would do this to her?"

"Go ask your husband," he says just as Corrine and another speech therapist are coming through the lot toward their cars. "And be careful," he adds before he turns and leaves. It takes a moment for his words to register with me. They make no sense. I must have gotten it wrong. I get it wrong a lot. Especially if I don't know the person who's speaking well.

Go ask your husband.

Can that be right? Peter's crazy. He has to be.

I open the driver's-side door, climb inside and lock the door. With shaking hands I fumble for my keys and manage to start the car. Stitch is in the passenger seat next to me, still barking. *"Utisit, utisit,"* I say over and over until Stitch has calmed. *Hush, hush.* It really isn't Peter whom I'm afraid of. It's what he said. *Go ask your husband. Be careful.*

I don't know what to do or where to go. So I just drive, turning down random streets, winding my way through parts of Mathias that I haven't been to in years. My vision blurs and I realize that I'm crying. Why would Peter tell me to ask David about how Gwen was hurt? As far as I know, David barely even knew Gwen. It's true we were friends, but we almost never spent time together with our husbands, and while Gwen was a nurse at the same hospital where David worked, she shifted around departments and floors. Besides, how did Peter know whom I was married to anyway?

I wipe away my tears with my forearm and glance in the rearview mirror almost expecting to find Peter following close behind. No one is there.

Stitch is finally calm but I have no doubt that he would have ripped Peter's throat out in order to protect me.

I don't want to go home. I'm not thinking straight. Is Peter dangerous or just crazy? Maybe he's both. He does seem to have a strange obsession with Gwen. The news articles, the hidden scrapbook. And what about David? I'm still sure he was the one who left the glass of wine on my kitchen counter. Could he really have been involved with Gwen? Involved in her death? The very idea is ridiculous. Isn't it? David delivers babies and takes care of Nora. He doesn't kill people. The thoughts are ricocheting around my skull so furiously that I itch for a drink. Something to calm my nerves, something to quiet the storm in my head.

Before I even realize it, I find myself back on familiar roads. In the end, this isn't about me at all. It's about Gwen. It's about her daughter. It's about making sure that a very bad person can't hurt anyone else. I have to go to the police department and tell Jake everything. He'll know what to do.

15

I wait for Jake in one of the hard plastic chairs in the waiting area. When he finally appears, he signals me to follow him into his office. I do and when he shuts the door behind us I'm positive he's going to give me hell for trying to insert myself into the investigation.

I take a seat and Stitch sits at my feet, watchful, as if expecting McNaughton to come through the door at any second. I wait for the ass-chewing to begin. Instead, Jake signs, "Now tell me exactly what happened."

I take him step-by-step through each of my encounters with Peter but conveniently leave out how I ended up in his garage going through his things. I also leave out the part of the story when Peter says, "Go ask your husband." Why, I'm not sure. I guess despite our past and our differences, I don't want to accuse David of murder without one shred of evidence.

"So," Jake signs, "you just happened to be walking Stitch down the exact street where McNaughton lives?" Jake doesn't give me a chance to respond. "This is the same guy who you saw leaving flowers at the river and this is the same guy who took off from Gwen's funeral when he saw you?"

I nod.

"And while you're walking Stitch on the same street where Peter McNaughton lives, Stitch just so happens to escape from his leash and runs onto his property? And then today, out of nowhere, Peter McNaughton follows you to speech therapy, corners you and starts yelling and then apologizing and crying?"

I nod again.

"And that's the entire story? When we bring McNaughton in to talk to him, he's not going to have a different story?"

"You're going to arrest him?" I ask. "I don't know if you should do that."

"Well, let me tell you a few things about Peter McNaughton. We have a file on him about this thick." Jake holds his thumb and forefinger about five inches apart. When he sees the alarm on my face he adds, "No, it's not what you think. Peter calls *us* about once a week complaining about something or reporting some sort of crime. A neighbor making too much noise, someone loitering around his bookstore, kids knocking on his front door and running away, a lady on his property with a dog running around without a leash." He slides his eyes toward Stitch and I feel my face grow hot. "Peter is a one-man Neighborhood Watch. He really is harmless."

This matches what Marty told me, as well. "He has a bookstore?" I ask. "Which one?"

"A used bookstore over on Depot Street. I think it's called The Book Broker."

I've heard of it, driven past it a million times but have never been inside and had no idea that it was owned by Peter McNaughton.

"If it will make you feel better, we can talk to him. Remind him it's not a good idea to corner women in parking lots and start yelling at them. Besides, we can tell him that you're harmless too." I give him a sour smile.

"I should get home," I say. "The weather is supposed to get pretty bad."

"It already is. There's an ice storm advisory. Why don't you crash at my place tonight?" Jake signs.

"I don't know . . ." I begin, but the offer is tempting. The roads out to my place can be pretty treacherous and I'm still a little freaked out about the whole wine bottle fiasco. I haven't told Jake about it. I'm afraid he'll start putting me into the same category as Peter.

"Come on," he says, "I can take off now." Jake stands and grabs his coat from a hook on the back of the door. "We'll go to my house."

I look at the clock on the wall. It's almost seven thirty.

"Seriously," he says, seeing the doubt on my face. "It's okay. We'll grab some food and watch the Hawkeye game."

I won't say it out loud, but I'm relieved. "It's probably safer," I concede.

"Then it's settled. Let's go," Jake says.

Stitch and I follow Jake out of the station and to my car. Night has fully fallen and the streetlights have come on. The snowplows have made their rounds, turning the newly fallen snow grimy along the fringes. The temperature is at that level just above freezing when the skies don't know if they are supposed to rain or snow. Sleet falls in icy sheets and I hold on to Jake's arm until we reach my Jeep. I carefully follow Jake's SUV to a sub shop where we pick up dinner and then to his house, the one he shared with Sadie.

It's a two-bedroom craftsman in a quiet, tree-lined neighborhood just a few blocks from where we both grew up. If Jake and Sadie had children they would have gone to the same elementary school that we did. I park behind him in his driveway and together we walk up the slick steps to the front door.

Inside, not much has changed since Sadie died. He still has the same sofa and love seat, the same pictures on the walls, the same books on the bookshelves. I don't know how he stays in this house. How does he walk across the same floors that Sadie once walked? How does he sit in the same furniture, sleep in the same bed without feeling her presence? Maybe he does feel her there. Maybe that's the entire point.

Despite its unaltered appearance, despite all the cozy furniture, the house has a neglected air about it. Maybe that's because I knew Sadie. Knew that her very presence filled a room. Sadie was sweet, beautiful, kind, and she and Jake were inseparable. In crowds she was always searching for him. *My Jake* she called him. Even when all the eyes in the room were on her, Sadie was always looking for her husband.

What did she see in the murky waters of Five Mines that compelled her to leap from the train bridge? I don't know how she could leave a world that held someone whom she so clearly loved and who so clearly loved her.

I kick off my shoes and take off my coat. Jake takes it from my hands and opens the closet door. As he reaches for an empty hanger I see Sadie's red, ankle-length, woolen coat. Four winters have passed since Sadie killed herself. I wonder if Jake presses his nose into the scratchy fabric in search of some lingering essence of her. It makes me sad thinking of Jake this way, held captive by a ghost. A small voice in my head scolds — *who's the one holding on to the past?* I'm the one still clutching on to the eroded edges of my marriage.

Jake presses a button on a remote and the TV comes to life. He tells me to take a seat and tosses me a throw blanket and the remote. "Rookie," he signs and moves to somewhere in the back of the house. I take this to mean that he's going to let Rookie out of his kennel.

I switch on a light and settle onto Jake's couch and arrange the blanket around my legs. I know that Jake doesn't let Rookie on the furniture, so I don't invite Stitch to join me. Instead, he spends a few minutes sniffing each corner, each chair leg and a discarded pizza box left on the coffee table.

Jake and Rookie come into the room setting Stitch on edge. With his broad chest and regal stature, Rookie is definitely the alpha male. Stitch waits rigidly while Rookie sniffs at him and assesses Stitch with his sharp eyes. When Rookie is satisfied that Stitch is no threat to him, he looks at Jake, who orders him to go lie down. I notice that Rookie complies with each of Jake's commands immediately and without complaint. I look down at Stitch. *"Lehni,"* I say. *Down.* He ignores me and begins to snuffle the pizza box again.

I catch Jake laughing as he comes over to the couch, take-out bag in hand, and I stretch out my legs so he can't sit down next to me. He does anyway, and I scramble to move my feet before he sits on them.

When Jake finally stops chuckling I can see just how exhausted he is. He's been working 24/7 on Gwen's murder and it doesn't look like he's much closer to finding the killer than he was on that first day.

"You okay?" I ask, taking in the dark smudges beneath his eyes and the deep grooves that seem to have suddenly appeared in his forehead.

"I'm fine." He sets the sub-shop bag on the arm of the sofa and props his feet up on the coffee table. I'm well aware of how close we're sitting to each other — only inches apart. "All part of the job." He closes his eyes and folds his hands across his chest. I know this is true. Jake lives for his job. Since Sadie died it has become much more than a job really, more like a vocation.

"Now that you know Marty didn't kill Gwen, what are you thinking?" I ask as I begin to feed Stitch one of the sub sandwiches we picked up.

Jake opens one eye. "I can tell you what I'm not thinking. I'm not thinking it's Peter McNaughton. At least not yet."

I nudge him with my shoulder. "Come on, you must have someone in mind."

Jake sits up. "We've got nothing," he signs. "The ME says there are no signs of a sexual assault so the theory that she was abducted and raped is out the window. From all that we can find, Gwen Locke was simply a wife and a mom who worked as a nurse and ended up strangled and dumped in Five Mines." Jake looks defeated and this isn't like him at all. Jake doesn't give up.

"Hold on a sec," he says and gets up. He disappears into another room and comes back a moment later carrying a manila folder. I almost groan. I've had my fill of manila file folders as of late. "You're a nurse. Can you take a look at the ME's report and tell me if anything at all looks out of the ordinary. I've gone through it a million times and from what I can see it doesn't tell me a damn thing that will help me solve this case."

"Sure," I say, and he opens the file and pulls out a small sheaf of papers and hands it to me. Jake watches me as I read and he's right. There is very little to learn from the autopsy, at least initially, besides the fact that Gwen was strangled. Listed is the obvious injury from the blow to her head and the ligature mark around her neck but beyond this there doesn't appear to be much in terms of forensic evidence — no wounds on her hands to indicate that she fought back and no evidence that she was drugged. Plus the fact that Gwen's body was deposited in Five Mines means there is a good chance that any evidence left behind by the killer was washed away and was compromised by the millions of microorganisms found in a river's ecosystem.

I continue to read and my eyes stumble on a tiny notation that I almost miss. To me it's the most tragic piece of information in the entire report. "She was pregnant," I say, looking up at Jake.

"Yeah," Jake says. "About three months along."

"Did Marty know?" I ask. He didn't mention anything when we met.

"He says he didn't but he also said that they had been trying for a while and Gwen had a few miscarriages before then. Marty said that Gwen was probably going to wait until she was sure the baby was healthy before telling him."

"So he's sure the baby was his?" I ask.

"The lab is testing the fetus's paternity but there's absolutely no indication that Gwen was having an affair. She went to work, she came home. That's it."

But of course that wasn't just it. Whoever killed Gwen targeted her for some reason: for the way she looked, for something she knew or something she saw. If we can figure out what it was, her murder would be solved. In frustration, Jake tosses the file folder on the coffee table and the corner of a photograph slides out. The autopsy photos.

I reach for them but Jake gathers them back up. "You don't need to see those," he says.

"I'm a nurse, I found her," I say, gently tugging on the folder. Reluctantly, Jake lets go. The first series of photos are from the crime scene. Gwen floating in the water, hair tangled among the brambles, her skin starkly white among the fallen gemstone-colored leaves. The next set shows Gwen in the medical examiner's office laid out on a metal table. These photos focus more on Gwen's injuries: the three-inch gash on her skull, the broken blood vessels in her eyes, the bruised flesh around her neck. The marking is curious in its uniformity and the surprising lack of tissue damage. If the murderer used a wire garrote there would be deep narrow cuts in the flesh around her neck. If he used a belt or strap of some kind there would be unique, distinguishing marks or bits of fabric left behind. "Do you know what made these marks?" I ask.

Jake shakes his head. "The ME couldn't say for sure. Something smooth but strong enough that it didn't snap."

I gather up the photos and hand them back to Jake. I feel ill. He was right, I didn't need to see these. "Where do you go from here?" I ask.

Jake looks defeated. "We keep investigating. Keep asking questions." We settle back into the couch cushions and stare at the television, both of us lost in our own thoughts.

After a few minutes I say, "Gwen sent me

an email a few weeks ago. I think she . . ." I begin and look over at Jake. His eyes are closed, his mouth is slightly agape, his chest rising and falling evenly. He's fast asleep. Good to know I have that effect on people. I arrange the blanket around him and press the mute button on the television so it doesn't wake him.

Nothing about this past week makes sense and I have so many more questions and my one source of information is fast asleep.

I turn off the light and except for the glow from the television we are covered in darkness. I flip through the channels, finally deciding on one of the countless housewife shows. It's a good way to practice speech reading curse words. Next to me, Jake is still sleeping soundly. His thigh pressing against mine is warm and comforting. He looks younger while asleep, unguarded, vulnerable. All my life Jake was the tough one. He came from a home that I knew was filled with harsh words and violence. Came over to our house with more than his fair share of suspicious bruises. But Jake didn't end up taking the same path as his father. Jake was tough, but kind.

Hours later, I awake with a start. It takes a moment for me to realize where I am. On the television the housewives have been replaced with an infomercial and I'm stretched out on the couch with Jake's arms wrapped around me. I hold completely still, hardly daring to breathe. I don't remember falling asleep and I sure as hell don't remember shifting positions so that Jake's chest ended up pressed against my back. Stitch is lying on the floor next to us and raises his head so that we are eye level. He's looking at me as if I've lost my mind, which could very well be the truth. I do a quick mental check and as far as I can tell I still have all my clothes on.

Jake's warm breath sweeps across my neck, sending a jolt of electricity down my spine. *Be careful,* I tell myself. I know better than this. We're old friends, and we're both lonely. Every fiber of my being screams at me to get up, to put distance between the two of us, to stop whatever this is in its tracks. But I don't want to move. With Jake's solid form snug against mine I feel whole, safe and completely out of my element.

This is not supposed to happen. Jake is the one who told me that the Tooth Fairy was make-believe, that no boy in his right mind would ever want to kiss me. But when I was fifteen Jake was also the one who beat the crap out of the guy who got me drunk at a party, then told everyone I slept with him. He was also the one who drove all the way out to my house on Five Mines to pick me up for our sign language class once a week.

I reach for the remote, careful not to jostle Jake awake and turn off the television. We are plunged into darkness and for the first time in a long time, I'm not afraid of the dark. I match my breath with the rise and fall of Jake's chest, and with the weight of his arm around me, a ballast, I drift off to sleep.

16

I awake to the smell of coffee brewing and sun streaming through the window. Momentarily disoriented, I then remember Jake's breath on my neck, the feel of his hand resting on my hip. I'm alone on the couch and I wonder if Jake woke up this morning mortified to find us tangled together. I close my eyes again, giving myself a few more minutes to think about how I'm going to handle this. I could pretend it never happened. Two exhausted friends who accidentally fell asleep on the couch. It didn't mean a thing.

I open my eyes to see Jake standing over me, dressed in fresh clothes, hair still damp from his shower, a cup of coffee in his hand. "Good morning," he says.

"Morning," I say, sitting up and taking the mug from him and I wait for him to say something about last night. I try not to show my disappointment when he doesn't.

"David has been trying to get ahold of you," he signs. He's wearing his cop face. Unreadable. "He sent a text." Jake hands me my phone.

"Probably just something about Nora," I say because I can't think of anything else to say.

"Actually, it's about dinner Friday night," Jake says.

"Jeez, it's seven," I say. "I have to get ready for work."

"There are towels in the bathroom if you want to shower," Jake signs. "I went ahead and let Stitch out and fed him."

This is new territory for the two of us and I don't know how to act. I want to escape, get out of here but I don't have time to run back to my house and still get to work without being late.

Self-conscious of my messy hair and morning breath, I follow Jake through his bedroom and he opens the door to the master bath where he pulls a set of clean towels from a cupboard and sets them on the sink.

"And by the way, McNaughton is all kinds of weird but he didn't kill Gwen. He was at the emergency room with his eighty-five-year-old father during the time we think she was killed. He also said that next time he catches you on his property he's calling the police. Best if you stay clear of him."

"Did he say anything about who he thinks might have killed her?" I ask, thinking of our interrupted conversation the day before.

"No, just gave his alibi and let us know that you're a menace to society. I've got to get to the station. The roads are pretty bad out there. Be careful driving," Jake signs. "I have to get to work. Just lock up when you leave." Then he's gone and I'm left alone. This wasn't how I wanted this morning to go at all.

I shut Jake's bedroom door and strip the clothes from my body, fold them neatly and lay them atop a bureau. I wonder if anyone at work will notice I'm wearing the same outfit as yesterday and then decide I really couldn't care less.

The peaceful, sage-green room was obviously decorated by Sadie. A duvet in a white, soft blue and green floral pattern covers the bed along with a mound of matching pillows. The furniture is painted white and a dusty wreath of dried flowers hangs above the bed. Knowing that I shouldn't, I go to the closet and peek inside. My stomach drops. Sadie's clothes hang neatly from their hangers next to Jake's. It's been four years and still she's here. Always here. I slam the door shut, causing Stitch to flinch.

It's good that things didn't go any further with Jake last night, I tell myself. Nothing good can come from falling in love with someone who is still in love with his dead wife. Besides, I'm still married to David, but more and more I wonder if that's even what I want. I look at the text that David sent this morning, the one that Jake read. See you tomorrow night. Don't forget dessert.

Of course this text would be confusing to Jake. It's confusing to *me.* As far as Jake knows, my marriage to David is all but over. Countless times I've ranted to Jake about David's unwillingness to give me a second chance, his refusal to let me spend time alone with Nora. But now it seems David is softening, willing to let me back into his life. Into Nora's. See you tomorrow at six, hesitating only momentarily before hitting Send. I take a quick shower, dress in yesterday's clothes and run my fingers through my wet hair. I make sure that the house is locked up tight and spend fifteen minutes warming up the Jeep and scraping layers of ice from the windshield.

Jake's right, the roads are an icy mess. The only good thing is that everyone else in their right minds had the sense to stay home until the salt trucks have a chance to treat the streets. A trip that should only take five minutes from Jake's house takes fifteen but I manage to get us there in one piece.

When Stitch and I walk into the center it is nearly deserted. The waiting room lights are on but the rest of the clinic is dim. No nurses or doctors have arrived and Barb, the ever-present office manager, is nowhere to be found. Lori is behind the counter nodding patiently to a scarecrow-thin woman wearing a heavy pair of snow boots and who is nearly lost in the folds of an oversize down parka that falls below her knees. She has a stocking cap pulled down low over her ears and she has the round moon face of someone on heavy doses of prednisone. Angrily, she slaps the thick pocket folder she is holding down onto the counter and flips it open with trembling hands. Lori waits for the woman to shuffle through the papers to find what she is searching for but gives me a beleaguered roll of her eyes as if to communicate that it's much too early in the day for this.

The woman's eyes barely register our presence as Stitch and I pass by. Though I don't know exactly why she is upset, from her stack of papers it's probably an insurance issue. Being sick is obscenely expensive and when you are ill and can't work, every penny must be counted and saved. I can relate. Even though David and I had good insurance, the medical bills following my accident were staggering.

I go back to the file room and retrieve a stack of files from the cabinet, my thoughts turning back to Jake. He has been a lot of things to me over the years: my first crush, obnoxious big brother, best friend. Waking up together, with his arms around me, felt good. But confusing.

I open the first folder, eager to stop obsessing over the night before when Stitch leaves the room. I call to him but he doesn't return. I'm not too worried about him getting into mischief, but not everyone is a fan of dogs and some of the patients may be allergic or with their suppressed immune systems susceptible to illnesses spread by pets. I head back to the reception area to find Lori kneeling over the still form of the woman she had been talking to minutes earlier.

I order Stitch to stay and rush over to them. The woman is barely conscious and Lori moves aside so I can get a better look. Blood oozes from a head wound. I look to Lori for more information. "She just went down," she says, distress etched across her face.

"Has anyone else gotten here yet? Dr. Huntley or one of the nurses?" I ask. Lori shakes her head.

"Bad roads," she explains.

"Call 9-1-1." I get up and run to one of the examining rooms and grab as many supplies as I can hold, then dash back to the woman. My heart is pounding, but not because I'm scared. My nurse's instincts kick in and my adrenaline is in overdrive.

I quickly pull on a pair of rubber gloves. "Do we have a cervical collar?" I call out. I'm guessing she fainted and struck her head on the counter as she fell to the ground. She may have a neck or spine injury. She's bleeding heavily from a gash along her hairline. Head wounds bleed a lot, but I don't know if this is her biggest issue at the moment. I gently press two fingers into the soft groove at the side of her windpipe to check her pulse. It's faint but it's there.

I stanch the bleeding from her head with gauze and then I unzip her parka. I dig through the pile of supplies I grabbed and find a pair of scissors. I need to get her coat off her by moving her as little as possible. With difficulty I cut through the fabric in order to free her arms. I gently lift her T-shirt and see an eggplant-colored bruise spreading across her abdomen. Maybe a ruptured spleen. I'm guessing due to her chemo treatments she has thrombocytopenia — a low platelet count. Any injury, no matter how minor can be devastating to a cancer patient.

"She's bleeding internally," I say. "Where's the ambulance?" I ask, locking my eyes on Lori's lips.

"Ten minutes out." She holds up ten fingers so she's sure I understand. "The roads are a sheet of ice."

I nod my comprehension. I hope we have ten minutes. If I'm right and the woman doesn't get into surgery soon, she will die. I strip off my bloody gloves and toss them aside. Together, Lori and I carefully place the cervical collar on the woman, hoping to stabilize her neck and prevent any further injury.

"Let's get some fluids in her and treat her for possible shock until the EMTs get here," I tell Lori. "Go get an IV starter kit, a blanket and a few pillows." I pull on a fresh pair of gloves and check her pulse again. It's still thready.

Lori returns and hands me the IV starter kit and I tell her to tuck the blanket around the woman to keep her warm and to prop her legs up with the pillows in hopes of increasing blood flow to her brain.

I haven't inserted an IV in two years. I know I should wait until the paramedics or one of the scheduled doctors or nurses arrives, but I know I can do this. It's as natural to me as breathing.

"Hold this," I say to Lori and hand her the IV bag of fluid. I uncoil the tubing, puncture the bag with the tubing spike and pinch the drip chamber between my fingers. Once I open the roller valve and release the line the fluid will run down the length of tubing without bubbles. Bubbles in an IV line can be disastrous. I slip on the gloves and search for a prominent vein on the woman's arm and can't find one. I grab another sterile package, this one holding a narrow hose-shaped rubber tourniquet. I tie it tightly around her arm and a vein swells with the pressure. Her eyelids flutter and open. A good sign. I swipe her skin with a disinfectant wipe that Lori hands me.

I insert the needle and catheter in one smooth move and once I'm sure I've accessed the vein I remove the needle, leaving the catheter in place. I cover the catheter with Tegaderm, and I remove the protective cover from the end of the IV tubing and insert it into the catheter hub, screw and lock it into place.

I push myself to my feet and survey the bag of fluid that Lori awkwardly holds, making sure that the saline has started to flow into the woman's veins. It looks like it's going to work. There's nothing more I can do. We have to wait for the paramedics to arrive. I untie the makeshift tourniquet from her arm and already a tubular bruise is forming, momentarily reminding me of Gwen's autopsy photos and the garish marking around her neck.

Thankfully, the emergency workers push through the doors and I step aside. The EMTs will need all the information that can be given about the woman and I know that the time it will take for me to understand their questions will only put her in more jeopardy. Lori hands the paramedics the woman's purse and fills them in on what happened while I lower myself into one of the waiting room chairs and watch as they efficiently transfer the woman to a stretcher and roll her from the building.

The waiting room looks like a tornado has struck. Blood stains the carpet and discarded latex gloves, gauze, antiseptic wipes litter the floor. I feel a new pair of eyes on me and find that Dr. Huntley has arrived at the clinic. He looks pissed and I realize that I could be in trouble. I was not hired to act as a nurse here and I'm not even sure what I did was legal. I could open Dr. Huntley and his clinic to a lawsuit. I'm an office worker. I was hired for data entry and filing and in an emergency to answer a phone call or two. But it felt so good to be tending to a patient, to be making those split-second decisions. I don't question a single move I made.

Stitch must sense the gravity of the situation because, miraculously, he is still in the same spot where I ordered him to stay.

"Ke mne," I say, and he comes to my side. I massage the spot behind his ears that I know he likes and breathe into his ear, *"Hodney pes,* Stitch, *hodney pes." Good dog,* Stitch, *good dog.*

Dr. Huntley comes over to where I sit. I only catch every third word or so but I get the message.

I nod, the pit in my stomach expanding. Dr. Huntley goes out the clinic doors and off to the hospital to check on the woman. When he returns I'm to meet with him.

I spend the next hour helping Lori clean up the detritus of the morning's emergency. I gather up bloody gloves, the tattered remains of the woman's parka and the pillows used to prop up her feet.

"Do you think we should call someone?" I

ask. The thought of the woman at the hospital all by herself seems so wrong.

"I'll double-check her emergency info," Lori says as she picks up a wad of bloody gauze, "but I think she lives alone."

That could be me, I think. If something happened to me who would they call? David, I guess. But he doesn't really count, seeing as we're probably not going to be married for much longer. I think of Stitch and what would happen to him if I was hurt. Who would take care of him? It makes me wonder if the woman has a pet at home.

I gather up all the papers that fell to the floor when she collapsed. I've already decided that I'm going to stop by the hospital to see how she's doing and give her back the folder of paperwork she brought in with her.

I futilely sponge at the bloodstain left behind on the carpet. "I think we're going to have to get a steam cleaner for this," I say.

"Just leave it," Lori tells me. "Let Maintenance finish cleaning it up."

I drop my rag into the bucket of sudsy water and pull off my gloves. "I'm not looking forward to meeting with Dr. Huntley. I think I may have made a big mistake."

"Why?" Lori's eyebrows rise in surprise.

"You saved her. He should give you a raise."

I give a small laugh. "Yeah, but that wasn't our deal. I'm only supposed to be doing clerical work, no patient care. I blew it and I've only been here a few days."

Lori gives me a sympathetic smile as she takes the bucket from me, and I go back to the file room with the woman's jumbled mess of papers. I clear space on my desk so that I can sort through her paperwork and put it back in some kind of order.

I learn that the woman's name is Rachel Nava and she was diagnosed two years ago with multiple myeloma, cancer of the blood cells in plasma. Multiple myeloma is incurable and often deadly. To date, Rachel had three bone marrow biopsies and was prescribed monthly intravenous immunoglobin injections and a complex chemo regimen that seem to repeat itself every three weeks. Very aggressive treatment.

I organize the paperwork the best I can by date. Just as I suspected, the cost of Rachel's treatment is startling. Most appears to be covered by insurance but not all. After doing the arithmetic in my head, it looks like Rachel owes the center well over fifty thousand dollars in medical bills. I place the file in my purse and decide that I'll return it to Rachel at the hospital in the next day or so.

Stitch, who is lying beneath my desk and on top of my feet, shifts and I look up. Dr. Huntley is standing in the doorway.

"How is she?" I ask right away.

"She's stable. I'm going to go back over there in a bit and check on her. Come on back to my office and let's talk."

With dread, I follow him to his office and he unlocks the door and steps aside to let me in. I'm conscious of the bloodstains that dot my shirt. I fold my arms across my middle in hopes of covering them up. Dr. Huntley sits down behind his desk. A large tote bag filled with what appears to be file folders sits on the only remaining chair so I stay standing and wait for Dr. Huntley to speak. When he doesn't I realize he's expecting me to explain myself.

"I'm so sorry. I know you told me no patient care," I begin, mentally kicking myself for starting with an apology. *Fight,* I tell myself. I straighten my spine. "I came in early and there wasn't anyone else here to help. I saw her lying on the floor." Though I can't hear my own voice I know it's gaining strength, conviction. "She needed emergency care and I knew what needed to be done. I assessed her injuries, just as I would in the ER. She had a superficial head injury but she was bleeding excessively." He picks up a pen from atop his desk and begins to tap it on the wooden surface. He doesn't say anything so I continue. "But it was the bruising on her abdomen that most concerned me. I figured she had a low platelet count due to chemo and I was worried about internal bleeding. I thought there was too much of a risk not to give her treatment until the paramedics arrived."

Every word that Dr. Huntley mouths is unmistakable. He's beyond angry. "Your actions have opened my clinic up to a lawsuit, Amelia. Ms. Nava is my patient and I should have been called immediately. Don't you dare act like you are a nurse in this office again. I want to make sure you understand loud and clear that you are not a nurse, you are a file clerk. That is it, nothing else. You do not take a patient's temperature, you do not apply a Band-Aid, you do not touch a patient for any reason. Do you understand?"

I open my mouth to argue but I know I have no recourse. Tears threaten to gather in my eyes but I blink them back. There's no way in hell I'm going to cry in front of my boss. I may still have my RN license, but I was not hired as a nurse. What I did today could cause major problems for the center. "I understand," I acquiesce, though it pains me to say it.

"Good. You can go now."

I return to the file room somewhat surprised I still have my job. Dr. Huntley could have very easily fired me right then and there, but for some reason he didn't. I pick up my pace as I move through the hallway just in case he changes his mind. All I want to do is hide in the file room for the rest of the day. Unfortunately, that's not what happens. For the remainder of my shift, the nurses and other staff stop by the file room to tell me that they heard about what I did and congratulate me. I smile and thank them, but wish they would just let it go. I don't want the attention.

I can't get out of the clinic fast enough when twelve o'clock comes around. The temperature has risen and the roads are slushy rather than icy and I should have no trouble getting home. Hopefully, all the excitement around today's emergency will die down and tomorrow morning things will be back to normal.

17

I needn't have worried about any fuss surrounding my role in helping Rachel Nava yesterday. When I arrived at the clinic this morning it was business as usual. In fact, I was the only one to bring it up. I asked Lori how Rachel was doing and was assured that she was in stable condition and would most likely be able to go home sometime next week. No one else said a word.

At five thirty I stop at the cupcake shop and pick up an assortment of flavors to bring with me to David's. Snickerdoodle for Nora, cherry cordial for David and chocolate peanut butter for me. I'm not sure what I'm going to walk into tonight. Maybe David really is finally forgiving me for the hell I've put him through and wants to start over. Could be, but for all I know he might pull out the divorce papers and have me sign them over coffee and cupcakes. Plus, between the break-in attempt and what I think Peter was trying to tell me about David, I feel on edge. I'll have to pay attention, be on watch.

After the accident, not long after my leg had healed and the constant dull ache in my head seemed to subside, David decided to have a group of his colleagues over to the house for dinner. I tried, I really did. I showered, combed my hair, even put on a little makeup. David ran out to pick up a few things and the caterer arrived while he was still gone. She started asking me questions and I had no idea what she was saying. I kept saying, "Let's wait for my husband, he'll know what to do." It took him forever to return and by the time he got home, the caterer was completely irritated and I was on my third glass of wine. Things went downhill from there.

I don't remember too much of that evening but when I awoke the next morning I was alone in the guest bedroom, still dressed and covered in my own vomit. Within a month I was living on my own in the cabin and David refused to let me see Nora.

I pull the Jeep into David's driveway and see Nora standing at the living room window waiting for me. She's out the front door before I can even open my car door. Her dark hair is pulled into lopsided pigtails, she's wearing a skirt and her favorite sweatshirt that is a size too small. She's barefoot, her toenails painted a bright purple. I smile at the thought of David helping her paint her toes.

"Brrr," I say, looking over my shoulder as she yanks open the car door to let Stitch out. "Aren't you freezing?"

"Nope," she says but then runs on tiptoes back inside, Stitch at her heels. I grab the box of cupcakes from the passenger-side seat and follow Nora inside. This is the first time I've actually been inside the house I once shared with David and Nora since I moved out — since David threw me out.

David's redecorated. I think of Jake and how his home is practically a shrine to Sadie and I can't help but be hurt. The carpet has been replaced with hardwood floors, the sofa we used to snuggle up together to watch television on has been exchanged with one covered in leather. Even the television is different. I'm touched to see that at least one of our wedding pictures still hangs on the wall. David greets me with a polite kiss on the cheek that is at once both sweet and confusing. He smells like he always has — a peppery citrus scent that still has the capability to make me swoon.

The smell of David's famous chili wafts

out from the kitchen. He's remembered it's my favorite. In the kitchen there are new countertops and the kitchen cupboards have been refaced in a crisp white. I set the cupcakes down on the gray quartz counter and take in the new stainless steel appliances. A tall pot of chili simmers on the restaurant-grade gas stove. All this must have cost a fortune.

David catches me looking around and has the decency to look embarrassed. "The Realtor made me do it," he says. "She said it needed updating."

"Realtor?" I ask, not sure that I read his lips correctly. "You're selling the house?" My stomach knots. How can he sell this house? Our house? We have made so many memories here.

"I'm considering it," he says, not quite meeting my eyes. "The house is too big for just the two of us and, well . . ." He lets the sentence hang there, but I know what he's getting at — that since we're no longer together there isn't the chance of having more children. I turn away from him so he can't see the hurt on my face.

Nora pulls a package of bologna out of the refrigerator and tries to get Stitch to do an array of tricks, all of which he refuses. Somehow he still manages to get Nora to give him the treats anyway.

"You look beat," David says with concern.

"It was crazy at work," I say. I'm not sure how much detail I should go into. I settle on giving David the very basics about Rachel Nava.

"That's pretty impressive," David says.

"Yeah, well, Dr. Huntley wasn't particularly thrilled with me jumping in like that."

"Why? What did he say?" David asks, his face registering indignation. "He wasn't angry with you, was he? You know you don't have to work there, Amelia. I've known Joe for a long time and he can be a bit of a hard-ass." I'm a little bit surprised at the way David comes to my defense, but he never wanted me to work there in the first place.

"Not angry," I say. "More like concerned. I'm not supposed to be treating patients."

"Still," David says but drifts off. I decide to change the subject. I don't want to have this debate. I examine his face, carefully looking for any sign that he could have been the one to break into my house or worse. I just can't see it, and I can't help thinking that Peter's advice to ask my husband about what happened to Gwen was just the ramblings of a crazy man.

"Gwen's funeral was nice," I say. "Did you

get a chance to talk to Marty?"

"No, there was always a crowd around him. I sent a card."

I nod. "Me too. I was trying to remember the last time I saw Gwen. Alive, I mean. I think it was in the ER about a week before my accident." The memory sweeps over me and I can almost picture Gwen wearing her nurse's scrubs, her hair piled on top of her head, reading glasses on the edge of her nose. I can almost hear her bell-like laugh. "When was the last time you saw her?" I ask.

David stirs the chili, his forehead knit in concentration. "God, I have no idea. Probably on the ob-gyn floor at the hospital. Just in passing, though, and that was months ago."

"I found an old email from Gwen," I say, watching for a reaction. "She wanted to get together and catch up. Said she wanted to run some work problems by me. Did you hear anything about Gwen having trouble at the hospital?"

David pulls a ladle from a drawer and dips it into the pot and begins spooning the chili into bowls. The same bowls we had when we got married. At least he hasn't replaced everything.

"Christ, there's always some kind of

drama going on at the hospital. Did she say what kind of problems she was having?"

"No, it was probably nothing," I say, sensing that I am not going to get any more out of David on this topic but I can't tell if he actually doesn't know anything or doesn't want to tell me. "I just wish I would have had the chance to talk with her one more time."

"Are the police any closer to arresting someone? I thought I heard her husband did it?" David says and then calls to Nora to come and eat.

"No, he's been cleared," I say and cast a glance at Nora who has come into the room, pulling Stitch along by his collar. There will be no more talk of murder tonight. At least in Nora's presence.

We carry the bowls over to the dining room table. David has outdone himself in setting the table for a simple dinner of chili and corn bread. He bought fresh flowers. Pink and burgundy ranunculus and white anemones. Nora, in her lopsided print, wrote each of our names on construction paper place cards and placed them next to the napkins and silverware. She even made one for Stitch and set it on the floor next to the water dish she put out for him.

"To Amelia," David says, holding up his

goblet of ice water. "Congratulations on your new job."

"Good job, Mom," Nora says, raising her own glass and then laughing. "Good job on the job," she says and laughs.

We touch the crystal together. "Thanks," I manage to say through a film of tears. It's almost like old times.

Nora is so excited to share what life is like in second grade that I have to ask her to slow down and repeat herself several times so I can keep up with what she's saying. I eat two bowls of David's chili and give Nora my cupcake. She sits on my lap and plants sticky kisses on my cheek in thanks.

Stitch watches us warily from his spot on the floor. I wonder if he's feeling a bit neglected, so I call him over but he averts his eyes and pretends he hasn't heard me. Could Stitch be jealous of David and Nora? I smile at the thought. There was a time not so long ago when I thought Stitch hated me.

At eight o'clock Nora skips off to put on her pajamas, and David asks me if I'd like to read her a bedtime story. I almost start to weep with gratitude. I go up to her bedroom, still the soft pink that I painted it over two years earlier, and we settle side by side on her bed. I read two books to Nora and she reads one to Stitch before I tell her it's time for lights-out. She wraps her arms around my neck and presses her forehead against mine. I hold on to her until she pulls away wanting the moment to last as long as possible. I've missed this so much.

I go back into the kitchen to find David rinsing the dishes and putting them in the dishwasher. "She's finally settled in," I say.

"Nora's the queen of avoiding bedtime," David warns. "She'll be out three more times — she'll need a drink of water, have to go to the bathroom, need another kiss good-night."

I hand David a glass. "I kind of hope she does keep coming out. I've missed her . . ." I leave my last thought unspoken, that sometimes I miss him too.

"So, Nora mentioned someone named Helen. She told me she helped with her Halloween costume. Said she was a nurse at the clinic."

David nods, a smile still playing on his lips. "Helen was a nurse who now works for me, and she did help with Nora's costume. She helps me out in a pinch. Did Nora also happen to tell you that Helen is a sixty-two-year-old married grandmother?"

"She may have forgotten to mention that," I say, grabbing a wet dishcloth and scrubbing at a nonexistent spot on the counter.

David gently removes the dishcloth from my hands. "Come on," he says. "Let's go in the other room." He leads me by the hand to the living room, and we sit down side by side on his new sofa. I sink into the supple leather and think that this may be the most comfortable piece of furniture I've ever been on. "You know there has been no one besides you, don't you," David says.

"No one?" I repeat.

"Not a soul." The smile has dropped from David's face, his brown eyes have softened. No trace of the usual wariness I've seen in them the last few years. "I'm glad things are going well for you. You deserve to be happy."

I want to say that what would make me happy would be if our family was back together again. If I didn't have to ask permission to see Nora, if I could come back home, if we could just go back to the way things were before. But instead I ask, "Are you really going to move? You're not planning on leaving Mathias, are you?" The only thing worse than not being able to see Nora here in town, would be if David took her far away.

"No, no," David says in a rush as if the idea is absurd. "This house is just too big. Mathias is home. Nora loves it here. I love it here. The practice is doing great. You're here."

I have no idea what he means by this or what to say, but we're interrupted when David shifts away from me and pulls his pager from his pocket. He reads the message and then looks to me apologetically. "I'm sorry, but I've got to call the sitter. I've got to get to the hospital. Emergency delivery."

"Let me stay," I offer. David looks doubtful. "Come on," I urge. "I'm already here and Nora's fast asleep. What could go wrong?" Dumb question. David looks like he could list a thousand things that could go dangerously wrong. "Really, it will be okay. I've got my phone." I hold it up. "And Stitch is here. We'll be fine."

"Text me if you need anything," he says as he gets to his feet. I watch as he pulls a coat from the closet and then disappears through the garage door. It feels so domestic, I think to myself. So normal.

I look around the great room and I still can't believe that David is thinking about selling the house. Granted, it is too big for just the two of them. It was too large for the three of us back when David and I were first married, but we had hopes of filling it with more children. But time slipped away and then I had the accident. I wonder how things might have been different if the car hadn't hit me. Maybe I'd be in this kitchen, heavy with pregnancy making spaghetti for Nora and a little boy with David's dark hair and brown eyes that snapped with mischief. I'd hear each creak in the wooden floor, each groan as hot water flows through the pipes, every sigh and murmur of my children.

I know it doesn't do any good to dwell on what might have been. *Be grateful for what you have,* I tell myself. I look over at Stitch who has contentedly planted himself in front of the fireplace. I have Stitch. I have this time with Nora. For now, it's enough.

I pick up the empty aluminum cans that held the chili beans and pull open the door that leads to the attached three-car garage. I think it has more square footage than my cabin. As soon as I step into the garage a motion sensor light pops on to reveal the runner-up for most pristine garage in the history of the world. The grand prize, of course, going to Peter McNaughton. The concrete floor is swept clean, David's and Nora's bikes hang from hooks on the wall. The recycling bins, clearly labeled, sit in a corner next to a large garbage can. There is no lawn mower, snowblower, ladder or chain saw. A lone shovel hangs from a nail.

The strong smell of bleach hangs in the air. I toss the recycling into the proper bin.

I know the immaculate condition of the space has more to do with David's busy schedule than any obsessive compulsive need to be tidy. Between delivering babies and taking care of Nora, David doesn't have time to change a lightbulb let alone do any sort of yard work so he hires a service instead. Two of the parking spots sit empty. David's at work with his Lexus and then there's the space where I used to park my Jeep. A lone Rorschach test of an oil spot is one of the few reminders that I once lived here.

In the final spot, covered by a blue tarp, is a motorboat we would take out onto Five Mines on David's rare day off. We would pack a cooler and our fishing poles and spend a lazy day on the river. I'd slather coconut-scented sunscreen over Nora's fair skin, checking and double-checking that her life jacket was secured.

A for-sale sign is affixed to the boat cover, and I run my fingers over the shadow of script that once graced the side of the boat — *Nora~Amelia*. David added the *Amelia* once we were married, I'm sure so that I would feel welcomed to his little family. He's removed the black lettering. I guess it's easier to sell a nameless boat. A fresh start for someone else.

I remember how David used to stand with his chest pressed to my back, his arms wrapped around my waist, as I would steer the boat through the back channels. I release one of the tie-downs, step up onto the frame of the metal trailer and peel back one corner of the boat cover. For a moment I can almost feel the warmth of David's skin against mine. I step down and release the rest of the tie-downs and strip the cover from the boat. I hoist myself up over the side and into the boat, remembering. After a long afternoon in the sun, Nora would fall asleep in the shade beneath the boat's canopy. David would turn off the engine and let the boat drift and we would sit side by side, feeling the gentle rocking of the current, my head on his shoulder.

I am lost in a nostalgic daze when suddenly a shimmery filament on the carpet catches my eye. I bend over for a closer look. It's a long strand of blond hair caught on a small metal bolt. It could be anyone's hair, I tell myself. One of Nora's friends, a coworker from the hospital. Lots of women besides Gwen have blond hair. There has to be a logical explanation.

I remember what Peter said about asking

my husband about what happened to Gwen. I turn back to the boat. There's no way to know just by looking whether or not it's been taken out on the river recently. The smell of bleach burns my nose. *Stop it,* I tell myself. David probably just gave it a thorough cleaning before he put it away for the season. But how long does the smell of bleach linger? I start at the stern and carefully begin to examine every inch. There are no puddles of blood, no bleach stains. See, I tell myself, you're being ridiculous.

I hate that I'm doubting David. He's simply an ob-gyn trying to raise his daughter. He barely knew Gwen and said he couldn't remember the last time they worked together. Gwen was pregnant. Could she have gone to David's office for prenatal care? There are plenty of ob-gyn docs in Mathias, but David is known as one of the best and lots of health care professionals go to him because of this. Would Marty know if Gwen saw David for prenatal care?

I stare at the boat for a moment longer, thinking of the morning I found Gwen and the wake from a nearby motorboat that knocked me to my knees and Stitch into the water. It would be a little harder to identify a boat if it didn't have a name emblazoned on its side. But why would David kill Gwen? None of it makes sense.

I go back inside. The house has grown chilly and I take the liberty of turning on the gas fireplace. The flames instantly come to life, licking at the glass screen. I pull Gwen's calendar from my purse and settle onto the couch to examine the last year of my friend's life.

I flip through the pages, each square box filled with Gwen's distinctive handwriting. Every once in a while I come across something written in what I figure is Marty's hand. I first focus my attention on September and October of this year. I'm able to translate most of Gwen's shorthand. The obvious abbreviations are easy. QP means Queen of Peace, MR stands for Mathias Regional, ICU, OBGYN, PSYCH and ONC. A few are more cryptic and it takes me a few minutes to figure out that SC means the skilled care unit and RR means recovery room. All makes sense in relationship to the different areas where Gwen would work as a floater nurse. I think that WC could stand for Willow Creek, a hospital that I traveled to as nurse examiner in the past. Gwen most likely was also called there to work with a sexual assault victim.

But several abbreviations have me

stumped. I have no idea what DT, SL or GH could mean. I flip through the calendar skimming for any reference to David. I finally spot QP/OBGYN in the box for June 5 and my pulse quickens. But this matches with what David said about not working with Gwen for several months. I flip forward to just before Gwen sent me the email.

There. On September 27 at nine thirty in the morning. MOG — Mathias Obstetrics and Gynecology. The clinic where David sees patients. Not a shift at the hospital. An appointment.

I close the calendar and slide it back into my purse. So David did see Gwen, and not all that long ago. Why wouldn't he tell me about this? Maybe he thought he shouldn't due to doctor-patient confidentiality. But Gwen was dead and she was my friend at one time. But wait, there are several doctors that practice at his clinic. Four to be exact. Gwen could have had an appointment to see any one of them.

I look at my watch. Nine thirty. David will most likely be gone for at least a while longer. Maybe there's a way I can find out if Gwen was David's patient. I get up and move down the hallway to the back of the house where David has his home office and Stitch follows me. The door is open and the lights off. I find the light switch and flip it to the on position.

David hasn't gotten around to redecorating his office yet and everything is the same as it was two years ago. Many a night I would walk past this room and see David sitting at his desk, reading glasses on the edge of his nose, staring at the computer screen, updating patient charts and files. But he would always stop to give me a smile or wave me into his office to talk. He would slide his office chair next to where I sat on a small sofa and I would prop my feet up on his lap while we'd talk about our day.

Now I pull out the desk chair and sit down in front of his computer. What I'm planning on doing is not only unethical but in violation of HIPAA privacy laws. I wiggle the mouse, the computer comes to life and I am met with a log-in screen. This one is easy. I enter the password that I know David has always used for logging in to his computer since I've known him. Nora1115. I open the browser and go directly to David's bookmarks and find the link that will take me to Mathias Obstetrics' secure site where David is able to access patient information. I'm met with another log-in screen and I try Nora1115 again but get an error message. I try David's birthday. Again, the error message. I know I only have one or two more tries and then the system will lock me out. I type in my name and birth date and hold my breath when I hit Enter.

I'm in. I enter Gwen's name into the search bar and her information immediately pops up. David is her doctor of record and she did have an appointment with him on September 27. I click on the date and learn that Gwen was two months along in her pregnancy. I can just imagine how happy Gwen would have been to know that she was going to have another baby. David's notes from her visit showed that both mother and baby were healthy and he prescribed her with prenatal vitamins and twenty-five milligrams of B6 three times a day for nausea. Another appointment was scheduled for October 31 but according to a notation on the calendar she never made it.

A fissure of fear runs through me. David was Gwen's ob-gyn, and she was supposed to meet with him on the day she died. But this knowledge doesn't get me much closer to knowing what happened to her and what, if anything, David had to do with it.

I remember what Marty said about Gwen being worried about a patient with a name that reminded him of a bug or an insect and

I wonder if there's some connection between that patient and David. I browse the patient directory, looking for any name that jumps out. I scroll through the *A* names but nothing seems like a match. I click to view the *B* names and that's when I find her. Jo Ellen Beadle. Beetle. Could this be it?

I open the file and see that she's a twenty-seven-year-old woman who was six months pregnant in September. Her appointment date was listed as the same as Gwen's just fifteen minutes later. They would have been in David's clinic the exact same date and most likely were in the waiting room together. Okay, I'm getting somewhere.

Jo Ellen's next appointment was scheduled for one week later. I click on the visit summary. It's blank. Jo Ellen never made it to her next appointment, either. I decide to go back through each of her previous appointments. From what I can tell from the records, Jo Ellen had a high-risk pregnancy due to a history of Waldenström's macroglobulinemia, a cancer similar to multiple myeloma and non-Hodgkin's lymphoma. At the time she learned she was pregnant she was in remission. From what I can tell, throughout her pregnancy, David was watching Jo Ellen and her baby very carefully and by all accounts the baby was a bit on the small side but developing normally.

I go back a few screens and click on the tab that would lead me to any hospitalizations that Jo Ellen may have had. One is listed. Two days after the clinic appointment, Jo Ellen was taken to Queen of Peace complaining of contractions. It was much too early for the baby to be born. There are pages and pages of scanned records but it's the final one that says it all. Jo Ellen Beadle's heart stopped at 3:37 a.m. on September 29. The infant was declared deceased thirty minutes later. David was the doctor present at the time.

Stitch suddenly gets to his feet and starts barking. Oh, my God, David is home. I have no idea how close David is to walking into the house. He may already be inside. It takes me two tries to close out of the website and to log out of the computer. I try to get up from the chair as quietly as possible.

Stitch is still barking. "Stitch, *vpred, skoc,*" I order. *Go out, jump.* Stitch runs from the room, his paws sliding across the floor. I peek around the corner and see Stitch jumping up and down nearly knocking David over. I slip from the room and across the hall to the bathroom without David seeing me. I quietly close the door. While I try to calm my racing pulse, I flush the toilet, then turn on the faucet. What does it all mean? Did David do something that led to Jo Ellen's death? Did he try to cover it up and Gwen found out? Was David trying to play God and as a result a mother and her baby died?

I open the bathroom door, hoping that David won't be able to tell that something's wrong. I needn't have worried. David is still trying to ward off Stitch's leaps.

"Stitch, *lehni, lehni*!" I say sternly. *Down.* Stitch stops jumping and, breathing hard, lies down on the floor. "Sorry," I say to David, who looks a little shell-shocked.

"Sorry," I repeat. "I don't know what got into him."

David shrugs off the apology and rubs the head of a now calm Stitch. "It ended up being a pretty quick delivery. Thanks for staying," he says.

"It's nice to be able to spend time with Nora. Thanks for letting me do this, David. It means more to me than you'll ever know."

"I know what it means," he says. "I've missed you, Amelia." I search his face for any hint that this could be a joke but all I see is a sadness in his eyes. He lifts his hand to brush aside a strand of hair that has fallen into my face. My skin tingles at his touch.

But it's not a shiver of pleasure. I'm scared of him now. I'm afraid of what he might have done. What he might do. He steps even closer to me and I think he might kiss me. It's all I can do to not push him away. I don't want David to know I'm onto him. He leans in, his lips just inches from my own and I feel the warmth of his breath against my skin. My body tenses and David can't help but feel the way I've gone rigid beneath his touch. He pulls away, embarrassed, and averts his eyes and just like that, the moment is gone.

"Well, I should get going," I say, hoping that my relief hasn't reached my voice. "Can I just say goodbye to Nora? I promise not to wake her."

David lags behind while I move through the hallway and up the steps to Nora's bedroom. I crack open the door and the light from the hallway spills gentle shadows across her face. Nora is curled up on her side, and I go to her and drop a kiss on her forehead. "Thanks for a great night, Nor," I whisper. "Love you." She turns over, burrowing more deeply beneath the covers.

Back downstairs David and I say our goodbyes. "Thanks, Amelia, you were really a lifesaver tonight."

"You're welcome," I say, at once eager to

leave and wanting to stay for Nora.

This time, when David leans in to kiss me, it's a chaste, polite one on my cheek. "I'll call you tomorrow," he says. "Maybe we can do dinner again soon."

"Sounds good," I say, trying to keep my voice casual, but I'm quaking inside. I open the door and step outside. The cold, dark night soothes my flushed face but I'm conscious of David's eyes on me as I make my way to the Jeep. How can I leave Nora behind with a man who may have killed to protect himself? Is he a monster? I don't want to believe it. Is there a way I could have it all wrong? I hope I do.

David's still there, in the doorway, when I look up and start the car. It isn't until I put the car into Reverse and pull out of the driveway that he steps back inside and shuts the door.

18

I spend a quiet weekend at home recovering from my first five days of work. I'm exhausted. I'm used to being by myself and it's hard to explain, but trying to understand others can be draining. Forget the fact that I found a dead body not far from my backyard, had a woman nearly die in my arms and discovered that my husband might be involved in a murder. I've had enough excitement lately to last a lifetime.

I scan the Saturday paper for any more information on Gwen's case. Nothing. I'm tempted to call Jake, to find out if he has learned anything more, but my pride stands in the way. That morning was so awkward. I don't want our friendship ruined over something so stupid. I'll give him a few more days and then show up at the station at lunchtime with Chinese takeout.

As promised, the locksmith comes and installs brand-new locks on both my front and back doors. Stitch follows him around all morning while I try to find out more about what happened to Jo Ellen Beadle. I find her obituary online. It doesn't give much information. She died on September 29 at Queen of Peace Hospital. She was originally from a small town in South Dakota and worked at a local bank in Mathias for several years. No husband or significant other is listed. Survivors included her parents and a sister who still lived in Letcher, South Dakota. I wonder what brought her to Mathias. A job opportunity, a man? I wonder who the father of the baby was. There is no mention whatsoever of the baby in the obituary.

I search for her on Facebook and her profile picture appears, but she kept her account private so that's a dead end too. Next I pull up the Mathias Bank and Trust website in hopes of finding the names of some of her coworkers but the only names listed are the CEO and the board of directors. But what am I going to do if I do find someone I could talk with? What could they possibly tell me about what happened in that delivery room?

Since I couldn't learn anything from Jo Ellen's Facebook friends, a nurse who was present in the delivery room at the time of her death sure could help me. I know just about all of them. At least I did two years ago. Just like with all of my other friends and colleagues, I lost touch with them, but there were a few that I think I can still look up and they won't slam the door in my face.

I think of Elaine Flynn, a large, grandmotherly type who has been at Queen of Peace for going on forty-five years and if she has her way will be there for forty more. I used to joke that she probably helped to deliver me when I was born and she laughed and said, *Oh, Amelia, I would have remembered you.* I've never met a woman who loves her work more than Elaine. We used to meet for coffee in the hospital cafeteria when we had breaks. She was funny and sweet and was one of the people who tried on many occasions to be there for me after my accident. I shut her out too.

I have to be careful, though. If I come across as accusatory I'll get nothing, and chances are Elaine would go right to David and tell him that I was asking questions. I settle on sending her an email and giving her an update on what I'm up to. I ask after her husband and grandchildren and invite her for coffee. Having face-to-face conversations with people who aren't used to my deafness can be a challenge, but the questions I want to ask aren't something I can do in an email or over the phone.

Just as I hit Send on the email, Stitch comes to my side and nudges my leg and then goes to the phone to let me know that it's ringing. I recognize the number as the one belonging to Five Mines Regional Cancer Center. "Hello," I say.

"Hello, Amelia, it's Lori," scrolls across the phone display.

"Hi," I say, a little taken aback. I know the clinic is open on Saturday mornings for those individuals who might need an infusion or a radiation treatment, but I don't know why Lori would be calling me.

"I was just wondering if you have Rachel Nava's paperwork that she came in with the other day. Her sister called and wanted to come by and pick it up for her."

"Yes, I do have it," I say. "Is she doing okay?"

"She is. It looks like she'll be able to go home early next week," Lori says.

"I was going to take the file to her on Monday, but I can drop it off at the hospital today for her," I offer.

"No, no, that's not necessary. Just bring it

with you to the office on Monday and her sister will swing by to pick it up."

"Sure, okay," I say. "I'll bring it then."

"Thanks and have a good weekend," Lori says and then disconnects.

After a few hours I give up waiting around for Elaine to email me back. I don't know what I expected. I've neglected the people who cared about me for so long it's no wonder that they don't bother to make the effort. I lock up the cabin and Stitch and I go for a run in the woods.

Another snowstorm is scheduled for next week, but for now the temperature has risen to above freezing and much of the recent snow has melted and the earth is spongy beneath my feet. We make a five-mile loop of relatively level terrain. I like taking this route when I need to think things through since I don't have to concentrate so hard on each stride I take and worry about navigating over rocky spots or watching for tree roots and sinkholes. I'm able to focus on my own thoughts and enjoy the beauty of my surroundings.

Today I'm not looking at the scenery. I'm trying to make sense of the recent events of the past and still can't seem to wrap my head around all that's happened. Gwen's death, David's newfound interest in me, not to mention Jake's, the break-in at my house, the condition of David's boat and Peter McNaughton's strange behavior and his cryptic statement that leads me to think David is inextricably involved in all of it. The thing is, it still just doesn't quite all come together for me.

By the time Stitch and I make it back to the house, I'm not any closer to understanding it all. I use my new key to open the front door and look carefully around the house for anything that's out of place. All seems to be in order so I'm relatively confident that no one has been in the house during my absence.

The light on the phone flashes and I answer it as Stitch goes off in search of a drink of water.

"Amelia, it's David," he says and I'm immediately wary.

"Hi," I say, still a little out of breath from the run. "What's up?"

"I'm in my office getting caught up on some work things and I was wondering if you happened to be using my computer last night?" A stab of anxiety pierces my chest. How could he know?

"I'm sorry, that didn't come through on

my closed captioning. What did you say?" I ask, trying to buy myself a little more time to think of how to respond.

"I asked if you were working on my office computer last night?" he repeats. Again, there is no way to know if David is just curious or if he's onto me and angry.

Did I clear the browsing history? I think I did. If I didn't he could have easily gone back and seen the sites I had visited. No, I'm sure I cleared it. My next guess is that his clinic website has a feature that lets him know what time someone logged in and out of the site. I decide the only thing I can do is play dumb.

"Your computer? No, I wasn't using it at all. Why?" I ask, trying to sound as casual as possible. I hold my breath waiting for his response.

"Just wondering. It looked like someone was in my office. I must have moved a few things around without realizing it. Thanks again for coming over for dinner last night and staying with Nora. She really enjoyed it. I'd really like for you to be able to spend more time with her. I think it's healthy for both of you."

"Me too," I say, not sure where this

conversation is going. He has to know I was on his computer and in his patient files. This isn't just some casual call.

"Just take care of yourself," he says. "Keep making those good decisions and everything will turn out fine."

What the hell does that mean? I wonder. Take care of myself by not drinking? Take care of myself by eating a well-balanced diet? Or take care of myself as in don't dig around into something that is none of my business?

"I appreciate your concern," I say, trying to keep the edge out of my voice. But I can't help but add, "You know me, though, I jump headfirst into things."

"I do know you, Amelia, better than anybody. Just take care, okay?" David says.

"I will," I say, then disconnect. Well, that sealed it. David knows I was in his computer files. I don't know if he can tell exactly which files I was digging into, but he knows I'm onto him. This is getting out of hand and I have to be careful. I have Nora to think about.

It's time to eat crow and put aside the embarrassment I felt the other day with Jake. I need to fill him in on what's going on. I pull out my phone and send a text to Jake. You free tonight? Steaks on the grill and

Rear Window?

I wait, staring at my phone for his response. It comes almost immediately. I'm on call for the next four days. How about Wednesday night?

Four days feels like an eternity, but it'll have to do.

Wednesday works. How about at six?

See you then, but I've had your steaks. Don't touch them until I get there.

19

I go into work Monday morning still distracted with my visit to David's house on Friday and his strange phone call to me on Saturday. I keep rehashing everything that points to David having something to do with Gwen's murder.

I mentally tick off the facts that I do know:

- Both Marty Locke and Peter McNaughton have alibis for the time of the murder
- Gwen sent me an email saying that she had an ethical work-related dilemma she wanted to talk to me about, yet
- David told me he hadn't seen Gwen in months, but
- His medical records clearly show she had an appointment with him, as did Jo Ellen Beadle
- Jo Ellen Beadle and her baby died during childbirth when David was present

- Marty said that Gwen was worried about a woman she knew who was pregnant
- David's boat appears to have been thoroughly cleaned recently and there was a blond hair left behind that could have belonged to Gwen

All interesting information, but it proves nothing. Jo Ellen Beadle also had a history of Waldenström's macroglobulinemia, a rare blood cancer, so there is a good chance that she was treated by Dr. Huntley or his partner. I enter Jo Ellen's name into the computer system and her file appears. Jo Ellen was a patient here and Dr. Huntley was her oncologist. Beyond this, there is little information. It doesn't look like Jo Ellen's medical reports were scanned and entered into the electronic file yet. I get up and go to the standing file cabinets and pull open the drawer where the names beginning with *B* are stored. This is when I realize that I forgot to return Rachel Nava's file to Lori and will have to bring it in tomorrow. I find Jo Ellen's file right away. It's about six inches thick and it takes two hands to pull it from the drawer. I set it on my desk, feeling a bit guilty. This isn't what I'm supposed to be doing right now.

I flip to the final page in the file and see that Jo Ellen's last recorded visit with Dr. Huntley was approximately six months before she died. Her treatment protocol, in very basic terms, was administered in a combination of chemotherapy and a monoclonal antibody that targets and attaches itself to the cancer cell in order to mark it for destruction by the body's own immune system. Miraculously, Jo Ellen was in remission right when she became pregnant and was able to halt treatment.

Stitch nudges my leg, alerting me to a presence. I look up. Dr. Huntley is standing in the doorway, a pink slip of paper in his hand. "Phone message," he says. "I told Lori I was coming back this way and would deliver it to you." He hands me the slip of paper, and Stitch wags his tail happily as he pulls a dog treat from his pocket, feeds it to Stitch and then moves on.

I unfold the piece of paper. It's a phone message from David.

David forgot his cell phone at home. Wants to know if you can pick up Nora at 3:10 at school and take her home? Call his office if it won't work for you.

Once again, David's actions thoroughly

confuse me. I can't figure him out at all. I'm still suspicious and am convinced that he's hiding something but it's not enough to keep me away from Nora. Of course I'll pick her up.

At noon I log off my computer and return the pile of files I was working on back into the file cabinet, say my goodbyes to Lori and the others and head out into the cold with Stitch. We run several errands including a stop at Target and the grocery store to stock up on mom-daughter necessities for our afternoon together.

I arrive at Nora's school a few minutes before dismissal and park across the street to wait. The doors to the school open and a flood of children spill out onto the front walkway. I step from the Jeep and cross the street to meet Nora. She exits the building arm in arm with another little girl. I wonder if this is the little girl with whom Nora had a sleepover. Their heads are bent close together and they are both grinning widely, revealing a variety of gaping holes where they lost baby teeth. A sobering thought overtakes me. I've missed so many firsts in my time away from Nora. I wasn't there when she had her first visit from the Tooth Fairy, I wasn't there when she first tied her shoe all on her own or rode her bike without training wheels.

I fight the urge to run up the walkway to meet them and instead hang back, not wanting to be the overbearing mom. I don't know what she has told her classmates about me. Has she told them that her mother — stepmother, I amend — doesn't live with her anymore? Did she confide to her best friend that her father forced me from the home because I drank myself into oblivion every night? Did she tell her classmates that I can't hear?

Then a new fear overtakes me. What if Nora is ashamed of me? Maybe she's told her classmates absolutely nothing about me. Which would be worse? I wonder. Nora's friends knowing the truth about me or thinking that I never existed?

My fears are short-lived. Nora looks up and her smile widens when she sees me. She gives a hurried goodbye to her friend and runs my way, her backpack bouncing on her shoulders.

"Mommy," she says, the sweetest words I could ever read on someone's lips. She wraps her arms around my waist and presses her face against my stomach. I savor the moment. When she finally pulls away from me, she has a confused expression on her face.

"Sorry, sweetie," I say. "I didn't hear you."

"Helen," Nora says, and I turn to see an elderly woman walking toward us. Helen reaches for Nora's hand and pulls her close to her.

"Hello," I say. "We haven't met yet. I'm Nora's stepmom, Amelia. I'm picking Nora up from school today."

Helen's expression morphs from confusion to worry. She shakes her head and starts speaking so quickly that I can't understand her at all.

"David called me," I explain patiently. "He told me to pick Nora up at three ten and to take her to the house."

Again, Helen shakes her head and holds more tightly to Nora's hand. "Tell her who I am, Nora. Tell her it's okay." Nora looks embarrassed but begins to speak but Helen isn't listening, she's looking around. She catches the attention of a man wearing a badge that identifies him as a teacher at the school.

"It's okay," I tell him. "Nora's my daughter, my stepdaughter. Her dad asked me to pick her up." Parents and students walking by are giving us curious looks and I can tell the attention is upsetting Nora.

"Let's go inside the school and we'll figure it out," the teacher says, and we follow him into the building and to the main office.

"I'm sorry, ma'am," he says after conferring with the school secretary. "I'm afraid your name isn't on the pickup list."

"And her name is on the list?" I ask in disbelief, gesturing toward Helen, who looks thoroughly mortified.

The secretary checks her computer and nods.

Great. Why would David leave a message asking me to pick up Nora and then not even make sure I'm on the approved list?

Nora is near tears. This isn't her fault. I draw her close to me. "Don't worry, honey," I say. "You go on home with Helen. I'll call your dad and we'll get it figured out. It was just a miscommunication." Nora gives me a tight squeeze.

We all head back out to the school yard when Cole and Bennett, the two officers who apprehended Evan Okada outside my house, come up the walkway. My heart skips a beat. Maybe they've caught the person who tried to break into my house. Very quickly, I realize that's not the case.

"What's wrong?" I ask.

"Ms. Winn," Officer Cole says, glancing down at Nora and then back at me. "We need to speak with you for a moment. Privately," she adds.

I look at Helen and the teacher, horrified. Did they actually call the police? How could they have arrived so quickly? But they look as confused as I do. "Nora, honey," I say. "Go on with Helen and let me talk to the officers, okay? I'll call you later." Nora nods uncertainly, but releases my hand. To Helen I say, "Will you please tell David to call me when you see him?" Helen agrees and whisks Nora across the street as if she can't get away fast enough.

I turn my attention back to Cole and Bennett. "Is something wrong?" I ask.

"Have you been drinking this afternoon, ma'am?" Cole asks.

"What?" I ask in disbelief, not sure that I understood her correctly.

"We had a call a few minutes ago about a woman in a car with your license plate driving erratically. Have you been drinking?"

"No," I say. "Absolutely not. Who called you? Who told you that?" Nearby, a small crowd is forming. Across the street stands poor Nora, clutching tightly to Helen's hand.

"Ma'am, I'm afraid we're going to have to give you a field sobriety test," Cole says.

"What?" I cry. "I haven't been drinking. I

promise. Please, my daughter is over there."

"If you refuse, you could have your license revoked for one year. Is that what you want?" Bennett says. "Is there any reason other than being under the influence as to why you can't perform the field sobriety test?"

"Please don't do this," I implore. "Not in front of Nora. Please."

Cole looks at me for a moment as if deciding what to do then crosses the street to where the crowd watches. After a moment the group disperses, including Nora and Helen. I want to call out to her, to tell her that this is all wrong but I don't want to embarrass her any more than I already have.

Cole returns. "Okay, let's get this done." She has me stand on one leg with my foot six inches from the ground. Then instructs me to walk heel-to-toe for nine steps and then turn and walk back toward her. Finally, she holds a penlight in front of my eyes and moves it from side to side.

When she finishes she says, "You're free to go, Ms. Winn. You passed all the tests just fine."

"I told you," I say, trying to hold back my tears. "Can you tell me who made the call?"

"Sorry, we don't have that information. We just go where dispatch sends us. You have a good day now."

I get into my Jeep and the tears fall freely. How can a person just call and accuse me of drunk driving? It doesn't seem right. I will never forget the fear and confusion on Nora's face. No child should have to witness that. Cole and Bennett have returned to their squad car and are waiting for me to pull away from the curb.

I slowly inch out onto the road and, still crying, begin the drive home. This can't have been a coincidence. I know David orchestrated this. How could he do this to me? How could he do this to Nora? I have to explain to her that it was all a terrible mistake. But what if he doesn't let me get anywhere near Nora now? We were happily married before the accident and when we argued we did it fairly. Rationally. Does David hate me this much? Is he so desperate to keep me from digging more deeply into his connection to Gwen and her death that he's willing to completely destroy my life?

If that's the case, he's got another thing coming. I'm not going to cower in a corner and allow David to dismiss me so easily. By the time I reach the highway my tears have stopped falling. There must be some kind of recourse against someone who files a false report or makes a malicious accusation. As

I turn down the road that leads to my cabin, I've moved past having my feelings hurt and now I'm just pissed.

20

I tossed and turned all night, trying to figure out what I was going to do next. I've gotten too close to this and I know it's David setting me up. I've decided that I'm going to tell Jake everything that I've found out. David is playing a dangerous game. But first I need to get through this workday.

I balance the box of doughnuts in one hand and the cardboard tray filled with cups of coffee in the other as Stitch and I push through the front door to the center and set the box of doughnuts and coffee on the counter and head back to the file room. The door is already open and Lori and Barb are standing behind my desk. Lori won't meet my eyes but Barb's bore right through me.

"What's going on?" I ask and come around to the other side of the desk to see what Barb and Lori are looking at. My bottom desk drawer is standing open and along with an extra sweater and a bag of mini candy bars is a blue plastic water bottle that I've never seen before. "What's going on?" I ask again, miffed that my coworkers are going through my things.

Barb reaches down and picks up the bottle, unscrews the lid and hands it to me. I peek inside and see the amber-colored liquid and the scent of Wild Turkey fills my nose. My heart skips a beat.

"It's not mine," I say. Lori won't look me in the eye. She wants to believe me but I see her doubt. I try to hand the bottle back to Barb but she folds her arms across her chest so I quickly set it down on my desk, sloshing the contents across the wooden surface. Barb's mind is made up. "That's not mine," I repeat. "Someone put it in there." Heat rises up my neck as I begin to comprehend what's happening. There's a zero tolerance policy for having alcohol in the clinic. I'm fired. I could lose my nursing license.

"My husband did this," I say. "He's trying to make me look bad . . ." I almost add how I'm sure that it was David who called me to pick up Nora at school and then had the police stop me for suspicion of drunk driving, but quickly realize that this won't help my case. "David is behind this."

He knows I'm onto his involvement in

Gwen's death and he knows I'm an alcoholic. He is trying to discredit me. If I went to anyone about what I learned all he has to do is say that I'm a raging drunk who can't be trusted.

Barb is speaking and I try to concentrate on her lips so I understand what she is saying but I can't. It's clear from her face that she doesn't believe me.

"Please, call Dr. Huntley," I say. "I need to talk to him." Barb shakes her head.

I'm able to catch a few of her words. "Leave now."

My eyes shoot to Lori, who is now staring down at her shoes. "It's not mine," I say again, barely able to form the words. I now know there is no way back. Every move I've made the past few weeks, every word I've uttered will be examined and interpreted and judged. "You can take a blood test. It will prove there's no alcohol in my system," I say, presenting my arm as an offering.

Barb gestures toward my name badge and I know she's asking me to turn it in. By now the other staff are standing in doorways, not quite coming into the reception area but close enough to be able to witness my humiliation.

Lori absentmindedly starts stroking Stitch's head and for some reason this infuriates me. Even in this short time I've worked closely with Lori and there is no way that she could have seen me taking a drink, no way that I could have been intoxicated in her presence. How could she so quickly turn on me?

"Ke mne," I say softly to Stitch, but he stays put, contentedly basking in Lori's caresses.

I catch more snippets of what Barb has in store for me if I don't cooperate. "Nursing board . . . charges . . . don't come back."

What can I do? Am I just going to sit back and let David ruin my reputation? Ruin what's left of the tattered remains of my meager career? When I was drinking so heavily, the only consolation I had was that I wasn't nursing at the time. I didn't put patients in any danger. The only person I hurt was me, I tell myself. But I know this isn't true. I hurt my family. I hurt my dad and my brother by the way I isolated myself from them and cut off communication with them. I destroyed my marriage to David and most regretfully, I hurt Nora. She deserved a mother who was there for her every day. There for her when she woke up in the morning and went to bed at night. I blew it.

"Don't make me call security," Barb says, tilting her head toward the door.

Fight, I tell myself. David did this, I know it. But what proof do I have? Nothing concrete that I could hand over to Jake and say, "See, I told you." But Jake would never believe me. Why should he? I've been coming to him for the last few weeks with my half-baked theories of who might have murdered Gwen. He'd think I'm crazy, that I'm overreacting.

And David will get away with murdering Gwen and will never let me see Nora again.

"I'm going," I say, reaching into the file drawer for my sweater. It's still damp and I can smell the yeasty scent of Wild Turkey infused in the fabric. David doused it with bourbon for good measure just to drive home the point in case there was any doubt. Any functioning alcoholic knows that you don't hide the strongest smelling booze in your desk drawer. I wonder in what other ways he's sabotaged me. David is well respected in our community. There is no way I can combat that.

I place my identification badge and key card in Barb's open palm. Leaving the doughnuts and coffee on the counter I turn to leave. Stitch hangs back. I'm sure he's wondering why we're leaving already. We just got here. I don't want to have to call for him. I don't want to have to order him to follow me. This would be the ultimate degradation — me, begging my dog to come with me and Stitch refusing. By the time I reach the door, to my relief, Stitch is at my side.

"Houdny, houdny," I whisper through tears now falling freely. *Good, good.*

A light snow has started to fall. A storm is fast approaching. I hurry through the parking lot to my Jeep and unlock the door. I load Stitch into the car and climb in after him.

Now I'm convinced that Gwen had something on David. Maybe he missed something important during Jo Ellen's pregnancy. Maybe he acted inappropriately with his patients, maybe he acted inappropriately with Gwen and that's why he killed her. I don't know but now he's trying to silence me — not by killing me but by discrediting me in such a way that no one can take me seriously.

I don't know what to do. I consider driving straight to the police station and telling Jake what has happened and insist that he go after David but I know that he won't. I stopped short of telling Jake everything and even if Jake was to believe me he can't just start accusing David of murder. I have zero proof. I lay my head on the steering wheel and try to get my bearings.

Ten minutes later, when I finally raise my head the windows are completely covered by snow and the steering wheel is damp with my tears. I can't sit here forever and the last thing I need is for Barb to call security and have them come out into the parking lot and escort me from the property. Stitch has stretched out the full length of the backseat and, apparently oblivious to my distress, is dozing.

He's not going to get away with this, I tell myself. He is not going to ruin my life. I turn on the windshield wipers to clear the windows and begin to drive. David killed Gwen and I'm going to let him know that I know it.

I take a quick left in the direction of David's clinic and my tires slide on the slick pavement, nearly sending me into the back end of the car in front of me. I slam on the brakes and skid to a stop with a bump against the curb, and Stitch nearly tumbles off the backseat. *Slow down,* I tell myself. The last thing I need is to get in a car accident after being accused of drinking at work.

I ease the Jeep back onto the road and carefully maneuver through the icy streets well below the posted speed limit. There is no sign of David's car at his clinic so my next stop is at Queen of Peace. I crawl slowly along the dim parking ramp, past the parking spaces set aside exclusively for physicians, looking for David's Lexus. If he's delivering a baby he won't be able to talk to me, but he could just be making rounds. I know the hospital isn't the place to have this conversation but hell, everyone seems to think I'm a raving drunk anyway. At least our conversation will be in public and David can't hurt me here.

Despite the fact that it's daytime, the parking ramp is shadowy and deserted. I'm hesitant to leave my car. Maybe it's not enough for David to set me up, get me fired, make the world think I'm drinking again. Maybe he wants me dead too.

I open the car door and cautiously step outside. I have no idea if David is skulking nearby, car idling, ready to run me down. I want to bring Stitch inside with me but think better of it. Given the conversation I need to have with David, I'm liable to sic Stitch on him.

I stay as far away as I can from the driving lanes, hugging the parked cars. I feel the vibrations first, the shiver of concrete beneath my feet. I step into the gap left between two cars and jump back just as a car comes flying around the corner. I flash back to when Stacey Barnes and I were hit and think maybe this is how David is going to kill me. The car shoots past and right away I know it's not David's Lexus, just a van driving much too fast for the narrow lane. I rush toward the doors, swiveling my head to look around for any more oncoming cars and push through a second-floor entrance. I immediately duck into a bathroom. My eyes are swollen and red and my skin blotchy from my tears. I need to try and be calm and rational when I confront David. I take the nearest elevator to Maternity.

I stop at the main desk and ask for Dr. Winn. "Are you a patient of Dr. Winn's?" asks the nurse. I don't recognize the woman, and inexplicably, I feel a bubble of laughter rise in my chest. She has no idea who I am. David never had any intention of getting back together. The only reason he expressed a newfound interest in me, the only reason he invited me over for dinner was to find out what I knew about Gwen's death. He never even mentioned me to his coworkers.

"I'm Dr. Winn's wife," I say. "It's important that I talk to him."

"Can I take a message?" she says. "He's just finishing up with a delivery."

"I need to talk to him now," I snap, and she flinches.

"Certainly," she says. "I'll page him right away."

I pace the hallway, my stomach sour, and I'm grateful that I hadn't yet eaten one of the doughnuts that I brought to the office. I know I wouldn't be able to keep it down.

I'm just about ready to lose my nerve and leave when I see him, dressed in his blue scrubs and moving leisurely through the hallway toward me. He looks so nonchalant, so calm. How could I have ever married a man capable of such deceit? Not only did he give up on me after my accident when I needed him most, I'm confident that he's the one who killed Gwen.

When he sees the look on my face his expression turns to concern. "Amelia," he says, reaching for my hands, "what's wrong? Did something happen to Nora?"

I shake his hands from mine. "I know what you're up to, David. I know what you did," I snap.

People are starting to stare, and David pulls me into an empty patient room. "Jesus, Amelia, what the hell are you talking about?"

"I know Gwen figured out that you had something to do with Jo Ellen Beadle's death and you killed her. You're trying to make me think I'm crazy. You planted alcohol in my desk at work. You got me fired. I don't know how you did it, David, but you're not going to get away with this." I must be nearly shouting now because David shuts the door and puts a finger to his lips.

"Quiet down, Amelia," David orders. "I don't know what the hell you're talking about, but you can't come in here and accuse me of . . . of what exactly? Murder? Putting alcohol in your desk? Do you know how crazy you sound?"

"I'm not crazy," I say, knowing that I sound like a petulant child.

"Go home," he says and tries to go past me but I step in front of the door to block his exit. This is how it is with David. When he's finished with you it's like you don't exist.

"You lied to me. You said you hadn't seen Gwen in months but you did. She was one of your patients. She found out something about you. Something you didn't want anyone to know. So you killed her, put her in your boat and dumped her . . ."

David takes a step toward me, eyes narrowed in fury. I turn away but he grabs my chin, forcing me to look at him. "Shut the fuck up, Amelia. You are a sad, lonely drunk who needs to go home before I call the police." He drops his hand and brushes roughly past me and out the door.

I drop into a nearby chair. I can't believe I confronted him like this. He's right about one thing. I must be crazy — I just accused my husband of murder. But what if getting me fired from my job isn't enough for David? What if he comes after me? I need to make some kind of plan, but the only thing I can think of is to call Jake and I'm already on shaky ground with him as it is.

This has gone too far. This is my life. My family. David isn't going to get away with this. I get in my Jeep and when I pull from the parking garage onto the street the light snow has thickened into fat, lazy flakes that cling to everything they touch. Tree limbs and street signs are cloaked in a lacy white covering. This all begins and ends with Gwen and the only other person who seems to have made this connection to my husband is an obsessive-compulsive quasi-stalker who lives in his parents' house and spends his free time in a garage, pasting news articles about his murdered ex-girlfriend into a scrapbook. Peter McNaughton has to be able to provide some clarity. For some reason he thinks David is an integral piece in figuring out who killed Gwen and I'm going to go find out why.

21

I drive to Peter's bookstore, The Book Broker, in hopes of talking to Peter in a public place. Although by all accounts he's harmless, I want to see him where there are plenty of people around and no way he can go off on me again. I also bring Stitch in for moral support.

The Book Broker is on Depot Street, a neighborhood where daily trains still rattle through the heart of downtown Mathias carrying a variety of cargo: corn and soybeans, coal, chemicals and ethanol. The Depot neighborhood, as it's called, is equal parts run-down industrial and revitalized hip. This stretch of street has been refurbished and also includes an organic grocery store and one of those art studios where you can bring your own booze and for forty bucks can paint a masterpiece, led step by step by a professional artist. Two blocks north you'll find the crumbling facades of old businesses and factories with broken-out windows. I find a parking spot right out front of the narrow redbrick building flanked snugly by a law office and a bar.

I push through the door and except for the walls and walls of books, I could be back in Peter's immaculate garage. The books appear to be organized by subject and despite the vague smell of musty paper, they look like they are in excellent condition. There are several cabinets situated throughout the store with a variety of tomes and anthologies locked behind their glass doors. Peter emerges from the shelves with a stack of books in his arms. He looks up, his eyes widen in alarm and he begins to speak rapidly so I'm not able to understand him.

"Please slow down," I tell him. "You're speaking too fast and I can't read your lips."

"I said," Peter begins, exaggerating the movement of his mouth, "you can't bring a dog in here."

"Just slow down, but talk normally. And he's my service dog," I explain. "Legally I can bring him with me wherever I may need his help. He's friendly."

"I really don't want to talk to you," Peter says. "We're closed." He moves to the exit and opens the door, waiting for me and Stitch to leave.

"Wait," I call after him. "Peter, please, it's okay. I just need to ask you a few questions."

Reluctantly, he shuts the door and comes back to his spot behind the counter. "Listen," he says. "I'm sorry about the other day, when I was yelling at you. I really am. That isn't me . . ."

I hold up my hand to stop him. "That's not why I'm here," I say. "I'm sorry if I caused you any problems with the police but it's Gwen I'm thinking about."

"She's all I think about too. I can't believe she's gone," he says, and I feel a pang of sympathy for him. He truly is a lonely man. All he appears to have is a demanding father and this bookstore. No wonder he is mourning Gwen's passing so deeply.

"I promise I have just one question, then I'll leave you alone." Peter looks like he's going to refuse. I expect him to just send me away but he doesn't. He waits for me to ask my question.

"In the parking lot the other day, you started to say something and I just need to know what you meant by it. You said that I needed to ask my husband about Gwen's death. What did he do? How do you know it was him?"

Peter looks perplexed and then begins speaking. I need to stop him and slow him down again. "I didn't say anything about your husband. I didn't even know you were married."

I stand there stunned for a moment. "But you said, 'You need to ask your husband . . .' "

"That's not what I said," Peter says, coming out from behind his counter and taking a moment to walk through the stacks to see if the store is empty. When he's sure we are alone he continues. "I told you to ask Joe Huntley, your boss."

I stand there in stunned silence, my mind momentarily blank. "Say that again," I tell him. "More slowly."

I watch his mouth carefully as he repeats himself. "I said, I told you to go ask Joe Huntley."

A shiver slithers a path down my back. "Why? What does Dr. Huntley have to do with Gwen?"

"I probably shouldn't have said anything. Just forget it."

"Peter, this is important. Tell me why you think Dr. Huntley is involved."

Peter is quiet for a moment but when he realizes I'm not going anywhere he continues. "I saw them together. Last month. Gwen and Dr. Huntley. In front of the coffee shop across the street." I turn and look at the shop he's referring to. I've been there several times. The shop is spacious with high ceilings and mismatched tables and chairs, and colorful paintings and mosaics made from broken teacups cover the walls. The baristas behind the counter don't even bat an eye at the presence of Stitch.

"I was inside getting coffee when I looked out the window and saw Dr. Huntley and Gwen. They started talking loudly, arguing. I went outside to see if Gwen needed help."

Again, I make him slow down and repeat himself so I'm clear as to what he is telling me. "What were they fighting about?" I ask.

"I don't know. By the time I got there they stopped arguing but they both looked upset. Gwen said she was fine, but she didn't like it when people played God. Dr. Huntley left and then Gwen left and I came back to the shop."

I don't like it when people play God. This is exactly what Marty said that Gwen had told him in reference to a patient or a woman she knew who was pregnant. Jo Ellen Beadle.

"Thank you, Peter," I say.

None of this is making much sense. Hadn't Dr. Huntley told me he didn't even know who Gwen was? If this was true, why would he and Gwen be having words in front of the coffee shop? Is it possible that the connection between Gwen and Jo Ellen Beadle wasn't David, but Dr. Huntley? If I was going to find out, I'd need access to the center's files. The center I just got fired from. I needed to get back in there and I needed to get my hands on Jo Ellen Beadle's medical file.

22

The center closes at six during the week. Lori should still be there. Dr. Huntley, Dr. Sabet and Barb will most likely be gone, along with most of the other patients and staff. My hope is to convince Lori that I need to pick up a few more personal items that I left behind in my rush to leave the center this morning. I need to get my hands on Jo Ellen's files.

I stop at an electronics store and buy a high-speed 256 GB flash drive, hoping that I'll actually be able to get past Lori and to my computer in order to use it.

I pull into the center's parking lot just before six. It is nearly deserted and I'm able to park right next to the entrance.

The waiting room is empty and Lori, sitting behind the counter, startles when Stitch and I enter.

"Oh, Amelia, you shouldn't be here," she says. She looks around the room nervously as if Barb or Dr. Huntley might suddenly appear.

"I forgot to pack up a few of my personal things this morning. Do you mind if I go and grab them? It will only take me a few minutes."

She hesitates, then nods her head. "I'm so sorry about what happened, Amelia, but there was nothing I could do." She looks as if she might start to cry and she looks afraid. Afraid of me?

I want to tell her that she has it all wrong. That I'm the last person she should be afraid of. But instead I say, "Don't worry about it, Lori. The truth will come out soon enough." I walk back to the file room hoping that she doesn't follow me. She doesn't. Stitch has stayed behind with her and I imagine she is feeding him the last of the dog treats.

Once in the file room I shut the door and sit right down at my computer. I don't have much time. I dig into my pocket and pull out the flash drive and insert it into the port. I enter my user name and password. An error message pops up. I tell myself to slow down and try again, entering each character carefully. Again the error message appears. My permissions have already been scrubbed from the system.

I have to think fast. I remove the flash drive and pick up a framed photo of Nora that I keep on my desk and tuck it under my arm to prove that I came here to gather my personal items. I go over to the file cabinet. I have to find one or two files and smuggle them out of here without Lori noticing. Huntley fired me for a reason. He set me up in the best way possible in order to ruin my credibility. I'm close to learning his secret and my thoughts are spiraling in a hundred different directions and I can't seem to rein them in.

Jo Ellen's file is not in the section labeled A to B, where it should be. My heart skips a beat. I thought I put it in the new standing file cabinet the other day. I thumb through each of the files and still don't find it. I return to the battered file cabinet to see if I may have accidentally put it back in its original spot. Not there. I check again, in case I missed seeing it. Still not there.

I'm running out of time. I already should have grabbed my things and been out of here. Lori will get suspicious soon and come back to find me.

Think, I tell myself.

The other patients. The ones where I noticed odd discrepancies. The missing biopsies and the missing blood tests. I scan my memory for the names. Roberts, Rivera, Quigley. All the files are gone. What's happening here? I have to find Jo Ellen's file or I've got nothing. I need to slow down, retrace my steps.

I think back to the last file I worked with yesterday. Dennison maybe? I open the drawer that holds the patient files whose last names begin with *D* in search of Jo Ellen's file. Here it is. I accidentally gathered up Jo Ellen's file with the Dennison file. I pull it and stuff it into my purse, knowing that I can't walk out of here with it in my hand. I need to get out of here. Now.

But I feel like I should have something more. I know that I will never get the chance to look at these files again. My instinct is to follow the money and find any reference to insurance or patient billing. My eyes land on the file cabinet that Lori said I didn't need to worry about. The cabinet that contains "inactive" files waiting to be shredded. I remember seeing some billing sheets in there when I was looking for John Winthrop's file the other day.

Knowing I have zero time for this but not able to leave without at least checking inside, I go to the cabinet. It's locked. Strange. It wasn't locked when I looked through it in search of the Winthrop file.

Someone doesn't want me in this drawer but I'm not ready to give up. It's an old file cabinet and after two good tugs the drawer pops open.

Billing files. Hundreds of them. It would take me hours to go through all of these. What had Jake said at dinner the other night? Something about the motives for murder: *Greed. Hate. Revenge. Evil.* What if the motive all along has been money and the proof is somewhere in these insurance records? What I'm doing is highly illegal, but there's got to be something here that will help me understand why Dr. Huntley wants me out of this office for good. I shove a fistful of billing sheets into my purse and, hoping that Lori doesn't notice the sudden bulk of my bag, I step from the file room and begin to walk down the hallway back to the waiting room.

I find Lori and Stitch where I left them and join them behind the counter, acutely aware of the files that I have concealed in my purse.

"Did you get everything you need?" she asks.

I nod. "Thanks, Lori. You take care."

"You too," she responds and looks as if she wants to say more, but doesn't.

With my contraband stowed away in my

purse, Stitch and I exit the clinic for what I know will be the last time. The wind has picked up and the snow is coming down in swift dizzying spirals. Drifts form in stiff white peaks across the parking lot and I scan the area searching for anyone who might be nearby, watching, but I'm alone. I unlock the Jeep and toss my purse onto the passenger-side floor. I'm ready to get home and really dig into these files and figure out exactly what's going on.

Stitch has wandered off several feet and I'm just about ready to call him back when I see his ears perk up and head tilt in the direction of the clinic. Something has caught his attention. There's something in Stitch's stance, not fear but wariness, which makes me want to see what he's going to do next. He sniffs at the air and starts moving toward the back of the clinic, and I hurry to catch up with him.

The narrow roadway, lined by a wrought-iron fence, leads to the back of the clinic and is just wide enough for a delivery truck to drop off packages at the rear entrance, or for Dr. Huntley and Dr. Sabet to park their cars. Beyond the fence is the beautiful view of Mathias and Five Mines.

Stitch rounds the corner and that's when I see two figures standing beneath the bright lights over the rear entrance. I manage to snag Stitch's collar just before he takes off running toward them and I pull him back behind a Dumpster. It's Dr. Huntley and Dr. Sabet, both bundled up against the weather, and from the looks of it they are deep in conversation.

Dr. Huntley looks at Dr. Sabet in irritation and Dr. Sabet scowls when Huntley begins to speak. I pray to God that Stitch doesn't try to wriggle from my grasp and that he stays quiet. We are less than ten feet from the men and I know I should get back to the Jeep and just go home, but fear of making a noise and being discovered and something on Dr. Sabet's face keeps me rooted to my spot. He's angry and fearful all at once.

"I got a call from . . ." I can't quite catch the name. I squint and crane my neck to try and get a better view. "His wife is terminal," Dr. Sabet says. ". . . unnecessary treatments?"

Though I pride myself in being a pretty accurate speech reader, I know that even my overinflated estimate of my abilities can be less than 50 percent and probably less so under these conditions. I have to fill in a lot of the words I miss.

Dr. Huntley rocks back and forth on his

heels before speaking. "Not your business . . . I treat my patients. You treat yours."

"It's my business," Dr. Sabet says, ". . . it's wrong." Dr. Sabet begins speaking rapidly and I try to catch as much of what he's saying as possible and come up with only snippets that when I piece them together are chilling. "Unethical practices . . . unnecessary and aggressive . . . prolong suffering . . . fill your pockets . . . kickbacks." I want to turn away, but I can't. I need to know what they are saying.

"What is it you think you are going to do?" Dr. Huntley asks.

"Quit, walk away. I can't do this anymore."

"I think that's a good idea," Dr. Huntley says. ". . . keep up your malpractice insurance, Aaron. If I go down, you're going down too."

Dr. Sabet shakes his head in frustration. ". . . crazy."

Dr. Huntley roughly grabs Dr. Sabet's arm and I know that the next words that come out of Huntley's mouth could be the most important that I ever read. ". . . that's what the last person . . . got in my way . . . She's not a problem anymore."

Did Dr. Huntley just admit to murder? Gwen's murder? I can't believe it and by the shocked expression on Dr. Sabet's face neither can he. Dr. Sabet throws off Dr. Huntley's grasp and goes back inside the clinic.

Dr. Huntley lingers a bit longer and I hold my breath, hoping that his eyes won't turn to the spot where Stitch and I are hiding. Finally, he slowly makes his way to his car, starts it and unhurriedly begins to brush away the snow from the windows. Once he turns his back to me, I can't stand it any longer and I run from my hiding spot with Stitch at my side and don't stop until I reach my car. I get Stitch inside and climb in after him, fire up the ignition and flip on the windshield wipers to clear the snow that has accumulated since I've arrived.

I'm not fast enough, though. Dr. Huntley's car comes out from behind the back of the building and he stares at me as he slowly passes in front of my still-parked car. The flat, cold anger in his eyes gives him away. Fear snags the air from my lungs. It wasn't David who killed Gwen, it was Dr. Huntley. I just need to figure out exactly why.

The snow makes driving difficult and I keep looking for Huntley in my rearview mirror, expecting him to come barreling up behind me on the road. It takes me nearly an hour to get home and by the time I pull up next to the cabin my fingers ache from clutching the steering wheel so tightly.

Once inside the house, I get to work. Stitch, sensing my anxiousness, sticks close to me as I settle at the counter with my laptop, Jo Ellen's file, Gwen's calendar and my phone.

First I text Jake. I know he's supposed to come over for dinner tomorrow night, but this can't wait much longer. Can you call me later tonight? I have some info about Gwen. I keep it short and sweet. I don't mention anything about Dr. Huntley. It's too complicated to get into now. I'll save that for when we can talk in person.

And though it's the least of my worries right now, I leave a message for my attorney, Amanda, asking her to please call me back, that I need to set up an appointment with her as soon as possible. I'm hoping that she will be able to somehow make sure that Barb and the others at the center can't use the fact that a bottle of alcohol was found in my desk against me. I know it's a long shot, but my drawer wasn't locked. Anyone could have put the bottle there but now I'm pretty sure it was Dr. Huntley.

I spend the next twenty minutes reading through Gwen's calendar. I try to make sense of the more cryptic shorthand and see if I can find any connection between Gwen and Dr. Huntley. I'm just about to give up when a brief notation jumps out at me.

Linda W. 2:30.

This could be it. Linda Winthrop.

What was it she had said on the online forum? Dr. Huntley wouldn't listen to their concerns. Hardly grounds for malpractice. Her husband, John, had been diagnosed with a bleeding disorder. Idiopathic thrombocytopenic purpura. But why would Gwen have a meeting scheduled with Linda Winthrop? I can't help but think this woman holds an important clue; I need to speak with her.

I search online for a phone number for a John or Linda Winthrop and two options pop up. I dial the first and wait for someone to answer.

"Hello" appears on my phone display.

"Yes," I begin. "May I speak with a John or Linda Winthrop please."

"This is Linda Winthrop."

I'm not sure how to continue. Anything I say will sound intrusive and strange. But what do I have to lose?

"My name is Amelia Winn and it's my understanding that you had an appointment to meet with Gwen Locke on October 30."

The display remains idle so I plunge forward. "I was hoping to ask you a few questions about that appointment with Gwen and the treatment your husband was receiving for ITP."

"Who are you again?"

I'm losing her. If I don't get to the heart of this call she's going to hang up. She might anyway. "My name is Amelia Winn and I used to work with Gwen Locke, as a nurse. I think she had some questions about the treatment your husband was receiving from Dr. Joseph Huntley."

Again there is a long pause. "We were supposed to meet but she never made it. She said she was working on quality assurance documentation for local health care providers. She wanted to talk about the care John got for his ITP."

I don't know how hard to push. So I just wait for Linda to continue. "Dr. Huntley had John receiving infusions of an antibody twice a month for the past three years when he simply could have had John's spleen removed. My poor husband suffered years of headaches and back and joint pain when he could have had the surgery and his ITP would have been managed."

"Why do you think he did that?" I ask, though I'm pretty sure I know the answer.

"Money. Why else? Each round of treatment cost upward of twenty-two grand. Thank God we have decent insurance. I can't even begin to guess how much of that ended up in Dr. Huntley's pocket. We finally got a second opinion and the hematologist told us to get the hell away from Huntley. John had his spleen removed and now his platelet levels are in the normal range."

"I'm so sorry you had to go through this," I say. "Do you mind if I or someone else follows up with you on this in a few days?"

"I hope you do," Linda says. "I've been trying to get someone to listen to me about that crook for months."

I thank her and we disconnect.

Outside, the storm is picking up strength. At least three more inches have already covered the ground, bringing the total snowfall to about six inches. I can barely see Evan's house on the bluff through the heavy snow, and the wind is shaking the bare branches.

I pull out Jo Ellen's medical file. I go

through it page by page and a sad picture slowly begins to form. Jo Ellen was a seemingly healthy twenty-seven-year-old when she went to her doctor complaining of feeling tired. The blood tests came back a bit off and Jo Ellen was referred to Dr. Huntley for follow-up. Dr. Huntley diagnosed her with Waldenström's macroglobulinemia. I'm not an oncology nurse, but I know that as cancers go, Waldenström's is relatively rare. I do a quick online search to learn more about its symptoms and treatment. I thumb through Jo Ellen's lab work and find her initial IgM levels, which are found primarily in the blood and lymph fluid and are the first antibodies the body creates to fight infections. Jo Ellen's IgM is a bit high but not exceptionally so.

I spend the next two hours poring over Jo Ellen's treatment files and when I'm halfway through I think I have an idea of what Dr. Huntley was up to. Based on what I know about Waldenström's and after a quick internet search, it appears that most doctors who encounter patients with similar labs and symptoms to Jo Ellen's would simply watch and wait. If the IgM levels increased, treatment would begin. But I still need more proof. I pull my dog-eared copy of the *Physicians Desk Reference.* A few years old, but it's still the go-to reference for pharmaceutical warnings, dosages and side effects. Based on Huntley's treatment protocol and the dosages and the number of rounds, Jo Ellen's lungs and liver would be fried. Jesus, Jo Ellen didn't have a chance.

Stitch nudges me with his nose, letting me know he needs to go outside, and I step out into the yard with him. The snow continues to fall but instead of the lazy fat flakes of earlier this afternoon, it has turned to small sharp pellets that scour my skin. Stitch sniffs around a tree trunk and then his ears perk up, suddenly alert. Here we go again, I think as he tears off in the direction of the woods. *"Ke mne!"* I shout. *Come here.* Stitch ignores me. The surface of the snow has formed a shiny crust and with each step it collapses beneath his paws. If I weren't so irritated with him and on edge I'd laugh at his comical trek. *"Ke mne!"* I call again. Stitch pauses briefly to look at me but then continues toward the pines.

I glance up at Evan's house and the wind and snow have calmed enough for me to see his silhouette in the window looking down at us. Chances are he won't come down and try and help me this time. I can't blame him.

Stitch disappears into the dark, and I

squint in hopes of catching a glimpse of his silver fur. “Dammit,” I say in frustration.

Just as quickly as he vanished, Stitch reappears and gallops back to my side. I look back up at Evan’s window and give him a wave that he returns along with a shake of his head. I grab Stitch by the collar and lead him back inside. “You have to stop doing that,” I say as he slides his eyes guiltily away from mine.

We go back inside, and I toss more wood into the fireplace and pour more kibble into Stitch’s dish. He sniffs at it but instead of eating he lies down on his dog bed. I flip on the television to check the weather forecast. More snow through the night with clearing early tomorrow morning.

All along I thought that Gwen found out that David did something that endangered Jo Ellen Beadle and her baby but now I’m confident it had to do with Dr. Huntley and Jo Ellen’s cancer diagnosis from before she was even pregnant.

Huntley overtreated Jo Ellen, leaving permanent damage to her body. Gwen figured it out and tried to confront Huntley at the coffee shop. Did she confront Huntley, and he killed her for it? Possibly. But there has to be more to it than what’s in Jo Ellen’s file.

I think maybe there is something else that *isn't* in the file that would lead me right to Dr. Huntley. I went through dozens of files in my short time at the clinic that appeared to have missing paperwork. Maybe that wasn't an oversight. Maybe Huntley didn't want a record of Sharon Quigley's lung biopsy or Mitchell Rivera's CBC report.

Why would a doctor want to make sure that certain tests weren't seen? Because they made a mistake and didn't want to get caught? No, doctors did make mistakes, but dozens? And those were only the files I had a chance to go through. The center performed thousands of procedures a year under Dr. Huntley. Maybe he wasn't trying to hide an honest mistake but trying to cover up something intentional and so evil that it's nearly incomprehensible? Maybe he was treating perfectly healthy people for cancer they didn't have.

Jo Ellen's file isn't going to be enough, though. If Dr. Huntley finds out I stole these files, then just like Gwen I'm in danger too. At least the bad weather will keep him away from me for the time being.

Next I tackle the billing files that I swiped from the office. They are billing sheets and patient records. Dozens of them. And from what I left behind in his office there were hundreds and hundreds more. What I find in these files is mind-boggling and bone-chilling.

One patient's file shows that Dr. Huntley was ordering chemo treatment for a cancer that was in remission. The accompanying billing statement had the cost being upward of eight thousand dollars per month for the drug. Several files are for end-of-life patients who are clearly listed as terminal and yet are being administered chemo treatments that cost thousands and thousands of dollars.

When I look up again, it's after 1:00 a.m. After reading through all these documents I feel dirty and ill. The scope of Dr. Huntley's malpractice is overwhelming.

But I still feel like I need more. Rachel Nava. She had dropped her files all over the floor when she collapsed in the waiting room. I meant to take the file to her while she was in the hospital. At first I thought that Lori was just being thoughtful when she called me to return the contents to the clinic so they could take care of getting it to her. But maybe it wasn't even Lori who called me. I couldn't actually hear the voice on the other line, just saw the words across my phone display. It could have been Huntley for all I know.

Rachel Nava's file is still in the Jeep; in my hurry to leave the clinic today after being fired I didn't even think about giving it to Lori. Maybe there is something in there I'm not supposed to see.

The yard is a swirl of white. At least three more inches have fallen and there's no sign of it letting up.

I root around in the backseat and I pull Rachel's thick file from the floor where I left it. I go back inside and begin to read.

I flip through the various billing paperwork again and find a curious coincidence. I had assumed that because Dr. Huntley was affiliated with Queen of Peace, he would have used the Q & P pharmacy. Not the case. The pharmacy listed on the billing record is named Midwest Comprehensive Pharmacy Services or MCPS. I compare this to Rachel Nava's records — same pharmacy. I've never heard of it. Though I need to dig deeper, I'm willing to bet that Dr. Huntley is a silent but very profitable partner in MCPS.

I go back to the beginning of the file and read each page word by word. Rachel was diagnosed with multiple myeloma, incurable, often deadly, but manageable with immunoglobin injections and chemo.

It takes me the better part of an hour, but

I finally find Rachel's earliest lab results, the results that led to her diagnosis. I read the pages over and over again. No plasma cell tumor, no high blood calcium levels, kidney function is fine, no abnormal MRIs, no elevated plasma cells in the bone marrow. Except for a slightly low red blood cell count or anemia, there is absolutely no indication that Rachel Nava had cancer. Ever. Despite this, it doesn't appear that anyone questioned Dr. Huntley's diagnosis. But why would someone question the judgment of a well-respected, brilliant oncologist whom patients and colleagues love?

I thought it was bad before, but this is nearly unimaginable. Once Dr. Huntley realizes that some of his paperwork is missing — that this particular paperwork is missing — I'm in deep trouble. I send Jake another text. Call me, please. Doesn't matter what time. I'm not going to be able to sleep at all tonight so I also decide to document all that I've learned in an email and send it to Jake.

I sit down again at the computer when Stitch comes to my side. He wants to go outside again. I let him out and then step into the pair of snow boots I left by the door to go out after him. "Stitch, *ke mne*!" I call. The snow has stopped, the sky has cleared and the moon is glowing as brightly as a lantern.

That's when I see the tracks. It's the unmistakable teardrop-shaped impressions that can only be left by snowshoes. They appear just at the tree line and wind around to behind my house.

Who is snowshoeing on my property? My mind tries to lock on any logical explanation. Could it be Evan enamored by the first big snowfall of the year and impatient to try out his snowshoes? I look up at his house on the bluff. It is dark and still. No, it isn't Evan. Someone camping and caught out in the snowstorm trying to get to shelter? No. That doesn't make sense.

Curiosity pulls me around the corner of the house and there, lying in the snow, I find Stitch writhing on his back.

"Stitch, *ke mne,*" I whisper. *"Ke mne."* He can't get up. I go to his side and drop to my knees. "Please," I say, but still he thrashes in pain. A new terror crashes through me. He's here.

The man comes around the corner, dressed all in black, his face obscured by the shadows and the hood pulled up over his head but I know who it is. I have to get inside. I have to leave Stitch where he is. I get up and scramble to the door and manage to get inside, sliding the door shut and inserting the wooden stick just as Huntley slams his gloved hands against the glass.

My phone. I need to call 9-1-1 and get help. I pat my pockets, frantically looking for it but it's not here. I've had it with me all night. I spin around, searching, scouring the living room for any sign of it. Huntley and I see it at the same time, in the snow, just off to the right of where Stitch's spasms are just starting to ease. It must have fallen out of my pocket. A slow grin spreads across Dr. Huntley's face and I watch in horror as he snowshoes over next to Stitch, bends over, picks up my phone and puts it in his pocket.

He then holds up another object. A gun, I think. He points it at Stitch and presses it against his flank. A stun gun. Again, Stitch squirms piteously and I'm useless in helping him.

My landline is just a room away. I turn and dash toward the kitchen counter. All I need to do is dial 9-1-1 and help will be on the way. I try not to think about the snow-covered roads and how long it will take for help to arrive. I reach the phone and just as I pick up the receiver the house goes black. The small green light on the phone that shows me I have a connection is gone. He's pulled the power on the outside of the house.

The dark, to me, is something dense and viscous. It fills my throat and my lungs. My limbs feel heavy with the weight of it. Though I can't hear it, I feel the desperate moan of fear emerge from deep within my chest. My heart begins to race, a pulsing throb. I hold my hand against my chest as if hoping to still the thrum. Blindly, I run my hand along the neck of my lamp, feeling for the switch. No matter which way I turn the knob, the room remains steeped in darkness. I can't see or hear anything. It feels like being in a black hole.

I know he's here to shut me up. I try to calm my ragged breathing. I'm getting lightheaded and dizzy. The only thing worse than having a panic attack in the dark would be having a panic attack and then passing out in the dark. I try to fight the surge of fear that sweeps through me but I know the more I claw against it, the worse things will get.

My flashlight. It's upstairs. I scrabble up the steps, tripping as I go, knocking my knees against the wood. I reach my room, throw the door shut and lock it. I feel along the walls until I find my bedside table and open the drawer. My hands land on the flashlight and with relief I switch it on. A narrow beam of light appears. I inch my way to the head of my bed and pull aside the curtains, knowing there will be light on the other side.

I peek out the window, hoping to get a sense of where Huntley is. The snow has stopped and the sky has cleared. The light from the full moon spreads out across the yard like a silver cloak. The feathery branches of the pine trees that skirt the property are flocked in white. A stunning sight under normal circumstances. There is no sign of Huntley. If he's intent in getting inside he will. There's nothing to stop him unless Evan Okada realizes that someone is trying to break into my house.

Stitch has disappeared. My hope is that he crawled off into the woods and to safety.

I scan the room. My hiding places are limited. I can squeeze beneath the bed or hide in the closet. I'm fit and strong. I could try and fight off Huntley. I'm confident I can take him on, but I have no idea what kind of weapon he might be carrying in addition to the stun gun. I think of Gwen. Her death was drawn out and brutal. There's no way I'm going down without a fight.

My eyes swing back to the window. I have no idea if he's in the house yet. How long will he wait until creeping up the stairs to come for me? I look at the window. What if he's outside, hiding in the shadows, waiting for me to try to get outside to my Jeep? "Shit," I say out loud. My car keys are downstairs. Never have I missed my hearing more than now. It's enough to spur me into action, and I grab a down running jacket from my closet and pull it on.

I unlock the window and push up on the sash but it doesn't budge. *Come on, come on,* I urge. Cold air bites at my fingers and I push harder until the window rises slightly. Inch by inch I force the window upward until I think it's wide enough that I can squeeze through the opening.

I look around the dim room for something with which to cut the screen. I don't want to have to kick it out with my feet. I know the noise will alert Huntley and shave away precious seconds from my escape. I find a ballpoint pen rolling around in the drawer of my bedside table. I wedge the point of the pen into one of the tiny mesh openings and wiggle it around until it rips. I pocket the pen and use my fingers to pull at the ragged edges of screen, the thin metal wires poking sharply into my skin, drawing blood. *At least I'm leaving evidence behind,* I tell myself. I work at widening the tear, almost ready to give up and kick it out, no matter the noise it makes, when it finally gives and the opening is big enough for me to crawl through.

I turn and stare at the door. I still don't know if he's got into the house yet. I lower myself to the floor to peek through the narrow crack between the bedroom door and the floor. It's too dark to be able to see if anyone is coming up the steps. I try to steady my breathing, close my eyes and lay my cheek against the hardwood and spread my fingers flat against the floor.

He knows I can't hear him. But I feel each step he takes. I feel the tremor in my jaw first. It's barely perceptible, but it's there. It slowly spreads to my fingers. I try to be patient. The vibration grows stronger with each of his footfalls. He's coming.

I leap to my feet and shove the flashlight into the pocket of my jacket and pull the hood up over my head and tuck my hands into the sleeves to protect myself from any more cuts and scrapes. I scramble over the bed and squeeze through the slit and slide out onto the snow-covered window box. I pray to God it holds. I reach inside and try to pull the curtains back together to conceal my handiwork, and pull the window shut. Maybe the darkness will confuse him for a few minutes before he realizes I'm gone.

The window box sits about fifteen feet above the ground. My feet dangle over the precipice and I try to decide how best to get the rest of the way down. As a teenager, my bedroom was on the main floor, so sneaking out of our house in the wee hours of the night was no problem. I could tuck and roll, easily popping up and onto my feet or I could simply leap from the window box and hope for a soft landing in the newly fallen two feet of snow below. I discard both thoughts. I'm forty and I have a feeling that one misstep will end my escape before it barely begins.

I twist my body so that I'm facing the house and then clutch onto the edge of the window box and lower myself so that I'm dangling the remaining nine or ten feet above the ground. I take a deep breath, knowing that there is no going back now. I brace my body for the impact and release my fingers from the wooden box. I fall fast, the soles of my feet breaking through the snow and striking the ground beneath. A concussion of pain radiates through my legs and they crumple beneath me. I lie on my back for a moment, stunned that the window box held.

I know I have to keep moving. Huntley

had to hear the clatter from my fall. He'll be coming soon. I get to my feet and plan my next steps. The quickest route is to make a dash up the bluff and directly to Evan's house. But that means coming out into the open. If Huntley has a gun I will be spotted in an instant. Dead in an instant. My best bet is to head into the woods and come up the bluff from the other side under cover of the trees.

I sidle up as close to the house as I can. The shades are drawn so I can't see inside but I do see how Huntley managed to gain entrance into my house. He has removed the screen from my laundry room window, knocked through the glass and climbed inside. With Stitch incapacitated, Huntley knew that Stitch wouldn't bark or react when he broke in. Stitch wouldn't hear a thing. And neither would I.

I want to find Stitch, tell him how sorry I am. I know that Stitch wouldn't leave me alone if our positions were reversed. He would stay by my side and protect me to the death. I want to tell him that this was my way of protecting him, that I will go get help and come back for him as soon as I can but there isn't time.

Right now, besides Huntley, the snow is my biggest enemy. Just as Huntley had left his snowshoe prints behind, I will give away my location through the trail I leave. Imagining Huntley behind me, gun in hand, the back of my head in his crosshairs, I zigzag the fifty yards toward the tree line. The snow is deep, coming up to just below my knee in some spots and it's all I can do to stay upright. In this one brief moment I'm thankful for my hearing loss. If death is coming I'm hopeful it will come instantly.

I duck behind a snow-covered white pine, jostling its branches so that a flurry of snow showers over me. I peer through the branches to see if Huntley is in pursuit. No sign of him. His snowshoes sit casually up against the house as if he were just a passerby stopping in for a visit. I wish I had thought to take them. If he puts the snowshoes back on to hunt for me he will be at a great advantage. He will be able to cross distances much more quickly than I will. Snowshoes, while they appear large and cumbersome, actually distribute your weight over a larger area so you don't sink completely into the snow, like my size-eight snow boots are doing now.

The moon, while a godsend in my bedroom, has now become a detriment. Huntley will have no problem seeing me beneath its bright, full face. I don't dare turn on my flashlight.

At last count I now have at least four strikes against me. No Stitch, the deep snow, the bright, full moon, my inability to hear. But I do have one thing that I'm pretty sure Huntley doesn't. I know these woods, the paths, the bluffs, the way the river cuts through the land. I know it with my eyes closed, I know it by the feel of the earth beneath my feet.

My bedroom curtains sway and then open. A dark figure stands in the window. It's impossible to see his face but I know it's Huntley. He is dressed in dark clothing, his head covered with a black stocking cap, his coat zipped up and a scarf concealing the lower half of his face. Though I know he can't see me in my hiding spot, he can see my footprints. It's time to go. My first instinct is to stay just inside the tree line, just out of sight and to make my way toward Evan Okada's house. I know the floodlights will go on the minute I step foot into his yard. I will be safe. But I need to be smart about this, because murderer, monster that Huntley is, he's smart too. He is sure to anticipate that very move. There is only one passable way up to Evan's house and all he needs to do is wait for me to try and take it.

"Help!" I scream over and over again,

hoping beyond hope that Evan will hear. "Please!" No lights appear on the bluff. Has Evan gone out? Or maybe he can't hear me. I look to my cabin. Huntley has come back outside. He sees my tracks, he hears my shouts. "Evan, help me!" I yell. Calmly, as if he has all the time in the world, Huntley puts on the snowshoes and starts toward me. Still no movement from Evan's house. Where is he?

I can think of only one thing to do. It could be the craziest plan, it could be the deadliest, but it's my only choice. I turn and start running toward the river.

23

Going down to the river may be what kills me but right now it feels like my only option. The more deeply I go into the forest the thicker the trees become, making it impossible for Huntley to squeeze between the brush and he'll have to take off his snowshoes, putting us on more even ground, so to speak. By following the river, I also have more of a chance of losing him. There are dozens of channels and paths that I know inside and out. If I can just make it a mile upriver, there's an old abandoned access road nearby that will eventually take me to Old Highway 3 and to help.

Though one mile doesn't sound like a very long distance, I know that the deep snow and my inadequate gear will make it treacherous. I need to put as much space as I can between us, and the only way I know how to do that is to run. My gait is awkward at first. I try to step high, lifting my knees so that my feet clear the top of the snow but I know I won't make much progress at this rate. Next I try to shorten my stride and keep my feet lower to the ground. Though the snow is deep, it isn't particularly heavy and I move a bit more easily through it. It takes me about five minutes but I find a decent rhythm. The deeper I go into the forest the darker it becomes. The low-hanging, naked branches cast long gnarled shadows across the snow. Occasionally, I slip and grab onto a branch or tree trunk to steady myself.

I try to stay aware of my surroundings without losing precious time glancing back over my shoulder to see if Huntley is catching up to me. I see no other signs of life. No deer or raccoons, no owls. My guess is that despite my best efforts, I'm making a hell of a lot of noise and scaring everything away. If this weren't so terrifying, it would be a beautiful night for snowshoeing. My biggest fear is tripping over a tree root or rolling my ankle on the uneven terrain. Both likely to happen more than once by the time I reach the old access road. If I break an ankle, it's over.

The trees are closer together here. A mix of pines, birch and pin oaks. I look down at my feet and figure that if there was a spot where Huntley would have to ditch his snowshoes, it would be here. The trees are too close together and there's no way he can maneuver his way around them in the awkward snowshoes. Though it's gradual, I can tell that I'm moving on an upward incline. I'm breathing so hard I can feel the air rattling through my chest and I'm sweating beneath my down jacket. My feet are warm but heavy with the weight of my boots. I have to stop, though I don't think I've even gone a half mile yet.

I bend forward, my hands on my knees, try to catch my breath while searching the woods for Huntley. In my periphery I catch movement. About fifty yards below me, it's him. I don't think he sees me. He is bent over and struggling to release his feet from the snowshoes.

I make a split-second decision. I know there is absolutely no way that I'm going to make it a half a mile farther to the old access road and then even beyond that to the highway. Already my lungs are screaming and my muscles are protesting. Instead of heading more deeply into the woods I'm going to head back in the direction of the house. To do this I know I can't take the exact path from which I came, I'd run directly into him. I continue upward for another fifteen yards until I can't see him anymore. I make a quick left and move deliberately, picking my way across fallen logs and rugged shelflike slabs of limestone. I use this time to catch my breath, bring my heart rate back down. I know that I'm going to have to use every ounce of strength that I have once he realizes I've turned back.

I start to jog again. I have to get home. If he catches me I'll never see Nora or Jake again. I'll never see Stitch. I pick up my pace, trying to ignore my fatigue when the blow comes from behind. I'm knocked off my feet and onto my stomach.

I try to squirm away but he is too strong. My mouth and nose fill with snow. I manage to reach an arm up behind me and clutch his wrist. I dig my nails into his skin, trying to embed as much of his DNA under my nails. He yanks his arm away, allowing me a split second to scramble out from beneath him and stagger to my feet. I reach into the pocket of my jacket trying to find the flashlight but it must have fallen out when he tackled me. But the ballpoint pen is still there. The only weapon I have. I wield it like a dagger and face Huntley.

"Why?" I ask him, hot tears warming my cheeks. "At least tell me why."

24

Huntley quickly gets to his feet. We are both breathing heavily and begin to circle one another warily. I'm struggling to fill my lungs with the air that Huntley knocked from me, and he rubs his wrist where I gouged him with my nails. In his hand he holds the stun gun. Oh, God, he's going to send fifty thousand volts of electricity through my body and then kill me. I wonder if this is how he immobilized Gwen before he strangled her to death.

With one hand, he pulls the stocking cap from his head, stuffs it in his pocket and unwraps the scarf from around his neck. Is this what he's going to strangle me with? I don't know what I expect to see when I can clearly see his face. I thought he was a good man. A man willing to take a chance on letting me work in his clinic, a man who would do anything to save his patients.

"Why?" I ask again, hoping to keep him

talking and lower his guard. "I don't understand."

I try to follow what he's saying, but I can't. It doesn't matter, I'm just stalling for time. "Why Gwen?" I ask and take a tentative step backward. Through the trees a ghostly crouched figure comes into view and my heart leaps hopefully. Stitch. He creeps slowly toward us, as if stalking his prey. He's still a bit unsteady on his feet but he's alive and he's here.

I continue to inch backward. I won't be able to outrun Huntley, but if I can get a few good punches in and with Stitch here, I might be able to slow him down enough so that we can get away.

"You're a doctor. You're supposed to save people," I say to him.

Huntley's eyes fill with something like regret but I know he isn't thinking about the men and women he poisoned with unnecessary or excessive chemotherapy and radiation treatments. He doesn't feel remorse for killing Gwen. He just feels bad because of the inconvenience of it all. He's upset because he was caught.

Stitch continues to move toward us, waiting for me to give him the command.

"I won't say anything. No one else knows," I try to reason with him. "We'll just go back." I tuck the pen back into my pocket, hoping it will lower his guard. "I'll keep your secret." I take a tentative step toward him and reach my hand out to him. Our fingers touch. He grabs my wrist with one hand, yanking me toward him and tries to press the stun gun against my chest. I'm ready for him.

"Stellen," I shout. *Bite.* Stitch propels himself toward us and I step toward Huntley and lift my elbow, forcing him to release my wrist, then thrust the heel of my hand into his face. Blood explodes from his nose in a crimson arc, splattering my face and the snow between us, he drops the stun gun and staggers backward. Then Stitch is upon him.

I turn and run. Wispy clouds have rolled in, covering the moon in a gauzy film, now, making it difficult to see the ground in front of me. I stumble over fallen limbs concealed by snow and I look over my shoulder to see Huntley kick Stitch in the chest, stunning him and causing him to retreat back into the woods. My blow to his face and Stitch's attack slowed him down but didn't stop him. He's searching in the snow for the stun gun but quickly gives up and heads my way.

I force myself to pick up my pace but my sore muscles protest. I try to keep the images of those I love in front me, incentive to get home: my dad and brother, Nora, Stitch. Jake.

I don't want to lose precious time or energy checking to see how close Huntley is to me but I do anyway. He is gaining on me, so close that even in the dimming light of the moon I can see his bloodstained, rage-filled face. *I'm going to die tonight,* I think, but I won't go quietly. Stitch is nowhere to be seen.

I am so close to the house. But something isn't quite right. Though it's gradual, I can tell the path I've chosen is winding upward. I've miscalculated. The only way home is downward. We've reached a precipice — the top of a crumbling bluff. To my right is a steep, rocky switchback portion of the trail that winds like a corkscrew and ends in a bed of jagged limestone and the river. Evan's house is a mere quarter mile from there. To my left is a steep, but more manageable incline that will take me back to the spot where I broke Huntley's nose but much farther from help. I go right.

I've hiked this switchback, named Nohko-metha — the Sauk word for *grandmother* — several times but never in winter and never alone. The limestone face is ridden with deep grooves and sits at a brutal angle that doesn't allow for much error. I don't have time to think about the consequences of climbing down; I know what will happen if I stay put. Huntley is stronger than I am but I'm lither.

The ledge I have to walk on is narrow and uneven. I put one foot in front of the other as if walking a tightrope, knowing that one misstep will send me falling six feet down to the next rocky shelf.

I've got a head start on Huntley, but I take little comfort in this. He's above me on the winding trail and at some point he will be directly above me by a mere two yards. Using the limestone face to help keep my balance I make slow but steady progress downward. I have to pause in my trek. It's the only way I can get my bearings as to where Huntley is. I don't want to stop moving but I also don't dare take my eyes from my feet, and even though my boots have decent treads that help me navigate the snow-covered ledge they are cumbersome and bulky.

I can't hear his approach but if I can catch a glimpse of him I'll feel a lot better. Even a falling rock or a shower of snow from the trail above will give me an idea of the amount of distance between the two of us. I see no sign of Huntley above me but when

I look over my shoulder I see him round the curve in the trail. He's gaining on me.

I have to think fast. I can try and pick up my pace, I can stop and face him head-on to see who can manage to stay on the trail. Our own sick version of King of the Mountain, or I can get creative.

Spindly but resilient trees sprout from the rocky soil of the bluff and I consider grabbing on to one rooted to the trail below and sliding down its trunk. It's tempting but a sure way for me to break my neck. Instead, I keep moving down the circuitous trail until I arrive at a portion of the trail that is slick with ice. I can't move forward and I can't go back. Below me about six feet is another section of the path that looks passable. I just have to get down there. I turn so that I'm facing the bluff and carefully lower myself to my knees. Clutching on to protruding rocks and exposed tree roots, I begin to inch backward.

I step, grab, step, grab, clinging to the footholds and crevices with all my might. Slow and steady, I tell myself. If I get careless I will fall. Huntley isn't far behind.

Above me, his left leg swings out, and for a moment I think he's going to stumble and fall and I flatten myself against the rocks so that he won't take me down with him. He steadies himself and keeps coming. I've gained a little ground but once again he's upon me and thrusts his foot in a downward motion. He hasn't lost his footing. He's trying to knock me off the bluff.

He strikes out again, clipping the top of my head and knocking me off balance. My hands slip and I begin to slide, the rough limestone sloughing away the skin on my face and where my pants and sweatshirt have crept up. I scrabble at the wall, desperately trying to grab on to something to stop my descent. With one hand I manage to grab a snow-dusted shrub that juts from between the cracks. The branches are dead and brittle and snap almost immediately in my hand but slow my momentum enough that I'm able to find my footing.

My mouth has filled with warm, coppery blood from where I've bitten my tongue. I gag and spit and the snow next to me blooms red. I look up. My slide has actually lengthened the gap between us. I'm about twenty feet from the ground — still too far to jump. I try to steady my breathing and not panic. I'm so close. "Step, grab, step, grab," I whisper to myself over and over until I only have about fifteen feet to go.

Almost there.

If I had time to enjoy the view I probably

would be able to see Evan's house from here. A shadow passes over me and hope rises in my chest. Huntley has fallen. Hopefully, in a way that has broken his neck. I look over my shoulder. He's lying on the ground in a crumpled heap. "Be dead, please be dead," I say. The muscles in my arms are shaking violently and I know I can't hold on much longer. Step, grab, step, grab. I glance down again, hoping that Huntley will stay down but to my horror he's already staggering to his feet. He leaped so he could be at the bottom waiting for me or he fell and it's to his advantage.

He didn't land unscathed, though. His face is a pale mask of pain and he's favoring his right ankle. I'm still ten feet from the ground, too high for him to reach me. He's hurt and I don't think he could climb up after me if I tried to hike back up. I cry out in frustration. There's no way I can gather the strength to climb back to the top of the bluff.

My hands are raw and bleeding and my muscles are tight and sore. I look back over my shoulder. Huntley is saying something to me — his mouth contorted with anger. I have to do something. I can't stand here forever. My feet securely stationed on a ledge, I release one hand, reach into the pocket of my jacket, and by some miracle find the ballpoint pen is still there. With shaky fingers, I place it between my teeth and then hold on again. I take three measured breaths and think of all those I love. I'm not ready to die.

I release one hand and slowly, very carefully, I begin to turn. Inch by inch, I rotate, sliding my feet until only my heels rest on the narrow ledge and my palms press uselessly against the face of the bluff. I have nothing to hold on to now.

Below, Huntley watches me, trying to figure out my next move. I remove the pen from between my lips and squeeze it into the scraped and bloodied palm of my hand. I leap then, pushing off the ledge with my feet. I belly flop right on top of him and as our bodies collide I feel his breath, warm and wet against my neck being forced from his lungs.

And then, pen in hand, I begin to stab at his face, aiming for his eyes but landing on his forehead, his cheeks. Blood, sticky and wet, coats my hand and the pen slides from my grasp. But the damage has been done. I push myself off him and almost get away when he snags my calf. I fall back to the ground and with my free leg kick out, making contact with his already broken nose.

His grasp relaxes and I manage to crawl a few feet until I'm just inches away from the river. The newly fallen snow covers the water in a pristine, downy quilt.

I try to push myself up, my hands leaving bloody prints in the snow, but find that my limbs aren't cooperating. I can't give up now, I tell myself. Nora needs me. Stitch needs me. Jake needs me.

I feel a painful tug on my hair and am pulled forward a few inches. Again, another jerk and I howl in pain as Huntley drags me by a chunk of my hair into the river. We immediately crash through the thin layer of ice, and the frigid water penetrates my system like a million bee stings.

Above me, Huntley thrusts my head beneath the surface and I clutch at his wrists, trying to loosen his grip. The water isn't deep here and I twist and writhe, trying to gain my footing on the rocky river bottom. My lungs are screaming for air and I know that I will quickly lose consciousness. I force myself to relax. I let my hands drop away from Huntley's wrists and I stop struggling. Above me, Huntley stands, his hands firmly holding my head beneath the water. My body has gone completely numb from the cold and lack of oxygen — a not so unpleasant feeling. He finally releases his grip and with every last ounce of strength I have, I wrap my arms around his knees and push, knocking him off balance.

I burst from beneath the water and flail, blindly searching for the riverbank. My hands strike solid ground and I struggle to pull myself up onto shore, my sodden clothing heavy and cumbersome. Dr. Huntley is right behind me. He grips my ankles, pulling me backward toward the water. I grab onto a fallen tree branch when I see him, his gray eyes stare out at me from behind a copse of snow-covered broom sedge.

Stitch.

I blink, thinking I must be imagining things. But when I open my eyes again, he's still there.

"Ke mne," I try to say, not sure if the word has made it out from my swollen, bloody mouth. *Come.*

Again, Huntley tries to pull me backward, and I try to grab tufts of dead grass, exposed tree roots, anything to keep him from yanking me back into the frigid water.

Suddenly, Huntley drops my legs but I can't move. Small pinpricks of light dance behind my eyes and the earth beneath my body tilts. I'm going to pass out or maybe even die. Stitch comes to my side. Hackles raised, tail high and bristled, ears forward.

The last sliver of moon glints off the whites of his eyes and bared teeth. His entire demeanor has changed. My normally silly and gentle dog is now a snarling, vicious creature I barely recognize.

Huntley drops down next to me, lowers his face so that I can see him. His once handsome face is mangled. His nose has swollen to twice its size and there are deep gouges in his skin from where I stabbed him with the pen.

"Call him off, Amelia," he says, casting furtive glances at Stitch. I take pleasure in seeing that I knocked one of his front teeth out. I know that Huntley can't hurt me anymore with Stitch here. He knows that all I have to do is give Stitch a command and it's all over.

I just blink up at him, wondering how so many people could have been so fooled by him. Was he always so greedy, so willing to sacrifice others for financial gain? I didn't think so, but maybe the evil has always been there, lying dormant, waiting for the right moment to emerge. I have no doubt that Huntley will drown me in Five Mines and find a way to hide my body so no one can find it. I have no doubt that he will try to find a way to discredit me and make my account of what happened here suspect. He's a respected doctor in Mathias. He has money and clout. But I have something more powerful, the will to live and a petri dish worth of Huntley's DNA beneath my fingernails.

I can order Stitch to back off, to stand down. Stitch and I can leave Huntley behind and stagger out of here together. Battered and bruised but alive.

"Sedni. Klid," I tell Stitch. *Sit. Quiet.* Immediately, Stitch's jaws still and he sits. He keeps one eye on me, waiting for me to tell him what to do, and the other on Huntley.

He's on my back before I have the chance to even get to my knees. His fingers wrap around my throat, squeezing. I reach one hand out to Stitch who's waiting for me to give him a command. I try to peel Huntley's fingers from my windpipe.

"*Zabit,* Stitch," I manage to breathe. *"Zabit,"* I say again. *Kill.*

25

Stitch leaps to his feet. I close my eyes. My last image of Huntley's face is of pure fear. I should feel something — sadness, regret, anger. But I feel nothing. With difficulty, I get to my knees and then to my feet. I don't want to witness what is happening behind me and I'm thankful for the silence. I start walking. I'm less than a mile from home. The moon has set and the sky is darker than it has been all night. What was the old saying? It's always darkest before the dawn? Despite the black morning I know what to do. I know which direction to go. Follow the river.

I unzip my sodden running jacket and drop it to the ground. Despite the cold, in my long-sleeve T-shirt I immediately feel lighter, freer, I can breathe more easily.

The going is slow but I employ the strategy that has served me well the entire night — one foot in front of the other. My eyes are trained straight in front of me. I have to get up and over this ridge and I'm counting each excruciating step. I estimate that I have about five hundred steps to go. I feel a familiar presence limping at my side. Stitch. I start to cry with relief. I know we can make it together.

It would have been a circuitous journey, our tracks a jumbled mess but still Stitch found me. *Two hundred seventy-seven, two hundred seventy-eight steps. Over halfway there.* I try not to think about the blood dripping from Stitch's mouth. What's going to come next? Will there be enough evidence to prove that Dr. Huntley killed Gwen? Will there be enough of a paper trail to prove why he murdered her?

My wet hair has stiffened in the frozen air and my face has gone numb. Sharp knives pierce my feet with each step and though the pain brings tears to my eyes, I'm grateful. It means that the blood is circulating through them and I may have avoided frostbite. I hope the same holds true for the tips of my ears and my fingers.

The early-morning sky is just beginning to brighten. Ethereal seams of pink and tangerine peek between the trees. I follow the curve of the river and when it straightens ahead of me I see an ambulance, fire truck and three police cars with headlights ablaze in front of my still-darkened house. Three hundred ninety eight steps, three hundred ninety-nine, four hundred steps. Dark figures move purposefully in and out of the cabin but no one seems to notice me staggering toward them. I want to call out but my throat feels raw, my tongue too heavy. *"Stekej,"* I manage to say. *Speak.* Stitch's mouth opens and I lay a hand on his throat and feel the strong, sure vibration of his bark beneath my fingers.

Heads turn and then a half a dozen people start running in our direction. Evan Okada reaches me first and immediately removes his coat and wraps it around my shoulders. I lose sight of Stitch and search desperately for him in the crowd.

"Stitch," I say through swollen lips. I can't understand what Evan's trying to tell me, but he gets jostled aside and I feel myself being lifted and gently laid down onto a stretcher. Warm blankets cover me and I moan at their weight pressing against my ribs. They are trying to load me into the back of the ambulance. "No," I say, my earlier panic has returned.

I try to sit up, but firm hands keep me pinned to my spot. Mouths are moving but no one is looking directly at me. I have no idea what is being said. Hot tears of frustration seep from the corner of my eyes and roll down my temples. I spy Evan and I reach out for him, nearly tumbling from the stretcher to get his attention. He comes to my side, takes my hand and squeezes it. He speaks to the emergency workers and then disappears again. Why won't anyone listen to me? I'm lifted into the back of the ambulance and then suddenly Stitch is there. I struggle to sit up, and the EMTs don't bother to fight me.

Stitch goes right for my tears and licks them away. I rub one hand along his face. Huntley's blood still clings to his fur and he's panting heavily.

"Thank you," I say to Evan, who is standing in the doorway, watching. He raises one hand, smiles and then steps away. "Can he come with me?" I ask the EMT. "I'm deaf. He's my service dog."

"Of course," she says, looking straight at me. "There's someone else here to see you too." She moves aside so I can see.

It's Jake. He has the exact same look on his face that he did twenty-five years ago when he crashed his dad's car, sending both him and Andrew to the emergency room. He showed up at our back door two days later, wearing his arm in a sling and an expression of shame and regret.

He climbs into the ambulance and squats down next to me so I can see his face. "Earhart," he signs, his chin trembling with emotion. "I should have called you back right away. I'm sorry." I want to reach up and touch his face. I want to kiss away his apologies.

Instead, I speak. "Stitch saved my life."

"Yeah, and so did Evan Okada." Jake runs a hand down Stitch's back. "Evan looked out his window and saw the screen and the tracks and called the police."

"Dr. Huntley?" I ask, not sure if I want to know the answer.

"Dead," he says, holding my gaze. "Stitch took him down."

I feel my stomach churn. Now that I'm safe I'm questioning what I did. Can one word result in murder? I wonder. "I told —" I begin but Jake interrupts me.

"You did what you had to do."

"We really need to get going now," the EMT says. "The dog is staying I take it?" she asks. "What about this guy?" She nods her head at Jake.

Jake looks at me, awaiting my answer. I reach for his hand. It's warm and strong and I never want to let it go.

"Zustan," I say in Czech. *Stay.*

26

The afternoon May sunshine is hot on my neck as I paddle my kayak through the still-chilly water of Five Mines. In front of me sits Nora. Two tight braids snake out from beneath her baseball cap and flop over the straps of her bright pink life jacket. She's given up on paddling and instead lets her fingers graze the surface of the water. I don't mind. I could watch her all day.

Up ahead of me in a second kayak are Evan and Stitch. Stitch gladly ditched me for Evan but at least he glances back at me once in a while to make sure Nora and I haven't lagged too far behind.

It's taken months for the police and the medical experts to piece together what Gwen had already started to figure out — the enormous scope of Dr. Huntley's crimes. From interviews with those who surrounded Gwen and through the medical records that Dr. Huntley tried so hard to conceal and falsify, a disturbing trail of evidence had emerged: aggressive and unnecessary treatments, deliberate misdiagnoses, all for financial gain. And it was a profitable scheme. After painstakingly reviewing files and insurance forms, it looked like Huntley had made millions of dollars and counting through his fraud.

Jake surmises that Gwen figured it out and came to Dr. Huntley's office to confront him with what she had learned, and he killed her. He knocked her down momentarily stunning her. When she came to Huntley was on top of her, strangling her. They think with IV tubing from an IV starter kit, much like the one I used to help Rachel Nava when she collapsed at the center.

According to Jake's theory, Dr. Huntley tried to force Gwen to reveal who else she had told about what he was doing. When she wouldn't or couldn't tell him, he pulled the tubing tight again until she suffocated to death.

David wasn't completely innocent in all of this. He knew about Huntley's questionable diagnosis and treatment of Jo Ellen Beadle. But turned a blind eye.

According to David, Huntley showed up at his house asking to borrow his boat for a day of fishing out on Five Mines. David readily agreed.

Huntley took the boat out onto Five Mines and dropped her body into the water, hoping that her body would eventually make it to the Gulf of Mexico. He didn't count on Gwen getting tangled up in the brambles and he sure as hell didn't count on me finding her. David became suspicious when he discovered that Gwen was dead and Huntley returned the boat to him smelling of bleach. He didn't quite get it all cleaned up, though. Forensics found Gwen's hair and miniscule drops of her blood in the boat and in Huntley's office at the clinic.

David figured it out and Huntley kept David quiet by threatening him with Nora's and my safety. This was why he ended up offering me the job. He wanted someone close to David nearby as another leverage point — a threat to hold over David to ensure his silence. This was why David was so opposed to me working for Dr. Huntley. I guess I should be flattered.

Both David and Huntley underestimated me, though. They expected that I would simply enter patient data into the computer system and not look too closely at the files or ask any questions. They were wrong. Huntley was diagnosing healthy people with cancer and pumping them full of chemo and radiation for the insurance money. He was overtreating the sick ones and giving false hope to terminal patients — telling them that he could save them if they just trusted him. He administered treatments that would in no way lengthen their lives and in most cases were unbearably painful and destroyed their quality of life. Somewhere along the line, Dr. Huntley decided to act in direct opposition to his Hippocratic oath — especially the section that reads, "Most especially must I tread with care in matters of life and death."

How did he get away with it for so long? That's the question everyone is asking. But the thing is when you are sick or think you are sick, you trust your caregivers, your nurses and doctors. You have to.

David was charged as an accessory after the fact and goes to trial next month. His medical license has been suspended pending the outcome of the trial. To his credit, David still allows me to see Nora and has even set the wheels in motion for Nora to legally live with me if he is convicted and is sentenced to prison time.

I'm hopeful that Nora's biological mother won't come out of the woodwork and cause yet another upheaval in Nora's life. It's been five months and she hasn't shown up yet. I pray she never does but if she appears on my doorstep one day, she better be ready for the fight of her life.

The police found a copy of my house key on Huntley's body and are sure it was Huntley who broke into my house and set out the bottle of wine on my countertop. They think that he was also planning to use it to get into my house the night he tried to kill me. He hadn't counted on me changing the locks. I think back to the day he was in the file room, checking on how I was doing. He could have grabbed my keys without me knowing, had a copy made and returned my keys without me being any the wiser. Not David like I first thought. Huntley lured me to the school to pick up Nora and then called the police saying that a woman driving a Jeep was driving erratically. He's also the one who planted the alcohol in my desk. At first, according to David, Huntley just wanted to scare David through scaring me, but then the news reports alluded to the fact that I might have actually seen a boat fleeing from the scene. That must have put Huntley on high alert. Then when I started digging and trying to figure out what happened to Rachel Nava and Jo Ellen Beadle he was trying to make sure that everyone thought I was a drunk and not to be taken seriously. He underestimated me.

There's no reason to believe that Dr. Huntley had anything to do with my hit-and-run accident. That's one case that's still unsolved and I'm resigned to the fact that I probably will never learn who was driving the car that killed Stacey and left me deaf.

I've got another job. Working for my neighbor Evan in his outfitter business. I lead groups down the river on paddleboards and in kayaks. Of course Stitch is right there with me. I haven't given up on nursing but I'm still trying to figure out how I can be deaf and a nurse. I know it's possible. I'll make it happen.

In the meantime, I'm working on fixing up my cabin, but progress is slow and every little project takes longer than it should. Right now we're working on the addition, which will include a bedroom just for Nora and a new bathroom decked out with a state-of-the-art shower and a claw-foot tub.

I've been nervous about going out on the river all alone with Nora, but Evan's been great. Just having an extra set of ears and eyes makes me feel better for the time being. Slowly, Five Mines is becoming my safe haven again.

Evan starts paddling faster, which means

he's challenging me to a race to see who can get to the dock first. "Hold on," I tell Nora, and she clutches the sides of the kayak. I can't hear her, but she tilts her face up to the sky and I know she's letting out a war cry for Evan and Stitch to watch out, here we come.

It's not even close. Evan beats us by two hundred feet and he and Stitch are already up on the dock to greet us. Evan is looking at his watch and yawning. I slap the water, a wave crashing over them and sending Stitch scurrying. They're not the only ones there to greet us. Jake is too. He's walking down from the cabin, dressed in his detective's uniform: dress pants, dress shoes, button-down shirt and tie. He reaches his hand out to help Nora out of the kayak first. She gives him a quick squeeze and then she and Stitch are off and running.

He extends his hand out to me but I ignore it and climb from the kayak on my own accord. Jake just shakes his head. Evan tells us that he'll take care of the kayaks and that I owe him a beer because he won the race.

Jake throws an arm around my shoulder, and I slide an arm around his waist. We move as if one as we head back up toward the house where Stitch and Nora are waiting.

Jake stops midstep and turns to face me. He kisses me on the lips and runs his hands up and down my arms, causing me to shiver. I lean into him and close my eyes. He traces the familiar letters over and over on my back with his finger until they feel almost engraved into my skin. *I love you.*

I could stand this way forever. Not a sight, not a sound. Just Jake. But I open my eyes and kiss him back, grab his hand and we head up to the house together.

AUTHOR'S NOTE

Not a Sound could be the most personal book that I've written to date. The serious issues of cancer and health care and the profound deafness of the main character are topics near and dear to my heart.

Having had family members and friends, including my son, battle cancer, I have nothing but the utmost respect and regard for the doctors, surgeons and nurses who treat patients. We put our trust and faith in the expertise of skilled professionals, and thankfully my son received top-notch care. For this we are eternally grateful. I believe this stellar standard of care to be true for most families.

Writing *Not a Sound* from the point of view of a profoundly deaf character has been a daunting and challenging endeavor. In researching the novel I learned that there are many resources available to aid the deaf in communication: interpreters, technology, sign language, service animals and more. Amelia, like many who are faced with hearing loss, has a variety of aids to utilize. Based on the circumstances and the personality that I created for Amelia, a woman with her own challenges and demons, as well as for the benefit of keeping the swift pace of the novel, the resources I opted to have Amelia use were limited to only a few of the many possibilities. As someone who is hearing impaired myself, I am grateful to know that many resources are available when and if I'm in need.

I hope I was able to do Amelia justice.

ACKNOWLEDGMENTS

As always, I have so many people to thank for helping me bring this story to life. Much gratitude goes to the early readers who offered suggestions and encouragement. Thank you to Julie Spahn, who shared her expertise and background with me in working with those who are deaf and hard of hearing. Her insights and advice were priceless. Thanks also to Anna Gudenkauf, Kristina Gruber, Amy Doud and Ann Schober, who got an early peek and provided priceless feedback. Extraspecial thanks goes to Jane Augspurger for her countless readings of the manuscript and the many phone calls fielded to talk through scenarios and strategies. Immeasurable thanks to Laurie Schmid — I am beyond grateful for the gifts of your time and wisdom.

Many thanks to Mark Dalsing for all things law enforcement, and to Dr. Tami

Gudenkauf, Dr. Milton Schmida and Rose Schulz for being available at a moment's notice for medical and health care questions.

Words can't express how grateful I am for the faith and confidence that my publisher, Park Row Books, has in me. I am thrilled to be a part of this amazing family. Thank you to Erika Imranyi, my insightful, gifted editor. I thoroughly enjoy our brainstorming sessions and so appreciate your ideas and spot-on suggestions. I can't wait to see where our next projects take us. Thanks also to Margaret Marbury, Emer Flounders, Natalie Hallak, Gina Macedo and all the talented folks at Park Row.

Special acknowledgment goes to my wonderful agent and friend, Marianne Merola. Thank you for being there for me and always believing in me — I couldn't do this without you. To Henry Thayer, Lina Granada and all the folks at Brandt & Hochman Literary Agents, Inc., thank you for the behind-the-scenes support.

The idea for this novel was born during a birthday celebration and a paddle-boarding excursion down the Galena River with Cathie Kloft, Jennifer Peterson, Rose Schulz, Sandy Hoerner and Laura Trimble. Thank you for the inspiration and the fun!

Thank you to reader Tara Mitchell for supplying the perfect name for who could be the most endearing hero in the novel — Stitch.

I'm so blessed to have a family who supports and encourages me: my treasured parents, Milton and Patricia Schmida, and my siblings, Greg, Jane, Milt, Molly and Patrick — best sibs in the world. And of course much thanks to my husband, Scott, and my children, Alex, Annie and Grace Gudenkauf — love always.

ABOUT THE AUTHOR

Heather Gudenkauf is the author of the *New York Times* and *USA TODAY* bestselling novels *One Breath Away, These Things Hidden,* and *The Weight of Silence,* which sold more than half a million copies and spent 21 weeks on the *New York Times* bestsellers list. She lives in Iowa with her family.

The employees of Thorndike Press hope you have enjoyed this Large Print book. All our Thorndike, Wheeler, and Kennebec Large Print titles are designed for easy reading, and all our books are made to last. Other Thorndike Press Large Print books are available at your library, through selected bookstores, or directly from us.

For information about titles, please call:
(800) 223-1244

or visit our website at:
gale.com/thorndike

To share your comments, please write:
Publisher
Thorndike Press
10 Water St., Suite 310
Waterville, ME 04901